A Bridge Apart

A Novel by

JOEY JONES

Hardcover: 978-1-948978-03-3

Paperback: 978-1-948978-04-0

E-Book (.mobi): 978-1-948978-05-7

E-Book (.epub): 978-1-948978-06-4

For my entire family.
Life with you all is the best.

Also by Joey Jones
Losing London

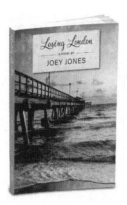

Losing London is an epic love story filled with nail-biting suspense, forbidden passion, and unexpected heartbreak.

When cancer took the life of Mitch Quinn's soulmate, London Adams, he never imagined that one year later her sister, Harper, whom he had never met before, would show up in Emerald Isle, NC. Until this point, his only reason to live, a five-year-old cancer survivor named Hannah, was his closest tie to London.

Harper, recently divorced, never imagined that work—a research project on recent shark attacks—and an unexpected package from London would take her back to the island town where her family had vacationed in her youth. Upon her arrival, she meets and is instantly swept off her feet by a local with a hidden connection that eventually causes her to question the boundaries of love.

As Mitch's and Harper's lives intertwine, they discover secrets that should have never happened. If either had known that losing London would have connected their lives in the way that it did, they might have chosen different paths.

Also by Joey Jones
A Field of Fireflies

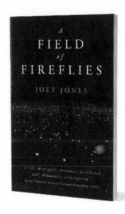

Growing up, Nolan Lynch's family was unconventional by society's standards, but it was filled with love, and his parents taught him everything he needed to know about life, equality, and family. A baseball player with a bright future, Nolan's on his way to the major leagues when tragedy occurs. Six years later, he's starting over as the newest instructor at the community college in Washington, North Carolina, where he meets Emma Pate, who seems to be everything he's ever dreamed of—beautiful, assertive, and a baseball fan to boot.

Emma Pate's dreams are put on hold after her father dies, leaving her struggling to keep her family's farm. When a chance encounter with a cute new guy in town turns into an impromptu date, Emma finds herself falling for him. But she soon realizes Nolan Lynch isn't who she thinks he is.

Drawn together by a visceral connection that defies their common sense, Emma's and Nolan's blossoming love is as romantic as it is forbidden, until secrets—both past and present—threaten to tear them apart. Now, Nolan must confront his past and make peace with his demons or risk losing everything he loves . . . again.

Emotionally complex and charged with suspense, *A Field of Fireflies* is the unforgettable story of family, love, loss, and an old baseball field where magic occurs, including the grace of forgiveness and second chances.

Acknowledgments

Bridge Apart, my first novel, would have never made it to print without the loving support of many amazing people. First, I know I need to thank God. Then, Amber, thank you for always encouraging me to pursue my dreams. To Branden, my son, you have been a true inspiration in my life, and I am a better man because of you. I will be forever thankful to God for placing both of you in my life. I love you with all of my heart. Branden, you are the most amazing son a dad could ever ask for, and I love you BIG.

I also would like to thank my family. To my parents, Joe and Patsy Jones, thank you for providing me an incredible amount of love and support throughout the years. Dad, even though you're gone, your love remains with me every day. Mom, thank you for being one of my best friends. To my brothers and sisters, DeAnn, Judy, Lee, Penny & Richard, thank you for your faith in me and for always having my back.

My editors Rebekah Jones, Kim Jones, and Pam Gray are not only family but are very talented at their work. This book is better because of you.

Lastly, I would like to thank some people who have been influential in my life throughout the years. You all know the part you've played: BJ Horne, Billy Nobles, Diane Tyndall, Gail Spain, Josh Towne, Kenny Ford, Meredith Walsh, Mitch Fortescue, Nicholas Sparks, Ray White, Richard Banks, Tom Pike, Steve Cobb, and Steven Harrell. I am honored to call each of you my friend.

A Bridge Apart

Prologue

It was almost four o'clock on a Friday morning when Andrew Callaway's dream about baby bibs and rocking horses was interrupted by the sounds of moans and groans caused by his wife's contractions. If it were up to him, the moment could have waited a few more hours, but like a volcano raining down on a sleeping city, a baby doesn't understand that it would be considerate to wait for mommy and daddy to brush their teeth, take a shower and stop for breakfast on the way to the hospital. The only option the little fellow left his parents was to grab the suitcase—the one that had been sitting by the front door for weeks—and jump or in his wife's case plop into the car that Andrew had once again habitually backed up near the house last night after dinner. As the engine cranked and adrenaline rushed, he was amazed at how awake he suddenly felt, even though the clock on the dashboard reminded him that it had only been about five hours since he had watched his wife fall asleep to the steady rhythm of his fingers massaging her aching back—another pregnancy-related tradition.

A thin fog covered the rural roads as Andrew quickly yet cautiously drove his nervous wife toward the city limits. In all honesty, he was probably more nervous than she, but he had been trying not to show it. *Just stay calm, cool and collected*, his brother, who'd been through this before, had advised on more than one occasion.

There were a couple of routes that led to the hospital, but one meant crossing the drawbridge into downtown. The plan was to steer clear of that bridge, in case a boat or barge were passing through, although highly unlikely at this time of night. After passing the *Welcome to Historic New Bern, NC* sign, blinking stoplights guided them to a nurse and a wheelchair waiting on the curb in front of the hospital. When Andrew had made the call from his speed dial to let them know he and his wife would be there shortly, he was almost certain the baby would come out as soon as she opened the door.

Six hours later, the baby still hadn't shown his face, and Andrew couldn't find a comfortable position in the dingiest and ugliest green chair he'd seen in his entire life. He'd tried to move the nice leather one from the corner closer to his wife's bed, but when he'd tugged on the armrests, it wouldn't even budge, which led him to wonder why in the world the hospital would think that someone might actually consider stealing a chair from the maternity ward. Allowing that thought to occupy his mind once again, he shifted for what seemed like the millionth time.

As soon as he settled, Andrew felt a tingle shoot up his right leg. Immediately, he looked to his wife, asleep on her left side, facing him—the position the doctor had said would be most comfortable for both her and the baby. For a moment, he froze, not sure if his leg had fallen asleep or if the cell phone he'd slipped into his pocket earlier this morning was vibrating. The nurse had asked him to turn the ringer volume off. "Mama doesn't need distractions," she'd bluntly suggested. He'd known she was right, but he also knew that family and friends would be calling, and

Andrew wanted to be available; he would be a dad before day's end, and he wanted the whole world to know.

Quietly, he reached for the phone and checked the caller ID. *Why was Barry calling*, he contemplated before whispering "Hello" into the phone.

"Andrew, we're at the hospital," his older brother announced.

Why? Andrew wondered. Earlier, when he'd talked to Barry's wife Marie, he'd agreed to let them know when the contractions got closer. They hadn't, so he hadn't called, and he hadn't expected them just to show up, but there was something else. Something seemed off.

Before Andrew could ask any questions, Barry spoke again. "You need to get up here right away," he insisted.

Something *was* wrong, Andrew decided. His brother's tone of voice didn't match the occasion. Instead of anticipation or excitement it resembled—fear. What did he mean by *up here*?

"Up where?" Andrew asked.

On the other end of the phone, Barry could hear Andrew's breath growing heavy, the suspicion building with each moment that passed without further explanation. He didn't want to be the bearer of bad news, but he knew he had no choice in the matter.

"Mom . . . ," he finally forced himself to utter, ". . . had another heart attack."

Andrew covered his face with the hand he had used to write the largest real estate contract of his career a week ago today and listened quietly as Barry told him everything he knew in a matter of minutes. There was no way this was happening, Andrew told himself, not today. It had to be a dream, a very bad dream. He glanced at his wife; neither the phone vibrating against the keys in his pocket nor the sniffles he was trying to cover with the tissues he'd taken from the box on the nightstand after hanging up the phone had awoken her. After such an early morning, he didn't want to wake her now, especially not with this news. It would upset her, and it would upset the baby, too.

❦

The heavy hospital door closed behind Andrew as he sprinted for the elevator at the end of the hallway; the white-bricked walls seemed to be collapsing all around him, and if the nurse screaming "Slow down" (the same one who'd asked him to shut off the ringer on his phone) wanted to catch him she would have to follow the trail of tears that started in Room 209. Andrew hadn't wanted to leave his wife there all alone, but after a short moment of contemplating the situation, he'd tapped her on the shoulder, and she'd told him to go, and go fast. She had a bad feeling about his mother; he could see that in the beautiful brown eyes he hoped his baby boy would end up with. Both he and his wife had brown eyes, but eyes, Andrew had been told, were a trait that came from the mother's side, not that it mattered in their case.

As he waited inside the empty elevator for the doors to come together, Andrew, too, experienced a bad feeling swirling in the pit of his stomach. The ride to circle number four on the elevator panel seemed twice as long as it had on the way up from the car to the maternity ward, and the only thing he knew to do as he listened for the ding and watched for the little orange light was pray.

"Not now, God," he begged aloud, glaring up at the flickering fluorescent light bulbs as if they were the doorway to heaven. "After what I've been through, you can't let this happen."

God, Andrew knew, didn't always ordain everything that happened in life, but he felt, nonetheless, like He did allow life to run its course. The direction in which this was headed, however, didn't seem fair, not to anyone. The mistakes Andrew had made nine months ago couldn't be blamed on God; those were his fault, and he knew that. But this, this he didn't deserve. He needed his mother. Caleb, the baby boy whose name he and his wife had finally decided on in the car on the way to the hospital this morning, needed his grandmother.

When the silver elevator doors split open, Andrew found Barry and Marie in the ICU waiting room just around the corner.

"Where is she?" he insisted.

"They took her back a few minutes ago, Andrew. They're working on her now," Barry answered, offering his arms to his younger brother.

"What kind of odds are they giving her?" Andrew needed to know.

"They didn't say," Marie answered through a face filled with tears, moving closer and touching Andrew's arm gently while offering a Kleenex from the box that had occupied her lap since the moment she and Barry had stepped into this dreadful room.

An hour later when family was cleared to enter the room where Rosemary Callaway lay with eyes closed and IV's attached to her arms and chest, Andrew felt his knees buckle at the sight of his mother. He studied her fingers, her toes, every inch of her body—motionless and surrounded by a cold and eerie room on the fourth floor of CarolinaEast Medical Center. When the reality of the moment finally took hold of him, it didn't matter that Barry and the doctor were also in the room (Marie had gone downstairs to sit with the mother-to-be as soon as Andrew had come up), he couldn't help but let his emotions spill all over the floor that smelled of dingy mop-bucket water. His mother had survived one heart attack, and he wanted a reason to believe she would survive this one, too.

Holding tightly to his mother's right hand, Andrew looked toward the doctor.

Clipboard in hand and eyeglasses perched on the tip of his nose, the seasoned doctor had settled in near the door he had discretely closed, allowing the family a few minutes with his patient. The sight of the two men, whom he assumed were the patient's children, each holding one of their mother's hands, reminded him why he had become a doctor in the first place, but it also reminded him that emotions had a place in his line of work. Although he wanted to show both concern and respect, it wasn't his place to display sadness or fear.

"Mrs. Callaway," he finally started, giving Andrew and Barry equal eye contact as he continued, "is in a coma. You can touch her; you can talk to her, but at this point she is not going to be able to respond. I can't say how long she will be in this state. We are monitoring her closely," he assured pointing to a cluster of machines that no one in the room other than himself had any idea how to interpret. "What I can promise you is that she is in the hands of an excellent team of doctors and nurses" were the words the man in a pale green lab coat left them pondering.

As the hinges pulled the door shut, Andrew glanced at Barry. He'd always feared that this would happen again, but he had always assumed he would have his wife standing by his side, holding his empty hand. Instead, his wife was two floors below in a bed almost identical to the one he was leaning on at this very moment. While he and Barry had waited the sixty long minutes in what had seemed like the loneliest waiting room in the world, his mind had danced back and forth between his mother, his wife, and the baby boy he was so eager to meet today. Andrew had noticed that the other families who had been cooped up in the crowded space along with them hadn't seemed to know what to say or do either. He and Barry had tried to make light of the situation, but that hadn't gotten them very far.

Not much time passed before the doctor made another visit to the room, and this time Andrew remembered to ask the question he couldn't believe he'd forgotten to ask earlier: "What are the chances that my mother will die?" He wished Barry were here to help absorb whatever answer the doctor would provide, but he had taken the elevator down to the maternity ward a few minutes ago to give the wives an update and check on the baby. Marie had promised to call for Andrew the instant the baby made a move, but Barry had decided he needed a breath of fresh air, which had left Andrew alone in the room with his mother who'd given birth to him in this very hospital twenty-eight years ago. He'd been raised in this quaint southern town, and other than the four years he'd spent two hours down the road in Chapel Hill, he'd lived here his entire life. Everyone he loved was here, most of them in this hospital at this very moment.

As Andrew processed the doctor's answer to his question, he found himself crying until he couldn't muster up another tear. When the pain that accompanied the thought of losing his mother on March 14, 2014—the same day his son would be born—began to eat at his stomach, the constant hum of the monitors produced the only sound in the room. He reached across the thin white sheet for his mother's other hand and held her tighter than he ever had, even tighter than the day his father died of a heart attack.

1

Approximately Nine Months Earlier

ndrew Callaway felt a cool breeze drift across his bare back as the curtains in his bedroom danced. This was unusual for a summer morning in eastern North Carolina. Instinctively, he reached down to pull the covers higher, and he couldn't help but wonder if the air-conditioner had malfunctioned. At times like this it would be nice to have someone to snuggle up next to, he thought, someone to share body heat with. A simple smile eased onto his face as a moment of reality suddenly struck him—in less than two weeks there would be someone to fill the empty spot his bed had known for so many years. His dream of finding a woman to share the rest of his life with would be fulfilled, and now as he shivered even with the blankets wound tightly around his body, he couldn't think of anyone he would rather take that journey with than Meredith Hastings.

When she'd given him a kiss goodbye beneath the front porch light late last night, he couldn't imagine life with anyone else. It seemed like she was the only woman he'd ever kissed, the only woman he'd ever loved, and the only woman he wanted to share intimate moments with. Even though he'd dated a handful, maybe a couple handfuls, of other women, the memories he'd made with them seemed so faint compared to what he'd shared with Meredith. When out and about, he still noticed other beautiful women; otherwise, he would have to question if he were a man. After a few months of dating Meredith, it was like a light had blinked on in his head and he'd known she was the one. He couldn't even remember what an attraction to another woman felt like, and it made him feel pretty confident about his decision to be able to admit that without having to cross his fingers and hide them behind his back.

The two of them had spent the entire day together yesterday; it began with breakfast downtown at Baker's Kitchen—a local favorite touting the best French toast in town—and the evening ended with a glass of wine beneath a Carolina moon on Andrew's back deck. If they'd poured a couple more of those, it might have ended in this bed, and instead of him being alone and freezing this morning, they might both be freezing and beating themselves up for giving into an act they'd chosen to save for the honeymoon. Andrew still couldn't fathom that they'd actually made it to this point in their relationship without having sex. Although there had been plenty of times where they'd come close, a whole lot of times, actually. Belts had been stripped off; clothes had flown across the room; and hands had traveled to places that are hard to pull away from, but somehow they'd managed not to totally give in to the natural urges of the human body.

Parting ways at the end of the night had always been the most difficult part for Andrew, especially lately. He seemed to be just as excited about falling asleep with Meredith every night and waking up with her every morning as he was about making love with his soon-to-be bride. In fact, a kiss from Meredith's sweet lips would have been a much more pleasant way to wake up this morning. Hopefully, her breath would smell better than his did today, he thought, catching an unwanted whiff.

As thoughts of his fiancée continued to flood his mind, he peered across his king-sized bed and discovered the source of the cold air. If Meredith were lying next to him, he was sure she would ask him to brave the cold, wooden floor, which at the moment looked like an ocean, to shut the windows, but for obvious reasons—namely the goose bumps that had joined the hair on his arms—he didn't feel like Columbus, at least not this early in the morning. He wished now that he would have let Meredith buy him those slippers she'd wanted to get him in May for his twenty-eighth birthday. "Men don't wear slippers," he had told her, but if he had a pair right now, he knew they would be wedged between the floor and his bare feet, although he probably would have left them in the bathroom where he left his shirt after brushing his teeth last night.

Suddenly remembering that the local weather channel had been forecasting a temperature drop for a week, Andrew let out an aggravated grunt. How had he forgotten that?

"Oh crap!" he suddenly shouted, abruptly breaking free of the cocoon tangled around his body, and in nothing but his boxers running past the open windows. *Forget the weather* . . . how in the world had he forgotten that he was supposed to be at Meredith's first thing this morning to take her and her mother to the airport? She was going to strangle him. Ten miles away, he could picture her now, flinging her arms in the air and shouting, "I booked the flight at nine o'clock instead of seven o'clock just so you would have plenty of time to get out of bed, take a shower, and get your butt over here." This wasn't good he thought for about the fifth time, as he jumped into the clothes he'd worn yesterday as fast as a teenage boy caught in bed with his girlfriend. He managed to skip half the steps in the stairwell and made it into the kitchen to get his keys before remembering that Meredith was supposed to be his wake-up call.

For a split second, he thought he might be off the hook, then he spotted the blinking light on the answering machine. No reason to bother checking it, he already knew it would play Meredith's voice, most likely saying something akin to *how do you not hear a phone ringing*? She'd said it before and he was sure he'd hear it again, so there was no sense in taking the time to listen to the message.

With his cell phone in one hand and keys in the other, he bolted out the front door.

The leather seats in Andrew's ten-year-old Land Rover Discovery reminded him why he should have left his shorts on the bathroom floor and snatched the pair of jeans Meredith had folded and put away for him yesterday afternoon. The third day of June had brought with it temperatures that felt like a brisk day in late autumn; it couldn't be one degree above fifty, he guessed, as he cranked the ignition and glanced at his cell phone. *Four missed calls*, all from Meredith. She'd always hated that he turned off his ringer volume when he went to bed. "This is why," he knew he would hear later. He figured Meredith had probably called the home phone twice as many times, but the only landline he had in the house was the one downstairs with the old answering machine hooked up to it, and it rarely woke him when he was sleeping soundly. Those were Andrew's lousy excuses along with the fact that he'd forgotten to set his alarm. The only person he would be able to blame for oversleeping was himself—and Conan O'Brien since he'd kept him up so late last night. Now he understood why people said that red-haired man was nothing but trouble.

The house that Andrew had quickly left in his rearview mirror could easily suit a family of six. The place hadn't been quite as appealing when he'd bought it five years ago, not long after moving back home to New Bern after college. He could still remember it at first sight—shutters hanging by a strand, shingles dangling from the roof, and a line of holly bushes that had grown higher than the windows on the first story. Every wall inside and out required a minimum of three coats of fresh paint before moving in. The house had been on the market for over a year when he'd finally decided to make an offer. As the listing agent, Andrew had gotten to know the seller, Mr. Lawson, well, and because no one else had made an offer on the place and Andrew had worked so hard to sell it, Mr. Lawson accepted his offer. At the time, a fixer-upper was about all he could afford, but this house wasn't just a fixer-upper and he knew that. The land alone was worth more than the price Mr. Lawson had taken for it. When Andrew bought the place he had only been in the real-estate business for a short time and hardly anyone in town even knew his name, at least not as a real-estate agent. He'd sold a small house to his high school math teacher and another to the youth pastor at his church. These days, however, the name *Andrew Callaway* circulated around town a little better, and as soon as he could close a deal on Gary Tyndall's place—one of the most luxurious homes in New Bern—he would be able to make a major dent in that thirty-year first-time home buyers loan he'd signed without knowing where the money would come from.

Just last week, he'd listed the gorgeous thirteen-acre estate in every real-estate magazine in the region and on websites that spanned the entire United States. His commission would allow him to build up the savings account he'd drained to make the needed repairs to his house the summer he'd moved in. He and his brother had spent countless hours fixing up the place; neither of them considered themselves to be a carpenter by any means, but they'd grown up hammering nails and rolling paintbrushes with their dad who'd been quite the handyman in his day. With a tool belt and a little bit of time, he could build just about anything. When Andrew made the decision to buy the house, he'd done so with the plan of it being an investment property, but after all the sweat and time he'd put into it, not to mention a few ounces of blood, plans had changed. Plus Meredith would have killed him if he had given up a three-acre lot on the river. Such property was hard to come by these days, even in a town as sparsely populated as New Bern. More and more tourists were hearing about this sweet little southern town, and it seemed waterfront property had tripled in price over the past ten years. Other than sitting on a goldmine, Andrew knew this place would be a nice place to raise a family, which was something he was looking forward to.

Weaving in and out of traffic, Andrew, cell phone in one hand and the steering wheel in the other, listened as Meredith rumbled nearly every word he had imagined she would. It didn't surprise him when she'd answered on the first ring, and he found out then that ten, not eight, was the number of times she had called the house trying to wake him. He'd been a heavy sleeper since childhood, and once again he found himself apologizing for oversleeping, and for some reason Meredith always seemed more intimidating than the school principal had. Before getting off the phone, Meredith begged him to hurry but made him promise not to speed.

Meredith's brother, Eric—decked out in a camouflage jumpsuit and a bright orange cap with a silhouette of an eight-point buck just above the bill—was standing on her front porch smoking a cigarette when Andrew's wheels ground to a halt. If only he could honk the horn and Meredith and her mother would come out, Andrew thought, it would save some sort of verbal altercation that seemed inevitable with Eric these days.

It didn't take long. "Mom and Meredith are pissed at you," Eric said, using more than a hint of southern twang. "Their flight is scheduled to depart at ten-thirty with or without them."

Andrew climbed the steps, rolling his eyes as he passed Eric. "Thanks, buddy. I didn't know that," he rumbled. What he thought about saying sounded more like: *If you weren't Meredith's brother, I would smack that grin right off that circle you call a face.*

A ball of chubby redness sat atop Eric's broad shoulders connected by a nearly invisible neck, making him close to six feet tall. At the ripe young age of thirty-one, he still lived at home with his mother, and since Andrew had started dating Meredith three years ago, he'd watched the man bounce around from one dead-end job to another. The highlight of his career to this point had been selling used cars at Ralph Hutchins' *Kar-Mart*. Spelling car with a "K" was Ralph's idea of a genius marketing plan, which he developed after taking one marketing class at the local community college. Similar to Eric, Ralph had dropped out after a semester, and when Eric joined him at the lot he came up with a marketing plan of his own—sell used tractors on the lot. Everyone in town knew Ralph as the epitome of a used car salesman, but somehow he managed to move enough cars to stay in business. Ralph, of course, loved Eric's idea in the beginning, but when three months passed and the ten tractors he bought at the auction in Greenville were still sitting on his lot, Eric once again found himself in his mother's rocking chair thumbing through the Sunday classifieds.

Eric had once told Andrew that his goal in life was to own a doublewide, which was fine if that was what he wanted. Instead of saving his paychecks for the down payment that he complained about not having enough money to afford, he blew his earnings on hunting equipment and supplies. The man had enough rifles to lead the Confederate army, and his knife collection looked like it could belong to the Smithsonian. In all honesty, if Eric spent any more time in the woods, he might turn into the tree that his attire resembled year round.

Once past the gatekeeper, Andrew began looking for Meredith inside the house. The smell of the oatmeal cookies she'd promised to bake and leave for him to eat while she was out of town lured him into the kitchen, where he found her mother, the one and only Sylvia Hastings.

"Hey, handsome," she complimented, greeting him with a hug. Her natural ability to flirt was a trait Andrew thanked God she hadn't passed down to Meredith. He couldn't imagine being with a woman who found it necessary to touch every man she talked to at least a dozen times during the course of one conversation. "How is my future son-in-law?"

Before Andrew could conjure up a response, she picked out the largest cookie, poured a glass of milk, and pulled out a seat. "Meredith said you haven't had breakfast yet." She paused. "I guess you already know she is upset with you for running late *again.*"

"The doorman reminded me," Andrew said laughing only a little, since Eric was her son.

"What are you wearing? You could have dressed up a little more."

Andrew glanced at his outfit wondering when a pair of khaki shorts, a heather gray T-shirt with a green stripe across the chest, and flip flops had become underdressed for a trip to the airport. At least he didn't show up at job interviews dressed in camos like her one and only darling son. That kind of attire paid dividends only when applying at gun ranges and outdoor stores. Unfortunately, Eric had already worked at every one of those within a thirty-mile radius, and now he had a plan to open his own hunting and fishing shop. When Eric had asked Andrew for advice on renting a small store, Eric had gotten aggravated when Andrew told him he'd be better off saving some money first, but Andrew had found out that the only way Eric knew how to save money was by changing his own oil.

Finishing his cookie, Andrew said, "Thanks," and then followed Meredith's mother into the hallway heading for Meredith's room.

"Here's your man," she said, delivering Andrew to Meredith, focusing on the mirror in her bathroom.

Andrew touched Meredith's shoulder gently and reached down to kiss the top of her head.

"Are you guys packed and ready to go?" he asked.

Meredith rolled her eyes, wanting to be angry with him for oversleeping and not hearing the phone ring, but knowing that she didn't want the little time they would have to spend together this morning to be ruined by a bad mood. "Yes," she said, drawing out the word. "*We* actually woke up on time this morning and got ready because *someone* has to make it to Tampa to finalize plans for *our* wedding." She decided that she couldn't let him off the hook without giving him somewhat of a hard time. "Remember us talking about all the things I have to do: check out the block of rooms we have booked for our guests and family, confirm times and locations for dinners and parties, and make a million other arrangements necessary to ensure an unforgettable occasion," she said with a painted smile.

Andrew and Meredith had picked Tampa, Florida, as the location for their wedding because ever since Meredith was a child her family had vacationed there regularly, and as a little girl, she had fallen in love with a quaint little white church on the bay. "I want to get married here one day," she'd said to Andrew the first time he visited Tampa with her.

"As long as you and the preacher are there, I can live without the other stuff," Andrew responded.

Meredith glared at him through the mirror as she continued to apply a light shade of lavender eyeliner. If she didn't love him as much as she did, she would pull a tube of lipstick from one of the bags on the countertop and fling it in his direction. *Better not*, she decided, he might decide not to marry her if she started acting like her mother.

Andrew stole a peek at his watch. "It's only a few minutes after nine. You have over an hour before takeoff," he said, giving her a kiss on the cheek.

He picked up one of her make-up accessories that he wouldn't be able to identify if someone were holding a gun to his head and began squeezing his nose with it. "What is this?"

Meredith tried not to laugh, but even in the midst of a morning filled with frustration, the sound of his nasal voice caused her to snicker. "Give me that, and it's called an eyelash curler," she said, straightening her posture while trying to wipe the smirk off her face. "If you think you can come in here and butter me up with your wit, you're wrong. You were supposed to be here an hour ago, Andrew Callaway, so we could get checked in before the plane actually starts rolling down the runway."

Andrew crammed the last chunk of his second cookie in his mouth as Meredith began to curl her golden blond hair. "I thought you said you were ready," he said. "You're going to the airport, not the *Grammy's*," he went on to remind her.

Meredith shook her head. "Don't talk with your mouth full, Andrew," she instructed as though he was six and she'd already told him twice. "I was ready, but I had to find something to calm my nerves since you are *always*," she said, making sure to emphasize the word *always*, "running late."

Standing close, he placed one hand on either side of her hips and gazed into her eyes through the mirror. "I'm here now," he sympathized, hoping his boyish charm would gain back her confidence in his ability to come through for her.

As he held a cheesy grin on his face, she smiled once more.

Andrew left Meredith to her primping and returned to the mountain of luggage nearly hiding the bricked fireplace. Once again, his eyes swelled as he counted six large bags next to a stack of firewood he'd chopped from the wooded area beside his house a while back. The pieces of oak served more as a decoration than anything, and they were so dry that he could almost hear them begging for someone to toss in a match which might not have been a bad idea on a morning like this. Above, the cherry oak glazed mantle held Andrew's and Meredith's engagement photograph and a few others from trips and holidays. Each one held a story— a lot of stories. Their time together had created many happy memories, and, of course, like all relationships, there had also been some they'd rather not remember, but those seemed to be few and far between. Overall, they got along well and in time they'd adjusted to one another's personalities and quirks.

"It's a vacation, not a month's stay in Paris," Andrew uttered, curling the first bag. "They won't let you take all this on one airplane," he informed Sylvia as she brought out another bag to add to the pile.

"I take this much every time, darling," she said with a wink. "My bags are the ones on the left. Be very careful with the black one, it has fragile items in it."

The screen door screamed as Eric walked through and then proceeded to stand in the doorway, watching Andrew strap a bag on each shoulder and pick up another with his right hand. He would've taken another in his left hand if he hadn't tweaked his index finger during a heated soccer match yesterday evening. He'd been running alongside one of the other team's players, attempting to steal the ball, when somehow his hand had gotten kicked in the process. Ice and an Advil had conquered the swelling, but the finger still throbbed if anything even so much as grazed it. He'd found that out the hard way this morning on the stair rail.

"Let me get the door, the one you haven't fixed for Meredith yet," Eric offered, propping it open with his foot. "I think I got some WD-40 out in the truck. It'll shut that squeal right up."

Andrew furrowed his brow. *Why don't you help with the*

*luggage instead? Or on second thought, spray that WD-40 up your—*Andrew took a deep breath knowing he needed to clear his thoughts before he said something he couldn't take back. Eric was Meredith's brother after all, and he had promised her that he would try his best not to argue with Eric anymore, at least not until after the honeymoon.

Keeping his mouth shut, Andrew went outside, and while he loaded the bags, Sylvia and Eric made themselves comfortable on the porch swing.

"Did you get a confirmation?" Eric asked his mother quietly, leaning toward her to make sure Andrew couldn't hear what they were discussing.

Sylvia plucked a Marlboro from the pack she'd opened at the table when Andrew was eating his cookie. "The plan is underway," she said as she rolled the lighter under her finger.

"This is going to be a great wedding present."

Sylvia lit one for Eric, too.

"I can't wait to see how they react," Sylvia replied through a cloud of smoke.

Andrew could see the two of them through the tinted back glass, and he couldn't help but wonder what they were scheming— probably some childish decorations for the rental car after the reception, like condoms on the antenna and windshield wipers, or *Honk if You're Horny* signs, not that he hadn't done similar things to his friends on their wedding days.

"Andrew," Eric called out "Got any WD-40 out there in your Land Labrador?" he asked, chuckling in between every other word as he spoke.

Knowing he was still shielded by his vehicle, Andrew shook his head and rolled his eyes again. "Land Rover, Eric. Not Land Retriever or Land Hound or any other of your poor hunting dogs that never get to chase the deer you can't seem to hit with your high powered sniper rifle with a telescope that could find a grain of sand on the moon." Whoops, he thought, that one slipped out. Thank goodness Meredith was still in the house.

Andrew knew the only reason Eric wasn't out in the woods now was because hunting season had yet to start. Once bow season kicked off in September, he would disappear from dusk until dawn. *Bummer.*

"Watch it buddy row. I almost tagged that ten-pointer last season," Eric reminded him. "And if you knew anything about hunting, you'd know it's illegal to hunt at night; that's when the moon is out, you know?"

It was always *almost*, Andrew thought, deciding not to respond to Eric's wisecrack about the moon. *And why did he always call people buddy row?* "That's good, Eric; maybe you'll actually shoot one this year, and we can have some meat to store in that freezer you bought—you know, the empty one sitting on your mother's back porch."

Letting that comment fly, Andrew knew that he now had two slips that he might have to explain to Meredith. It wasn't that he and Eric really disliked each other; they just seemed to clash. They'd actually had plenty of good times together. Andrew had been hunting and fishing with him on several occasions, and they'd actually had a pretty good time together.

Eric didn't respond, and for a short moment Andrew felt a little guilty about letting that one slip. Eric just made it so easy sometimes.

He watched Eric leave the porch and walk to his jacked up truck, the toy he spent his time and money on during the off-season. When cranked, the muffler sounded like a drag racing car, and the tires on his rig came up to his shoulders. In a swift motion, Eric dropped the tailgate and lifted himself into the bed where he began to dig through the toolbox. Inside the back window, Andrew could see a thirty-aught-six and a thirty-thirty rifle that occupied the two slots on Eric's gun rack at all times. On the duct taped vinyl seat below sat a digital camera that Eric spent a grand on just last week. His mother had been encouraging him to find a new hobby, and now he had one. Andrew hadn't yet been able to figure out what that was all about. After tinkering in the box for a few moments, Eric pulled out a blue can and went back to the porch. Andrew made two more trips from the house to his vehicle while Sylvia supervised Eric as he sprayed the hinges on the screen door. After the first trip to the car, Andrew had found himself wishing he'd known Meredith and her mother were going to have this much luggage, so he could have taken out his soccer equipment to make more room. Instead, he pushed it to the side and squeezed everything in as best he could.

2

The airport sat on the outskirts of town, and for a city the size of New Bern, the chain link fenced-in parking lot appeared close to capacity. When Andrew drove past the gate and swerved into the drop-off lane, he took a quick peek at the watch on his wrist. He'd gotten them to the airport in the time promised, and he could tell that Meredith was trying to ignore the proud look on his face.

By the time he could load all seven bags onto the baggage cart, a dressed up golf cart with a rectangular green light on the roof came cruising up to the curb. Out stepped a chubby little man with a bit of a limp.

"Andrew," the driver with a security badge on his chest proclaimed. "I was about to make sure you weren't going to leave this here vehicle unattended, but if I had recognized it was you, I wouldn't even have turned on the light."

Sylvia made sure to guard her mouth as she whispered to Meredith, "It's a good thing Andrew has connections with the Rent-A-Cop."

"Charles," Andrew replied to the man in uniform, "you've got to take any kind of action you can get, right?"

Charles had been the head security guard at the airport for as

22

long as Andrew had been coming here to pick up clients. Just last week he'd come here to escort a businessman from the Greensboro area over to the Tyndall estate, but like the other two people who had looked at the place since it hit the market, he too had seemed overly interested until he found out the asking price was non-negotiable. Andrew knew it was going to take someone with more money than he knew what to do with to buy the mansion.

"I'll watch your vehicle while you're inside," Charles offered.

Andrew and Meredith left her mother outside with Charles and a cigarette, and when they reached the circularly shaped ticketing booth inside the one-story red bricked building, they could barely see the thin-haired elderly woman on the other side. They waited patiently as she assisted the young couple in front of them. "She reminds me of a librarian," Andrew said in a whisper, and Meredith instinctively punched his arm. The attendant wore glasses at the tip of her nose with beads dangling around her neck, and if she was five feet tall, it was because of the heels.

"You better not get us kicked off our plane before we ever board it."

Meredith couldn't help but notice that the couple in front of them had one hand each tucked into the other's back pocket, and she had to smother her laughter in Andrew's armpit when the man squeezed the woman and said, "I love you, Baby Cakes."

"I love you too, Snookums," the woman replied, meeting his glazed eyes.

Andrew's eyebrows rose, and he tried to hide his snicker with his hand, but when Meredith purposefully snorted into his shirt, they both had to turn the other way. Meredith knew Andrew was thinking the same thing she was—nicknames like "darling" and "honey" were one thing, but if he ever, with a straight face, called her one of the pet names that had just spewed out of that couple's mouths she would be more than embarrassed. *Who wouldn't?* She thought.

Pacing the sidewalk, Sylvia finished smoking her cigarette before smothering it with the heel of her shoe. "You won't arrest me for littering will you, Charlie," she said with a wink.

Charles, puffing out his chest and sucking in his stomach, smiled. He'd always liked Andrew, but the reason he'd offered to keep an eye on his vehicle had more to do with the opportunity of chatting with the prettiest woman he'd seen at the airport in a month. Red-haired women had always been more attractive to him than blondes or brunettes, and something about the way Sylvia flicked the ashes from that cigarette turned him on. Now he found himself wishing that he hadn't stopped at the gas station on his way to work this morning for two jelly-filled Krispy Kreme doughnuts. Since his wife passed away four years ago, he had only been on one date, and he knew the fact that he'd been overeating probably had something to do with that. He could see himself taking Sylvia up on the offer he couldn't believe she had made just moments ago.

"No ma'am, I wouldn't think of it."

"Charlie, when I get back from Florida I'm going to expect an answer about that ride in your patrol vehicle. You won't mind if I smoke while we cruise the lot, will you?"

On the ride over, Andrew had enforced his *no smoking* policy on Sylvia, and the entire trip she'd wanted to pull her hair out. She figured he would have made an exception for her this one time since she would be on an airplane without a cigarette for over an hour. Trying to meet him halfway, she had even agreed to slide over behind Meredith in the passenger seat so the smoke would blow out the window as he drove. But no, Andrew never let anyone smoke in his car or house, he'd said. She continued to explain the dilemma to Charles as he walked her into the airport.

"I bet Andrew doesn't tell his clients they can't smoke," she said. "He even said he didn't have a cigarette lighter. All cars these days are equipped with cigarette lighters, Charlie. I bet your golf cart even has one." Before realizing that Sylvia was elaborating, Charles began to shake his head side to side, and Sylvia ignored him and continued talking. "You should have seen the look on Andrew's face when I pointed out the lighter below the climate control he had set on heat. Heat, Charlie. If he'd worn warmer clothing, he wouldn't need the heater, and I wouldn't have had to take off my jacket."

Andrew and Meredith stepped to the counter as the overly excited couple bounced away hand in hand as if they were off to see the Wizard, the wonderful Wizard of Oz. Meredith was glad to overhear that they would be spending their honeymoon in Hawaii; the thought of flying with the two of them any longer than the first leg of their trip seemed more life-threatening than jumping out of an airplane at thirty-five thousand feet—without a parachute.

"How can I help you folks?" asked the woman, surrounded by a counter that made her look like she was in a playpen, as she continued to eye the honeymooners she had wished off. Charles delivered Sylvia just as Meredith gave the lady her last name.

With one hand on the baggage cart, Andrew watched as the woman typed Meredith's last name into the computer one peck at a time.

"I'll need to see your ID's," the attendant requested before giving Andrew instructions for the luggage. "Freddie will make sure it gets loaded on the plane," she promised, pointing to a middle-aged man who'd come up and stood beside her while she'd been looking up the tickets.

Expecting him to complain about the amount of luggage for only two passengers, Andrew made small talk with the man. But as he reached for the last bag, it seemed he hadn't even noticed.

In the meantime, Meredith had handed the lady her license

and was now watching her hold the ID close to her glasses as if she were examining it through a microscope for fingerprints. When the lady finally began to peck again, they all waited patiently as the computer processed the information nearly as slow as she typed.

Eventually, the printer spit out two tickets, and then they headed in the direction the lady had pointed.

"We'll need to run or you'll never make it in time," Andrew said sarcastically, tugging at Meredith's arm.

Upon finding their gate, Andrew and Meredith also found Snookums and Baby Cakes, whom Sylvia had overheard them mimicking. "Who are Snookums and Baby Cakes?" she finally blurted out, loud enough for everyone within a thirty-yard radius to hear. The couple's tongues came out of each other's mouths for the first time since they'd taken their place in line.

Meredith turned her back and spoke directly into her mother's ear, "They are in front of us in line."

This time, Andrew smothered his laughter in Meredith's shoulder, and until the boarding call sounded over the loudspeaker, he couldn't help but snicker every time he glanced over at Snookums and Baby Cakes.

Clinging to his side, Meredith ran her fingers down his back, not sure which she was going to miss more, his crooked smile or the smell of his Old Spice aftershave. It had always made her want to rip his clothes off.

"I'll pick you up at the airport in Tampa on Sunday afternoon, okay?" Meredith reminded Andrew.

Andrew furrowed his brow, wondering what he was going to do without Meredith for an entire week. When she'd gone to Seattle last summer on a business trip for the bank, he'd spent most of his time at the office. Lately, he had been trying to work less. Fifty hour workweeks wouldn't cut it once he and Meredith tied the knot. She would want him home for dinner in the evenings, and he knew that is where he needed to be. Bachelors could spend countless hours working, but husbands had to be unselfish, and he knew he was ready to take that step. As for this week, the to-do list he'd made last night—starting with trimming the hedges and ending with building benches around the deck he and his brother built last summer—would keep him busy. He doubted the latter would happen, but he'd jotted it down just in case he ended up with extra free time.

"Thanks for bringing us here, sweetie," Meredith said, reaching out for a hug.

Ticket in hand, Sylvia made her way to Andrew. "Give me a hug, too," she demanded. "If it wasn't for you, I wouldn't have met Charlie," she said, patting him on the back.

Charlie? "You mean Charles?"

"I like to call him Charlie, and he said it's okay."

Calling him Charlie was most likely her first step in seducing him, Andrew figured. "Charles is a good man. You better not break his heart," he pleaded.

"I won't," Sylvia assured. "We'll miss you this week."

Andrew nodded.

"I'm sorry you can't come with us, honey," Meredith said with a frown occupying the face that won her first place in the local beauty pageant her senior year in high school.

"Me, too, but you know I have to stay behind this time, so I'll be able to have ten days in Cancun."

Meredith's eyes lit up at the thought of honeymooning in Cancun in less than two weeks. She wrapped her arms around Andrew's neck, pressing her body tightly against his. "I can't wait," she said provocatively, snatching a handful of his rear end.

Caught off guard by the visit from Meredith's hand, Andrew twitched. "Me, too," he reciprocated. "I hope you have fun until I get there."

Sylvia winked. "Don't worry about us, Andrew; we won't party too much, but two beautiful, single women shouldn't have any problem finding guys on the beaches. I won't let Meredith do anything she shouldn't do, though."

Yeah right, Andrew thought. Not once had he ever suspected Meredith would even consider cheating on him, but if he had to depend on her mother to discourage it, he might as well throw in the towel. She'd cheated on every husband and probably every boyfriend she ever had, including Meredith's father. Sylvia would meet men while in Tampa; there was no doubt in Andrew's mind about that. He just hoped she wouldn't attempt to drag his future wife into the middle of her charades. Actually, now that he thought about it, sending Meredith off with her mother seemed nearly as risky as cutting her loose with a group of freshmen sorority girls.

"Mom, I'm not single, and I'm not going bar hopping with you."

"You're single until you're married, and I don't see a ring on your finger."

Meredith extended her arm, bent her wrist ever so slightly, and stretched her fingers toward her mother's face—a motion that had become second nature since Andrew proposed six months ago. Most people probably thought she was showing off the diamond wrapped around her finger, but she was more excited about the man who would soon sleep beside her every night for the rest of her life.

"I mean an actual wedding ring, dear."

Andrew rolled his eyes, wondering how Meredith had turned out normal. At that moment, a crackly voice came over the PA system. The time for all passengers to board Flight 466 headed to Charlotte, where Meredith and her mother would spend their layover, had come.

Before Meredith and her mother walked through the narrow hallway that led them outside where they had to cross a piece of the runway before boarding a small jet, Meredith's and Andrew's lips met; they shared a long kiss goodbye.

On the plane Meredith found a window seat near the rear, and she stuffed her carry-on into the luggage compartment above her head. Her mother nestled in beside her and continued to ramble on the subject of promiscuity as Meredith silently counted the seats in front of them; twenty-four in total and only ten had been filled when the wheels began to roll. Thankfully, Snookums and Baby Cakes had chosen to sit up front, and before the pilot had a chance to ask passengers to turn off all electronic equipment, Meredith punched Andrew's number into her cell phone and told him where to look for her as the plane began to taxi the runway.

Andrew stood on the inside of a large glass window and waited until he spotted Meredith's face through one of the tiny windows on the side of the airplane. Waving the entire time, he watched the plane roll past the building. The distance between them began to grow, and Meredith couldn't help but think about the smile that had stretched across his tanned, unshaven face as her hand had fallen from his just minutes ago. "I love you," he'd said. "And I'll see you soon." She could still taste his lips on hers, and she found herself hoping the sensation would last the entire week.

3

ndrew woke up the following morning with the image of
Meredith's face etched in his mind. He thought about
how cute she'd looked peeking through the small window
in the airplane. He had to admit he missed her already, and he
found himself wishing he had given into the pressure to fill one
of those empty seats she had told him about. A week without his
future mother-in-law, however, had given him a valid reason to
lean in the other direction.

Andrew turned over in his bed to look at the alarm clock then
picked up his phone to see if he had missed anything.

"Ouch," he yelled, "ouch, ouch, ouch."

He started to squirm and shook his hand as if it would help
relieve the pain. After setting the phone back in place, he'd rolled
onto his back to stretch and in the process rammed his fingers into
the headboard. Groaning and staring at the speckles on the
ceiling, he held them tight, and the pain seemed to slowly fade as
his mind drifted back to Meredith.

Meredith . . .

She hadn't called, he realized, and all of a sudden the pain in
his hand seemed minimal. They'd talked during her layover
yesterday, which had stranded Meredith and her mother in

Charlotte until ten o'clock last night. The two of them had been irate about that, but Meredith was supposed to call when they landed in Tampa. *Maybe she called the landline?* Andrew thought as he caught a glimpse of the glow of the television on the dresser across from his bed. He must have fallen asleep watching Jay Leno.

He ran downstairs to the answering machine. The green light was flashing. Hopefully that was a good sign; he pressed play, and the robot-machine voice began to talk. It told him that there were twelve unplayed messages—not a good sign, he thought. That meant someone had been trying really hard to get ahold of him. With that thought in mind, he found himself hoping for the best yet preparing for the worst. His mind began to tell him all of the things a person didn't want to hear at a time like this. The television, he immediately thought, if the plane had crashed, it would be all over the news.

"Crap," he said as the first message began to play. He had forgotten to listen to the messages Meredith left yesterday morning. "Andrew, wake up sweetie," the first one started. He pushed save before it could play out. For the next, he listened only to the date and time, quickly pressing save once he found out it followed the first by only a matter of minutes. The following eight were also from Meredith, and all from yesterday morning. There was no need in listening to those messages right now; they could wait until later. Andrew glanced at the FOX News anchorman, doing a story on health care, and felt a sigh of relief. He flipped the channel to CNN, and as soon as he realized the reporter was covering an investigation on a Fortune 500 company, he pressed mute.

Then came message number eleven, a new voice, the frantic tone immediately grabbing Andrew's attention.

A confused expression covering her youthful face, Candice pushed through the door to Brooke's office. "I can't find Andrew anywhere," she exclaimed. "Do you know where he is?"

Brooke forced a smile. What was it with interns; did they not teach common sense in college these days? A month into the job and Candice still hadn't figured out Andrew's routine. Five days a week, he walked through the front door and directly by the reception desk, usually occupied by Candice, at exactly ten o'clock. That meant she had said hello to Andrew at least twenty times as she watched him walk toward his office with a cappuccino and a newspaper in his hand.

"Candice, Andrew works from home in the mornings, you know that."

"But he's not answering his phone. I've called him twice at home."

"He's probably in the shower or outside checking the mail. Is there something I can help you with?" Brooke asked, hoping she could calm Candice down before she had a panic attack. Brooke could see her now, sprawled out on the floor waving her hands and screaming to the top of her lungs. That was the type of person Candice was, a little—actually a lot—high-strung. The Ritalin must not be working today, she figured.

Candice hesitated before answering. "There's been kind of an emergency . . ." she trailed off, taking a moment to stare at her shoes as if conjuring up the nerve to continue.

Brooke waited impatiently. *Spit it out already.* "What kind of emergency?" she finally pried.

"Well, my neighbor keeps calling and complaining that my dog is digging up her flowerbed."

Brooke furrowed her brow. *An emergency involves blood or broken bones or interns beaten by a real estate sign like the one in the corner of her office. Not a dog searching for a cool spot to bury his body in the summertime.* "So go home and put him back in the fence or the house or on a chain or wherever it is you keep him," Brooke instructed. Did that really need Andrew's immediate attention? Had Candice actually called him at home over her dog? Brooke had to ask, "Are you telling me that you left Andrew two messages about your dog?"

Candice took a shy step backward trying to work her way to the door before Brooke could hurt her feelings. That had happened a couple times since she'd been working here. She'd only wanted to make sure she was following the rules. "I only left one. I hung up the second time."

Andrew pressed the erase button. Why in the world had Candice called to ask if it was okay if she went home to get her dog out of her neighbor's yard? He shook his head and waited impatiently for the next message.

"Hey sweetie, it's me, Meredith."

Andrew's eyelids sank shut, and he released what felt like ten pounds of air that had been building up in his lungs while he'd been praying for Meredith's voice to follow today's date. "I'm so sorry I didn't call you last night," she said. "My cell phone battery died; Mom couldn't find hers, and by the time we made it to the hotel, I figured you would be asleep. I hope you weren't worried too much. I set my alarm for seven-thirty this morning so that I could leave you a message for when you woke up. I don't know why I didn't just do that last night. I know you never wake up when the phone rings. Well, I'm here in sunny Florida; call me when you get a chance. I miss you and I love you."

Andrew took another deep breath. That had been way too scary. The thought of living without Meredith is a thought he never wanted to experience again. What would he do without her? He found himself wondering. He would definitely forget to pay his house payment, he decided, inspecting an envelope he'd picked up from the counter that Meredith had sealed, addressed, and stamped. Her handwriting was so beautiful, he noticed. He had always wished *he* could make cursive look like something more than chicken scratch. So did his employees, he'd found out from Brooke, and that was why he stuck to print these days.

Brooke Taylor was his right hand wo-MAN. She'd been by his side since he started the real estate agency after graduating from the University of North Carolina at Chapel Hill. He had managed to save up five thousand dollars waiting tables throughout college, but like everyone else whose parents weren't loaded, he had three times that much to pay back in student loans. Thankfully, the interest rate was minimal. The savings had afforded him a computer, business cards, and a few other necessities he'd needed to open the doors of the one and only Callaway Agency.

The note on top of the house payment reminded Andrew that he needed to drop it in the mailbox today since Meredith wouldn't be able to take the payment to work with her on the usual due date. Carolina Bank was lucky to have her as their branch manager, and he was lucky to have her, too. Now he was listening to and cherishing every word on all ten messages Meredith left yesterday morning. The latter ones weren't quite as sweet, but she still said, "I love you" before hanging up every single time.

With a smile on his face, Andrew skipped across the cool wooden floor as he headed to the dryer for a pair of socks. They felt nice on his feet, he thought, after slipping them on and filling the seat in front of his laptop computer to inspect a website on which he'd had the Tyndall home listed. The photo didn't look so great, he thought, but the write-up Brooke had put together made Gary's place sound as luxurious as it was. When Andrew closed that page, he began sorting through his email and, as always, discovered a SPAM filled inbox. Which left him wondering if anyone would ever find a real solution to that problem?

A few minutes later, he shut off the computer and headed upstairs where he found out that the sheets he had hastily thrown to the ground on his way to the answering machine were covering the floor. He tossed them across the bed, his alternative to making it. Why spend ten minutes neatly tucking corners and fluffing pillows, he'd always said, just to mess it up again tonight. Anyway, it wasn't like there was anyone to impress. Meredith was out of town, and if any of his guy friends came over, they wouldn't care.

After going back downstairs for a glass of water, Andrew leaned over the bathroom sink and spit out a mouth full of toothpaste. He always brushed his teeth before reaching for the shower nozzle to adjust it to just the right position. Luke warm is how he liked it, and as he slowly began to remove the clothes from his body, he listened as the water rained steadily onto the tub floor. He tossed each piece of loose clothing into the laundry basket in the far corner, missing the mark with his burgundy boxers. *I bet I couldn't do that again*, he thought, openly amazed at how they were dangling from the linen closet doorknob. He smirked and then pulled the shower curtain shut.

On summer nights Andrew liked to sleep in boxers and an old T-shirt. He had a drawer full of tees he'd received from sponsoring charitable events. Most of his business's marketing dollars went to help organizations like Relay for Life and Special Olympics. He'd always chosen to spend his budget on meaningful promotions rather than advertising with money-hungry television and radio stations. Not that sponsoring non-profits was a one-way street because it wasn't; he too benefited from what he put in, kind of like the basket at church. Those who give will receive, he'd always been taught, and giving to certain media outlets just didn't seem fruitful to him.

Statistics showed that they worked sometimes, but he had made a promise to himself that he would make a difference in the community. And he felt he was doing so. In fact, that is how he met Meredith. The two of them were donating blood at a Red Cross blood drive in New Bern one Saturday afternoon. The bank was a major sponsor with the Callaway Agency a little lower on the list. Fate, it seemed, would have it that their reclining chairs were next to one another that day, and Andrew would be fibbing if he said he hadn't noticed Meredith when he first walked into the gymnasium where the drive was being held. He hadn't summed up the courage to speak to her until a needle was about to be shoved into her arm. Whenever anyone would ask Meredith about what happened next, she would tell them that even until this day she wasn't sure why she'd reached for his hand and held it as tight as a woman delivering a baby might. It was frightening for Andrew at first, especially since the largest woman he had ever seen was holding a needle just above his arm, too. When Meredith yanked him, the needle had scraped across his arm leaving a nice cut for the nurse to bandage up. In the end that was what had started the conversation between him and Meredith which eventually led to dinner later that evening. He couldn't possibly hold a grudge over that.

As water trickled down the drain, Andrew wondered what mornings would be like once he and Meredith tied the knot. It would probably end up being a good thing that Meredith liked showering at night while he preferred to do so in the morning. Sure, the first few months they would probably shower together, maybe morning and night; but like every other stage that newlyweds go through, he was sure that one would fade as well. There were plenty of things he would have to get used to, little things for instance, like the amount of time it took Meredith to get ready for bed, more time than he spent showering and shaving before work each morning.

With that thought in mind, Andrew reached around the shower curtain for the razor beside the sink. The five o'clock shadow he'd sported yesterday had become more than a noticeable amount of stubble overnight. Razor in hand, he increased the water temperature, and a thin cloud of steam began to escape above the curtain rod, traveling across the ceiling as he bore a path in the small forest on his face.

⤙⤚

While Candice was out tending to her dog, Brooke assumed the role of greeting clients and answering the phone which had been ringing non-stop. Twenty minutes of this action reminded her why she had asked Andrew to hire an intern, and she decided against asking Andrew to fire the intern who had relieved her of her former duties at the front desk. Candice might not be the smartest cookie, but if she could answer the phones then having her was worthwhile.

"Thank you for calling the Callaway Agency; this is Brooke; how may I help you?" she said with ease.

A natural is how Andrew had always described Brooke — her voice as sweet as cherries. He often made comments about how she'd required absolutely no training in the customer relations department. Of course, Brooke tried not to allow his kind words to go to her head. Like Candice, she began her career working for Andrew as a summer intern, and she'd eventually been hired full-time two years ago. If you asked Andrew, he would say it was one of the best business decisions he'd ever made.

"Hey Brooke, I haven't heard your voice in a while."

Brooke picked up on the voice on the other end as instantly as he'd picked up on hers. "Don't get used to it, Barry. Candice is off rounding up her dog, and I'm just filling in for the time being."

"I won't ask," Barry said with a chuckle.

"Please don't." Even though she knew he couldn't see the gesture, Brooke shook her head.

In the time she'd worked for Andrew, Brooke had heard a lot of stories about him and Barry. They had grown up not just as brothers but best friends. Even now with their busy schedules, they managed to have lunch together a couple times each week which was probably why he was calling today. Andrew had told her that he couldn't remember more than a few times when the two of them had been mad enough at one another not to talk. The one time that always stuck out in Brooke's mind lasted only a little more than a week. It was Andrew's freshman year in high school, and Barry, the big junior on campus, decided to ask out the girl Andrew had his eye on—Lucy Lamm. Andrew only stayed mad for a week because that is how long it took Lucy to ditch Barry for a twenty-one-year-old biker with tattoos and a Harley. The girl had always been all over the map, still was.

"You guys having lunch today?" Brooke asked.

"Supposed to. Is Andrew around?"

Brooke peeked at her watch. Twenty minutes after nine. *Am I the only one that knows Andrew's schedule?*

4

ndrew stepped out of the shower and reached to a nearby shelf, seizing a Carolina blue towel. If it were up to Meredith, his Tar Heel décor would have been replaced with matching towels and washcloths a long time ago. She had been encouraging a trip to Pier One ever since she first showered in this bathroom years ago after a romantic swim in the river behind his house. Andrew could still remember the *what is this* look on her face when he handed her a washcloth embroidered with a UNC logo and told her to scrub hard. There had been some kind of seaweed in the water that day, and when he pulled a piece off Meredith's back as she stepped out of the river, she squirmed and ran into the house screaming. It wasn't that day or even the next time Meredith showered at his place that she questioned the college dorm look in his bathroom, but the conversation did come up a few weeks after he knelt down on one knee and proposed. Andrew had agreed that when they married the two of them could go shopping for something a little more grown-up, and he had even promised to move the autographed photograph of Jerry Stackhouse from his bedroom to his office. Meredith laughed and then shook on the deal. Of course, Andrew had joked that they needed to put it in writing; he even said he would have his real estate attorney work up the contract.

The day of the first shower was also the day Andrew made peanut butter and jelly sandwiches and surprised Meredith with a picnic on his back lawn. He'd had more than enough time to set up everything he'd planned since she had let the hot water run over her *icky skin*—as she later described it—long enough to wrinkle an ironing board. Thankfully, PB&J's don't go cold, and neither had the fire that started between him and Meredith when they were neck deep in the Trent River that afternoon. They finished lunch and later watched the sun sink beneath the tree line making way for the moon that lingered overhead long enough for them to wrap the checkered picnic blanket around their bodies while Andrew mustered up enough courage to tell Meredith Hastings, for the very first time, that he loved her.

After drying, Andrew wrapped the towel around his waist and snatched the boxers from the door handle, flinging them into the basket on his way out. On summer mornings, he liked to take in the picturesque view from his back deck, so he grabbed the pair of gym shorts he'd hung on the bedpost last night and headed down the stairs toward the sliding glass door. The sound of a ringing phone slowed his waltz through the kitchen, but then he picked up his stride after grabbing the cordless on the bar next to the answering machine. He slid the door open and let the phone ring two more times, wanting to take in the sound of two acres of dew filled grass, standing between him and calm blue water and crackling like Rice Krispies in a bowl of fresh milk.

"Good morning, sunshine," were the first words out of Meredith's mouth.

Her smile seemed to travel through the line, and sunshine was right, Andrew agreed, smiling as though she was standing a few feet away. No need for a light jacket today since that one-day cold front had been given the boot; it had to be at least eighty degrees already, he guessed. Only a light breeze wafted against his bare chest, and at the sound of her voice he was once again drawn to that summer night when Meredith had gently kissed his bottom lip and, for the first time, reciprocated the three most important words in their relationship.

"I got your message this morning. I was going to call you in a little while but looks like you beat me to it." Andrew considered bringing up how nervous she had made him this morning, but after thinking about the long day she'd had yesterday, he decided against it. While sipping a latte at the airport coffee shop during the layover, Meredith had told him about Snookums and Baby Cakes moving to the seats across the aisle from her and her mother. Ten minutes into the flight, they'd nosily overheard Meredith and her mother talking about wedding plans and just had to offer a few helpful hints. If the advice would have actually been about weddings, Meredith had said while gritting her teeth, that would have been fine, but all the couple had on their minds was sex, sex, and sex. They had gone on and on about the first night of their married life at the old Sheraton Grande hotel on the New Bern waterfront, and when Baby Cakes said she hadn't had to fake anything, that is when Meredith had faked being asleep.

"Did you get any sleep last night?" Andrew asked, "or did you have images of Snookums on your mind?"

"That's not funny, Andrew. I won't ever be able to get that story out of my mind," Meredith grumbled, making a face that looked like she had just tasted an onion for the first time in her life. "How's your day going?"

"Just another typical hump day—except you're seven hundred miles away."

A forced frown took the place of the smile that had occupied Meredith's bubbly face ever since the word *hello* had left Andrew's mouth and tickled the tiny little hairs in her earlobe. Only he could do that, and she didn't know how. He wasn't even breathing on her. He was four states away, but it felt like he'd jumped into the Neuse River, swam through the Inner Coastal Waterway that led to the Atlantic Ocean, and made his way into the Gulf of Mexico before ending up in Tampa Bay (the body of water of which she enjoyed a clear view from her hotel room window) and had snuck up behind her. "I miss you, too," she said, turning around just to make sure he wasn't there. The distance between her and Andrew had already affected her even though she had made a pact with her mother not to sulk over his absence this week. With that thought in mind, she brought back the smile, though not quite as authentic this time, and decided to lighten the mood. "Guess what I got to do at the airport last night?"

"What?"

"Watch *Castle,*"she said as excitedly as a little kid in a candy store.

"Really? Me, too," Andrew replied, in about the same tone as Meredith. "Not at the airport, though," he clarified.

"The TV just happened to be on TNT. I wondered if you might be watching the rerun, too."

"Your hunch was correct, dear."

"Can you believe Castle didn't kiss Beckett in that episode? I mean it's so obvious that they're both attracted to one another, and the mood was perfect."

Andrew smirked. Sitting alone on the couch last night, he'd remembered Meredith saying nearly those exact words when they'd first watched that original episode of *Castle.* During the show's regular season, he and Meredith had spent every Monday evening cuddled together on either his couch or her couch for as long as he could remember.

"Well, at least when watching it this time we actually knew what eventually happens between Castle and Beckett."

"They end up like us." Meredith had made her way over to the large glassed window and was staring through it, enjoying the view of waves crashing and people buzzing all around the beach, wishing again that Andrew was here with her now. "Do you remember on our first date when you asked me what my favorite TV show was?"

"Sure do," he recollected.

"I was absolutely thrilled when you said *Castle* was your favorite show, too." Meredith paused for a moment. Out on the beach kids were shoveling sand; adults were playing volleyball; and surfers were out in full-force. "But did I ever tell you that I thought maybe you were just trying to score brownie points?"

"I don't think you have—probably because you soon realized you were wrong," he teased, remembering how she'd tried to inconspicuously quiz him about the show on their first date.

Meredith laughed. "Once you mentioned Beckett and Castle, I knew you'd most likely watched the show a few times. Then as we continued to talk about the episodes and you knew Esposito and Ryan's first and last names, I figured you were probably telling the truth."

"What happened next?" Andrew quizzed. *My turn now*, he thought to himself.

"You asked me what I was doing the following Monday evening."

"You said, 'Watching *Castle*, of course.'" Andrew smiled, thinking back and forward at the same time, as the small ripples in the river seemed to have a similar motion as they found the shoreline at the edge of his property. "It was the perfect lead in for a second date." He paused for a brief moment watching a seagull land on the water in the distance. "I was so excited when you said you'd love to come to my place to watch the next episode."

Meredith relived that first evening on Andrew's couch in her mind. It was the first time they held hands, and after a couple months they were watching television together in their pajamas. She could remember thinking those nights were exactly how she wanted to feel for the rest of her life, which reminded her of the survey she'd taken at the office a while back. Meredith had asked nearly everyone—married and single—and none of them would admit to pajama parties with their significant other. When she told Andrew about her poll, he'd chuckled and said if asked he wasn't sure he would admit to it either. Andrew Callaway wouldn't have to admit how sweet of a guy he was, though, Meredith knew. Everyone at her office had found out that he was a romantic when he brought her a dozen roses symbolizing the first twelve days they'd spent together, but the romanticism hadn't ended there. Among other gestures, he'd also had a dozen roses delivered after twelve weeks, another at the twelve-month point, and she suspected he would do the same on their twelve-year anniversary.

Mr. Romantic and Meredith spent the next few minutes debating how many episodes of *Castle* they'd seen together. As Andrew watched a small boat glide effortlessly across the river's glasslike surface causing the lone seagull to take flight, he gave into Meredith's recollection of events fully supported by math and factual evidence. Meredith Hastings, he knew from experience, enjoyed a healthy debate as much as any politician or lawyer he'd ever met, and even though her degree wasn't in law, he'd let her defend him in a courtroom any day.

The fishermen in the boat waved in Andrew's direction, and Andrew waved back before bouncing down the wooden steps and rounding the back corner of the house. *Sure would be a nice day to be out on the water*, he thought. He'd always told Meredith that one day he would sell enough houses to buy them a sailboat, so they could go on weekend getaways or just sit in the cabin while the boat was secured to the dock that he hadn't sold enough houses to build yet either.

He followed the long gravel driveway to the mailbox while Meredith filled him in on her plans for the day—lunch at a little Mexican restaurant she and her mother spotted on an early morning walk on the beach, a favorite of the locals she said; and then a relaxing afternoon at the spa. Boy, did she have it rough.

"Oh, by the way, ask Brooke if she will sing *When You Say Nothing At All* at the wedding." For a moment the phone line seemed to go dead. Meredith waited for another second to pass before giving Andrew the final hint. "Alison Krause—"

"Oh, that one," he said, "I'll make sure to ask."

When Brooke sang at church one Sunday out of every month the pews were overflowing like it was Easter Sunday, even if the congregation hadn't planned a good 'ole Southern Baptist feast to follow the service. Andrew always joked with Brooke about a contract too, one that would state she wouldn't be allowed to audition for American Idol or record a demo CD to send to Nashville. Her voice was *that* good. The woman could bring a grown man to tears with her rendition of Amazing Grace or convince illegal immigrants to whoop and holler after a stellar performance of the most beloved song in America—*The Star Spangled Banner.*

"Don't forget," she encouraged. "Mom and I are supposed to meet with the DJ tomorrow, and he wants a list of all the songs."

After saying their goodbyes, Andrew, with a few pieces of mail in hand, turned and for a moment stood in awe at the sight of the three thousand square foot house he called home. Enormous prehistoric looking oak trees shaded most of the front lawn, and a few towered above the roof from the backside of the house. Gingerly, he made his way back to the deck, opening the mail as he walked, and then stood again on the weather treated boards he and Meredith had spent last Saturday staining. She always helped with projects like that, and that was one of the things he loved most about her. She wasn't afraid to get her hands dirty or hammer a nail. The only thing she was afraid of was spiders and snakes, and he didn't plan on having either as pets anytime soon.

☙

At the airport, the wheels on the plane that had carried Cooper McKay on the second leg of her journey from Fort Worth to New Bern touched down on a battered landing strip. The uncomfortable cloth seat and the motor-mouth sitting between Cooper and the window had kept her from getting even a wink of sleep; her brown eyes screamed of exhaustion and after catching the red-eye all she could think about was walking through the front door of her parent's house and crashing onto a mattress molded to the shape of her body. That's how she had left it anyway, before accepting the position at the law offices of Steen and Smith and moving out of her hometown.

When the wheels came to a stop, Cooper bent over and reached beneath the seat; her laptop had occupied the small space nearly the entire flight, ever since the longhaired guitar player dressed in all black—who assured her that fate was the reason he'd been assigned the seat next to her—tried to start a conversation about a string of emails she had pasted into a Word document. Her plan had been to review the details on the way here but so much for that. Now she couldn't wait to skip through the terminal to get away from Mr. Psycho and hug her dad's neck. He would be thrilled to see her, she knew, especially since his fiftieth birthday was this Sunday, which was why she was here—the main reason anyway. She still needed to get him a gift, something nice. After all, he'd sent her a dozen carnations and an all-day package to the day spa near her apartment for her birthday. Her *not* having a special someone in her life to take her out for a romantic evening, like her dad said she deserved, had something to do with the present, she figured. Though being single had been a relief, to be honest she hadn't even considered dating since Chris. Although if she changed her mind, there was always the Marilyn Manson look-a-like who had asked her out three times over the course of a one-hour flight.

Cooper strapped her laptop and her other carry-on over each

shoulder and found her dad waiting at the edge of the boarding gate. He was talking to a man she had never seen before, and on the ride home she found out he was an old high school buddy. The two had played on the football team together, and her dad said Charles was the fastest wide receiver in the state the year they had won the championship.

Andrew got into his vehicle and headed for the office. Dressed the same way he lived life, casually in a pair of khakis and a nice polo from J. Crew or Eddie Bauer made him feel like a million bucks. Today the polo was black, the khakis a light coffee color. Many of the other agents in town wore Armani suits, custom made Italian shoes, and gold watches, but that just wasn't Andrew's style. If he couldn't sell a house while being true to himself, he didn't want to sell a house at all.

Most of the other agents would also be irritated sitting in their air-conditioned Lexus or Mercedes, if they were stuck on the drawbridge waiting for a sailboat to pass through, but Andrew had always liked to get out of his vehicle and take in the view, so he did just that. From here, he could see Union Point Park, even the spot where he'd proposed to Meredith.

As the sailboat passed through, Andrew walked to the other side of the bridge and leaned against the concrete railing. He couldn't quite see his office building, but it was hidden behind a cluster of other buildings making up the serene cityscape.

When he eventually reached the two-story, red-bricked office that the Callaway Agency called home, Andrew dropped a dozen pennies in one of the meters that lined the curb and then waited on a few tourists to pass before crossing the sidewalk. Most likely they were headed to Tryon Palace or the Pepsi Museum Store, New Bern's most famous landmarks. Andrew's office building, shared by three other businesses, sat twenty yards off Middle

Street, the heart and soul of the historic downtown area. One of his very first goals after becoming licensed was to get a suite in this exact building; the phrase: "Location, location, location" had been coined by real estate agents many years ago, and this was definitely the place to be — near the water and near the people. It sure beat working strictly out of his home and car which he'd done for a few years.

A short bricked sidewalk connected the street to two wooden doors—twice the size of an average door—and on either side of the entrance three perfectly aligned windows framed in black shutters outfitted the building with cream trim. At first sight, it resembled a home but so did many of the other structures in the downtown district. Downtown New Bern, for the most part, was comprised of historic brick buildings and elegant nineteenth century homes, most of which stood two or three stories high. Many of the buildings were connected to one another and others were separated by small alleys decorated with flowers and antique wooden benches.

With two fingers, Andrew tugged open one of the massive doors and then used his back as a prop while he squeezed through the opening balancing a cappuccino in one hand, a Coke Zero in the other, and a newspaper and an oversized day planner under his arm. He laughed a little when he spotted Brooke at the front desk which meant the dogcatcher still hadn't rounded up Lassie. All four of the businesses in the building had their own reception desk, and the one Brooke occupied was in the back right corner of the perfectly squared lobby. As the door closed behind Andrew, she stood to her feet.

"Good morning, Brooke, I brought you a present," he said raising the miniature black, red and silver can.

Brooke met him halfway and relieved him of the planner and the newspaper. "You're so predictable," she smirked. Men, they always had to be problem solvers. She imagined Andrew's mind fast at work when the cashier at the coffee shop down the street handed him his cappuccino. Heaven forbid he would have to make two trips from his car like a woman would have chosen to do, then he wouldn't have a small coffee splatter on his shirt. Luckily for him he'd worn black, and she had baby wipes in her purse.

"Why don't you just bring your things in before you get your morning caffeine fix?" she asked, straightening his collar after wiping his shirt clean.

"If I did that, Brooke, you wouldn't have any advice to offer me each morning."

"Don't get ahead of yourself, we still have a lot of work to do on you."

"*We*?" he questioned.

"Meredith tells me the more I can take care of at the office, the less she has to worry about when you get home. I'm her assistant too, you know, especially while she's out of town. Somebody's got to keep an eye on you. A man who's used to having a woman around can't function without one."

The comment cracked Andrew up. Even though he appreciated help, he could manage just fine on his own at any given time.

Brooke continued. "I bet you can't even make a decent breakfast for yourself," she said, tapping her finger on her lip while pretending to think hard. "You probably ate a bagel this morning while watching Sports Center on ESPN, didn't you?" she added in a complacent tone.

"What does that have to do with anything?" *And how did she know about his morning ritual* he wondered, then it hit him. "Meredith told you I do that, didn't she?" Andrew didn't wait for an answer. "Oh, by the way, you're singing—

" he trailed off, racking his brain for the title of the song.

"I'm singing what?"

Andrew began flipping through his planner, unable to recall the name of the song Meredith had made him jot down. "*When*

You Say Nothing At All," he finally blurted out like he was on a game show and being timed. He looked up. "That is the song Meredith and I would like you to sing at our wedding."

"Allison Krause?" she blurted out. Of course, they couldn't have picked something easy, Brooke thought, the lyrics running through her head. They had to go and pick the artist with the purest voice in the music industry. "Don't expect my voice to sound anywhere near as sensational as hers, but sure, I'll do my best even on such short notice. By the way, it took y'all long enough to choose a song," she teased.

"You're awesome, Brooke."

"What is with the miniature Coke can?" she inquired.

Andrew handed it to her and wiped the sweat from the can off his hand. "It's for you."

"Oh, how sweet. Do I also get a dozen roses while Meredith is out of town?"

He shook his head. "She told you about that, too. I am going to kill her. Don't believe a word she says."

"The Coke?" Brooke questioned again, pointing at the can.

"Some vendor across the street from the Pepsi museum gave it to me; I guess he's trying to start a cola war."

He probably shouldn't be doing that in New Bern, Andrew had thought to himself as he'd taken the free can and given the man a *What are you doing?* look. New Bern was the birthplace of Pepsi-Cola, formally known as Brad's drink, which only New Bernians and historians would know. Almost any native could tell the story of Caleb Bradham, a New Bern, North Carolina, pharmacist who in August of 1898 renamed the carbonated soft drink he'd created to serve his drugstore's fountain customers to Pepsi-Cola. The downtown pharmacy where he'd sold the very first drinks was within walking distance of Andrew's office; he'd driven past it a thousand times in his lifetime but had only been inside twice.

Andrew lingered for a few more minutes of small talk with

Brooke and then in his office thumbed through the portion of the morning newspaper he hadn't read while in line at the coffee shop. After checking the scores he'd missed on Sports Center, he picked up a copy of the specs on the house he was supposed to show before lunch. "Why can't it be the Tyndall house?" he whispered to an empty room.

5

After a short nap at her parent's house, Cooper McKay opened an email that she had inspected at least twenty times since receiving it nearly three weeks ago. The words were as shocking today as they had been the first time she'd read them. *What kind of person in her right mind would ask another person to do something like this?* she found herself trying to figure out. Even the weirdo on the plane had agreed that this request was bizarre, although she hadn't been looking for his opinion. This wasn't the only email; there had been two others. The last arrived Monday night, and since she didn't have much time to look it over before catching her flight, she had copied all three of the emails into the Word document.

Cooper was scratching her head when her mother walked into the room. The bed, almost touching the desk Cooper was sitting in front of, squeaked when she sat next to her. "How was your nap, sweetie?"

"It can be summed up in one word: Replenishing," Cooper sighed.

"What are you up to now?"

"Just trying to figure out what to do about these emails."

"Just call him, Coop."

Cooper had received the first email after an evening workout at the gym, and she had spent over an hour on the phone that night with her mother talking about the content. Her mother advised her to call him then, but she didn't. She *did* pick up the phone a few times but couldn't talk herself into dialing the number. She was afraid of how he would react, what he would think of her, or if he would even believe her.

"Mom, I haven't talked to Andrew in years. I can't just call him and say, 'Hey, we need to talk.'"

For some reason that option hadn't seemed like the best scenario. Andrew Callaway was someone she once cared a lot about. Still cared a lot about. Which is why she knew she had to do something, she just wasn't quite sure what.

An hour after tossing the newspaper in the recycling bin, a knock came at Andrew's office door. With two women working for him, one trip around the clock for the long hand was about all the quiet time he could ask for these days. "Come in," he called out, letting the document in his hand fall to the cherry oak desk supporting his elbows.

The door opened, and with a grin on her face, Brooke closed it behind her and made herself comfortable on the black leather sofa diagonal to Andrew's desk. Two matching chairs faced the couch, and it reminded her of a psychiatrist's office she'd visited a few times after her son's father up and moved to Virginia without even saying goodbye. Maybe that is why she liked coming in here in the middle of the day just to talk. Andrew might not have graduated college with a psych degree, but Meredith and he had been there for her ever since Andrew went out on a limb three and a half years ago and hired her—an eighteen-year-old with an infant son—to be his errand runner. Now, Brooke's business card read Administrative Assistant, and he had told her that once she passed the real estate exam she could work under him as an agent.

"What are you grinning about?"

"Oh, nothing," she answered, kicking off her loafers.

"Make yourself at home," Andrew rumbled sarcastically. "Ooh," he sounded out, "I know what's on your mind. You had a date last night." *That* was why Brooke had been extra cheerful this morning. He'd known something was different; he just hadn't been able to put his finger on it until now. Her consistent smile had been even more consistent, and she'd actually offered to get him a second cappuccino when his had run out earlier. On a normal day she would have sent Candice, who'd finally returned to the office wearing a new set of clothes. Earlier, Andrew had overheard Brooke ask her what happened with the dog, and all she would say is that she didn't want to talk about it. Whatever had happened required a shower and even more perfume than she typically wore.

Brooke caught herself blushing just thinking about Roger Long. "Yep, sure did," she answered, a mischievous smile lurking on her face.

"This is the guy you met at the singles gathering, right?"

"It wasn't a singles gathering," she insisted. "One might call it a . . . young adult get-together."

She went on to tell Andrew all about the date, how Roger had picked her up at her place, and after taking her out for a nice dinner, the two of them had taken a ride through downtown in a horse and carriage. When she'd shown Roger where she worked and told him about what she did, he had insisted that she could pose as the model American businesswoman in almost any business magazine. When Brooke accidentally mentioned the part about Roger being a professional photographer to Andrew, she could tell he became a little hesitant, and she found herself sticking up for a man she barely knew.

"Brooke, honestly, you don't think it is a little odd for a man to bring his camera on the first date?"

Andrew couldn't help but ask the tough questions; Brooke was like the little sister he'd never had. She was the type who needed a big brother to talk with about these things. Danny, her big brother by blood, was serving life in a maximum-security prison in Nashville, Tennessee, for murdering one of her ex-boyfriends. After that happened, she'd met Sam, the Marine—now a deadbeat dad—and followed him to the base, fifteen miles down the highway in Havelock, which is how she'd ended up in New Bern.

"He's a photographer, Andrew; he carries a camera everywhere he goes."

"That doesn't mean he should ask you to model for him."

"You say that like I was swinging around one of the lamp poles on the sidewalk."

"I didn't mean it that way, Brooke. I know you better than that. I'm just asking you to be careful, that's all. Guys that have the wrong intentions can be very conniving sometimes. Just be careful. The last thing you need is for pictures of you to end up all over the Internet."

Andrew hadn't been able to figure out why, but Brooke had a knack for attracting shady characters. It wasn't like she was desperate or ugly; in fact, Roger had been right when he'd said her thin-framed black glasses charmingly accented her narrow face. Beyond the frames, her baby blue eyes were enough to catch anyone's attention. All of Andrew's friends thought she was sexy, and he had even tried to hook her up with a few of them, but it had never worked out.

After reaching for the *Modern Bride* magazine on the coffee table, Brooke hid her face behind it while Andrew fielded a call. She knew the advice he had given her was definitely worth mulling over. She just didn't want him to know that was what she was doing at this very moment. Maybe this guy was a little strange, she considered. When he'd asked her if he could have lunch with her today, he'd also asked if she would wear a nice suit and high heels. He said the heels would highlight her thin waist and add to the five feet and six inches that she already stood. She wasn't sure whether to feel attractive or used as she let down her silky brown hair—cut just above the shoulders—and started reading to get her mind off Roger.

"How are the wedding plans coming along?" Brooke asked when Andrew put down the phone.

He shrugged. "Meredith seems to have everything covered," he said. Then, he paused, as if the question had reminded him of something. "I did ask you about the song, right?"

"Yes, is that your only responsibility or do you get to help out with other things, too?" she teased.

"You couldn't pay me to plan even my own wedding as long as it involves getting in the middle of Meredith and her mother," Andrew said seriously but in a joking tone.

Brooke laughed. "I understand," she said nodding in agreement.

After the session with Brooke, Andrew left the office with his briefcase and met Mr. and Mrs. Avery at a home on the outskirts of town that had only been listed for two days. An hour later when he returned, Brooke could tell the showing had gone well. It was written all over Andrew's face. She shook her head in awe. In less than an hour, he'd shown the house for the very first time and made a sell. The Averys would drop by later this afternoon to sign the papers, he informed her.

"How do you do it?" she asked.

"These retired old men buy houses from me just so they can come in and fill out the paperwork with you."

Brooke laughed at the comment. Andrew had once told her a story about a client who'd said that if he had the money, he would buy a new house every day just to come in and see Brooke's smile. If that couldn't flatter a woman, even coming from a sixty-five-year-old married man, what could? Since the word flattering was on the top of her mind, Brooke decided to use it. "Flattering," she said, "I think you just have that special touch. You possess a persona that clients can't resist—a boyish charm, one might say."

His finger to his chin, Andrew mulled over her comment for a moment before responding. "Nope, I'm pretty sure it's you they're after. Take your pick, Mr. Avery can be your sugar daddy, or you can stick with Mr. Picture Perfect."

"Mr. Avery is old enough to be my granddad," she chuckled while rising from the front desk and handing him a note. "I think the old ladies like you, actually, but here's your chance to prove you're just a good salesman," she said handing him a note. "This might be the one!"

A puzzled look overcame Andrew's face as he studied the pink post-it note. "One o'clock?" he asked. "What does that mean?"

"That is when you are meeting a potential buyer at the Tyndall Plantation."

"Today?" he said peeking at his watch. "In fifteen minutes?"

"Yes."

"What were you going to do if I didn't make it back to the office in time?"

"I guess the sell would have been mine for the taking."

Hoping the sun would thaw out the tension streaming through his veins, Andrew shut off the engine and waited in the paved circle drive. Too bad he didn't keep one of those stress balls in his vehicle at all times; that should probably be a requirement of real estate agents, he thought, trying to find a way to keep his palms from sweating any more than they already were, but that was difficult for Andrew. Selling this home would make his day, his month, maybe even his year. Selling this house would mean he wouldn't have to consider putting his own home on the market. His payments were steep, always had been, and he'd been struggling recently to keep up with them. His savings account barely even existed these days, and if Meredith didn't work at the bank, they might have already closed it out. The commission on small houses like the one he had just sold the Averys paid decent, but they only ensured that food would be on the table and that the power wouldn't get cut off. Selling a home like the Tyndall estate, on the other hand, would allow him some wiggle room. He'd always heard that once an agent made one major sell like this one, many more would follow.

Two lion statues battling in the fountain in the center of the circle driveway were staring Andrew in the face when a reflection caught his eye. He watched a gold Honda Accord turn into the driveway and roll slowly in his direction. Instantly, his mind jumped back to the conversation he'd had with Brooke about the potential buyer just moments ago on his cell phone. Since he'd been in a hurry to beat the client to the property, he'd asked Brooke to call with the information as he drove. "The buyer is an attorney, a woman," Brooke had revealed. "But she was real hesitant about giving me her name, so even though I thought it was odd, I didn't pry." Brooke paused thinking back to the conversation she'd had with the woman. "From the sound of her voice, I predict she is relatively young, about your age, maybe," she added, and that was all she had.

Most attorneys, Andrew recollected, typically chose to drive Lexus's and BMW's, but hey, who was he to judge, he was just trying to make a sell. Honestly, it didn't matter to him whether a lawyer, a schoolteacher, or a social worker bought the mansion. He'd sold houses to all three in the past and treated every single one of them exactly the same. As long as they could afford it, he would help them make their dreams a reality.

Briefcase in hand, Andrew pushed his car door shut. He thought briefly about how he might approach the potential buyer since he didn't know her first or last name. Like Brooke, he thought it was weird that she hadn't given a name, but he hadn't had time to ask Brooke much about the conversation.

Now, it seemed like time was moving in slow motion as the client's car crept toward the circle. He figured she was probably admiring the elegant three stories and checking out the well-manicured landscaping, or maybe Andrew was just so nervous that it felt like an eternity had passed by the time the car finally came to a halt. At any rate, the sun was beating hard enough against the car's windshield that he couldn't catch a glimpse of the driver through the glass.

As he waited, Andrew noticed another car pull off the road and come to a halt near the real estate sign. Another potential buyer, he marveled. If the one he was showing now didn't work out, maybe the other person would call and he would show the house to him later.

After a moment more of suspense, the driver's side door of the car in the driveway opened, and Andrew suddenly had a pretty good idea why the lady had not given her name.

Cooper McKay watched Andrew's face turn as candy-apple red as the sixty-five Mustang convertible she had taken him on a ride in on the night they'd first met.

Andrew hesitated for a moment; he watched Cooper take a step in his direction, and when she smiled and said, "Hello, Andrew Callaway," he realized that her unforgettable smile and the sound of her sweet southern voice had never escaped his mind. Even though the time they'd spent together had been brief, he had neither forgotten the feel of love at first sight nor the silent stares and simple smiles that brought them together at the back wall of the local video store many years ago.

Cooper McKay—he couldn't believe his eyes. What was she doing in New Bern?

6

"I had no idea you were back in New Bern," Andrew said, meeting Cooper between their vehicles and offering his hand although the gesture didn't quite seem fitting.

He wanted to wrap his arms around her neck. Tell her he'd missed her and that it was so nice to see her again, but he couldn't. Things had changed. He was with Meredith now. Not just *with* Meredith, *engaged* to Meredith, and in less than two weeks he would be married and on his way to Cancun. So, then, he wondered why his stomach was cringing and his throat tightening as he searched for something to say. This wasn't a good time for old flames to reappear, he found himself thinking, still wondering what had brought Cooper to New Bern. Even more importantly, why had she chosen him to show her a house—this house, which brought up yet another question: Was she even interested in the Tyndall home? Maybe she had heard he was engaged and was here to take one last shot at being with him. *No, not Cooper*, he convinced himself.

He knew the sooner he told her about Meredith the better off he would be. Nonetheless, he couldn't help but compare her to the picture he had taken with his eyes and kept stored in his mind all these years. Her hair was different now, still light brown and straight but with a few curls reaching for her shoulders. Those hadn't been there before, but they looked nice, he thought, trying not to stare. He wondered if she noticed that his eyes had widened as if he'd seen a ghost, a ghost that he hoped would remove the pair of black sunglasses covering the eyes he assumed were still brown and making him even more nervous than he had been before she stepped out of the car.

Brown, it seemed, was her color of choice today. Her belt, looped through a pair of blue jeans, was brown and so were her shoes, he noticed as she walked toward him, a smile on her face. Beneath a thin button-up white shirt with pink, green, and brown vertical pinstripes, a white tank top covered her chest. Three small, matching wood pieces hung from her necklace as well as her ears, and he wondered if she had made those herself.

"I'm here for my dad's birthday; it's this weekend," Cooper said honestly, somewhat overwhelmed by Andrew's firm yet gentle handshake. She had forgotten how strong he was, and after a moment she caught her eyes following the thin veins on his flexed forearms up to a hint of his bicep peaking beneath the sleeve of his polo. When she heard his voice again, she shifted her eyes back to where they should be.

"It's been a while," Andrew acknowledged.

"Yeah, it has," she said, tucking a strand of hair, blown out of place by a gust of wind, behind her ear.

"How is Texas?"

"It's not here," she admitted, referring to New Bern. "But I've finally grown accustomed to city life."

"You're in Houston, right?"

"Fort Worth."

"I knew that," Andrew said, snapping his fingers. "When you called to say you had moved out there that was my third guess. I remember picking Houston, then Dallas, and finally Fort Worth."

Cooper thought back to that phone call. In a way, it seemed like it was just yesterday, and she could still remember how she felt when Andrew told her that he was seeing someone. She was mad but not at him—at herself. He hadn't done anything wrong, *she* had by waiting nearly a month to make the call. What had she expected? Andrew Callaway to wait on her? It wasn't like the two of them had been in a committed relationship, and until this day she regretted putting off that call even under the circumstances.

"So you are interested in the Tyndall mansion?" he probed, taking a step backward before turning to face it.

If Cooper could afford this place, it meant one of two things: either she had graduated top of her class and partnered with Robert Shapiro or she had married into money. Most likely, it was the latter, and if so, he would be happy for her because that was his only choice. Cooper McKay deserved the best, and this house was definitely the best. If she wanted it, with a smile on his face he would sign the papers with her and the husband that he assumed she must have.

"It's even more exquisite than the picture on the website," she remarked, avoiding a direct answer. If she'd known the place was this big, she would have chosen another to walk through. The picture on the website must have been taken from the sign next to the car sitting out on the road, and now she knew why a price tag hadn't been included.

As Andrew guided Cooper up six yellow-bricked steps toward a solid oak door, he noticed a camera flash from the road. A good sign, he thought. If the person was taking pictures, he was definitely interested. He only wished he could give him a business card since he'd noticed that he hadn't gotten out of the car to grab a fact sheet from the plastic box.

Cooper studied the antique brass door handle as Andrew reached for the key in his pocket. On the way up the steps, he had purposely fallen one step behind and taken a quick peek at her left hand.

"Are you married?" he asked even though it appeared his

second guess had been off. In his business, Andrew had learned not to assume anything, and for reasons he didn't quite understand, he had to know.

Cooper walked to the center of the great room, as bare as her ring finger, and glared at the cathedral ceiling. When she stopped, she rested her sunglasses atop her head, the arms slightly pulling her hair back in the process. When she answered, she looked Andrew square in the eye, "Still searching," she simply said.

Andrew wasn't quite sure how to respond. "Oh, okay," he finally uttered.

"I guess that leaves you wondering how I would be able to afford this." Her voice echoed as she admired the antique finish found on the inside of the house as well.

"I'm just here to show you a house, not question your financial status," he answered politely.

"That's a good line. Do you say that to all of your clients looking at homes that would require winning the lottery before signing a contract?"

Where was this going, Andrew wondered? "Last time I checked, attorneys draw a healthy salary, especially the good ones," he said with a wink. "If I know you as well as a person can get to know anyone in less than twenty-four hours, then my assumption would be that you are a good one, probably working for a high-profile law firm. Since you're not married, instincts would tell me that you are either trying to talk your firm into opening another office in New Bern, which would be good for me because not only do I have the opportunity to sell you this home, but I also know a prime spot for a law office." Reading her facial expression, Andrew paused. A good realtor knew when he was headed in the wrong direction. "Or you have already won enough cases to buy . . ."

Cooper stopped him there. "Actually, I haven't won any cases."

Andrew furrowed his brow. "Oh, I'm sorry, I didn't mean to . . ."

Cooper cut him off, again. "Andrew, I'm not an attorney."

Andrew furrowed his brow, again. "But you told Brooke that you work for a law firm."

"I do," she answered, "as a paralegal. I'm still working on my law degree."

"Are you planning on moving back to New Bern when you finish?"

"I'll figure that out when the time comes," she said, searching for the best way to say what needed to be said, her eyes locked on the wooden floor. "Andrew, I need to be honest with you about a couple of things."

"Sure," he said.

"First, I'm not interested in this home. It's amazing, but my salary isn't even enough to buy the guest house out by the pool."

Andrew snickered at the reference, again wondering where this was headed. "So, then why are *we* here?" he asked.

Had he been right? Cooper McKay had come all the way from Texas to ask him for a second chance? With that thought in mind, Andrew began racking his brain for a nice way to say that he wouldn't be interested. As beautiful as she was, he *wasn't* interested. He was happy with Meredith and even if Cooper got down on her hands and knees and begged him for even one dinner, he would be forced to say *No, thank you.* That, he knew.

"I need to talk to you about something important," Cooper said, lowering her head as though she was about to tell him that he was the father of a child he didn't even know had been born.

It was funny that that thought had popped into Andrew's mind. It couldn't be the case, not even a chance. He and Cooper had never been intimate. *What could it be though* he continued to wonder? *And how did it relate to him?*

Cooper waited for Andrew to meet her gaze. "Meredith sent me an email . . ."

7

A waitress wrapped in a checkered skirt held open the door as Andrew walked into Andy's, a 1950's style diner where the cooks wore paper hats and chimed a friendly hello as customers strolled effortlessly into the establishment. The joint, famous for their enormous hamburgers and tasty cheese steaks, promised a free lunch to any customer who didn't receive a smile and an open door. Andrew frequented the spot but had not yet been given the opportunity to cash in on that free meal, he once again realized, as he thanked the young girl at the doorway and then waved into the open kitchen. The cooks, though he didn't know them by name, knew his face and he knew theirs. This atmosphere had always made him wish he'd grown up in the days when the memorabilia that lined the walls—from pictures of Elvis to vintage model cars—wouldn't have been considered memorabilia. The collection was impressive, and even the kid's meals came in a cardboard box shaped like a 1955 Corvette convertible.

❧

From a booth in the far corner, Barry watched Andrew maneuver through a crowd that looked like it had packed into the hottest bar in town on a Friday night. The waitress had brought him a fresh glass of sweet tea fifteen minutes ago, and he had been sipping on that while he waited for Andrew to show.

"Where have you been?" Barry asked, neglecting to offer up a smile and a friendly hello, Andy's style.

"I had a showing and you'll never guess . . .," Andrew trailed off as a waitress kneeled at the table.

"What'll it be, Andrew?" she asked, wearing the name LUCY L. on the billboard attached to the shirt that might as well read: *Look at my fake boobs!*

Instead of taking her up on the offer, Andrew focused on the ordering pad as she copied down the usual—*a Chili Cheese Steak all-the-way and a side of onion rings.*

"I'm guessing you'll have sweet tea with that," she smirked, jotting it down before giving him a chance to reply.

Andrew nodded and then she walked away. "I guess you've already ordered?" he asked Barry.

"Of course I've already ordered; I've been here half an hour, and you know you're not supposed to be late when we come here. It's like the unwritten brother code. Neither of us is allowed to force the other to put up with Lucy Lamm alone. She's been to this table and sat in your seat three times already. I've been ordering extra stuff just to get her to go back to the kitchen," he said harshly.

Andrew couldn't help but laugh as his brother complained about a few unwanted minutes with the girl they had battled over in high school. "Why do we always get stuck with her?" Andrew said.

Barry glanced into the kitchen where Lucy was standing, and she smiled as if she had been hoping he would look her way. He forced a half smile and turned back to Andrew. "I think she likes you," he suggested, grinning.

"Who does she not like?"

"Good point."

Andrew peeked at Lucy who was still ogling over Barry as she talked to one of the other waitresses. "But you're the one she has her eye on, and you even took off your ring so she wouldn't know you're married," he said, pointing at Barry's wedding ring as it spun across the table and collided with the napkin dispenser. "You're going to lose that thing if you keep playing with it all the time," Andrew added.

"Lucy knows I'm married," he assured Andrew. "But I told her you were still single," he said, raising an eyebrow.

"You didn't!"

"You're right," he smirked, "but I did tell her she has less than two weeks to win you over," Barry laughed, sliding the ring back on his finger. "It won't be long before you'll have one of these, you know. And speaking of that, do you miss your future wife yet?"

Feeling an uncomfortable lull suddenly take over what had previously been a casual and relaxed conversation, Andrew contemplated the question.

Barry waited for a moment and when Andrew didn't reply, he began to pry. "What's wrong, Andrew?" he asked. He knew his kid brother well, and something, though he had no idea what, was definitely bothering him. "Did something happen between you and Meredith?"

"I don't think so."

"It's a yes or no question, Andrew."

"Not this time," Andrew answered, hesitant to continue. "Something happened today, something unexpected."

Barry sat up straight in his seat, offering Andrew his undivided attention. "Is everyone okay?"

"Physically yes, mentally and emotionally, not really."

"That's good—that no one is dead or dying or injured, I mean."

Andrew glanced suspiciously around the restaurant before scooting closer to the table. New Bern had its share of gossips, Lucy Lamm included, and if someone overheard your private conversation, you could bet it would have spread all over town by this time tomorrow.

Man to best man, Andrew held Barry's eye. "Do you remember Cooper McKay?"

"I remember the name, but I never met her."

Andrew reminded Barry how he and Cooper had met and then said something that confused Barry nearly as much as it had Andrew nearly an hour ago. "Meredith emailed her."

Meredith handed the waiter at the Mexican restaurant her credit card, and then she and her mother headed for a pier a short distance down the boardwalk. She hadn't been able to stop thinking about Andrew or maybe *worrying* was a better word. She had just spent an hour over a taco salad listening to her mother bash all men who had ever walked the face of this earth, especially the ones that had cheated on her. She had even gone so far as to classify Andrew as just another "One of *them*"—a man who would cheat if given the opportunity.

Overlooking the Tampa Bay, Meredith decided to confront her mother about what she had said. "Mom, why do both you and Eric dislike Andrew so much?"

As they leaned against the weathered wooden railing, her mother filled the gap between them. "Andrew's not a bad guy," Sylvia started. "I've just always had the feeling that he's not the one for you."

Meredith shot her mother an evil eye. "What?"

"I'm not sure if he's your type."

Meredith's tone increased with every phrase that followed. "The one? My type? If Andrew isn't, then who is?"

"When I meet him, I'll let you know."

"When *you* meet him—Mom, guys don't come much better than Andrew Callaway."

"That's one of the problems—he is too good to be true." She paused, gazing out above the waves. "The truth will come out, and you'll be glad your mother warned you."

"What is that supposed to mean?"

"A lot can happen when you leave a man alone for an entire week, Meredith."

From the size of marbles, Barry's eyes had grown to the size of—larger marbles. For a moment, he stared blankly through Andrew's skull. "What?" he finally asked. Had he misunderstood the words that had just come out of his brother's mouth? He asked a second time, "What did you say?"

"You heard right," Andrew confirmed, swiveling the straw in his tea making the chunks of ice circle like a tornado and clang together like lottery balls. When Lucy brought their food to the table, they said, "Thanks," in unison, but neither made eye contact. She shot them a funny look and walked away smacking her gum.

"But why?" Barry paused, trying to determine why someone would do such a thing. "Are you serious?"

"Shhh . . . ," Andrew gestured nervously, studying the faces of the other patrons through the mirrors that lined the four walls of the restaurant.

Barry lowered his voice to a whisper. "Let me get this straight. A few weeks ago Meredith sent an email to Cooper whom she, to your knowledge, doesn't know and has never spoken to before in her life. And in the email she asked Cooper to fly from Fort Worth, Texas, to New Bern, North Carolina, to find out if you would cheat on her—with Cooper?"

"As crazy as it sounds, that is what Cooper said."

"I just can't see Meredith doing a thing like that."

"Me neither, but Cooper has the emails to prove it."

"She showed them to you?"

"No, not yet, but she said she would if I wanted to see them. She said she really didn't want to get in the middle of the two of us and that she thought she should only tell me about the emails instead of bringing them to me to start with."

"Okay," Barry said, shaking his head and leaning against the red, vinyl cushioned booth. "So Cooper came here, not to see if you would cheat on Meredith, but to tell you that Meredith wanted her to see if you would cheat on Meredith?"

"Exactly."

"Why didn't she just call you?" Barry asked, suspicious of Cooper's itinerary.

"I asked that same question."

"And her answer was?"

"Her dad's birthday is this weekend; she had already planned a trip to New Bern, and she said she wanted to tell me in person rather than over the phone."

Barry took a deep breath. "Holy cow. This is the wildest thing I've ever heard in my life. I just don't think Meredith is that stupid, though; she knows you wouldn't cheat on her."

"Yeah, but her mom probably convinced her to put me to the test."

"That lady *is* nuts," Barry affirmed, "but I still can't see Meredith going along with it. Why would you put the person you love and are going to marry in less than two weeks in a situation like this?"

"You got me."

"Maybe Cooper is making up this whole thing. You have to admit it's kind of convenient that her father's birthday happens to fall on the same week that Meredith needs her to come seduce you."

"That was my initial thought too, but Cooper says she has the emails to prove it, and I can't think of any reason, other than my good looks and charming personality," Andrew joked, "that she would lie about this. She was the president of the FCA club in high school, and she even had a Bible on the dashboard of her car today."

"Why don't you just call Meredith and confront her about it?"

"I thought about that, but don't you think I should get the evidence first?" Andrew paused, thinking of the plan he'd thought about on the ride here. "If Meredith doesn't know about this and I catch her off guard with it, how's that going to relieve a future bride's normal stress level just before her wedding?"

"You're right. You need to get your hands on those emails. Make sure they came from Meredith, then you'll have something to go on other than what Cooper told you. That is what I'd do, just in case Cooper has an ulterior motive."

8

fter lunch, Andrew drove to Union Point Park, parked the car, and then zigzagged through a maze of children toward a wooden bench. Their giggles and shrieks reminded him of his own childhood—no responsibilities, no decisions to make, not a care in the world. He'd give anything to feel that way right now, for his biggest concern to be whether he or one of his classmates would occupy the next empty swing.

When he closed in on the river's crest, he plopped down on *the* park bench and stared aimlessly across the choppy water, thinking about the night he knelt in this very spot and proposed to Meredith. How could she do this to him? He contemplated as the sun worked its way through an assortment of oak trees behind him, shading the serene landscape.

From his viewpoint, Andrew could see both the Neuse and the Trent River. If he picked up a rock he could hit the drawbridge where he'd been standing earlier today. At his feet, three rows of steps led from the sidewalk to the water's edge where waves were crashing into large brick pillars, drowning out the sounds of the children playing in the background. *Why?* He continued to ask himself, even out loud a couple of times. *Why?* Why had Meredith done this? He had never even considered cheating on her. Like every other human being on this planet, he'd had his chances, but he'd never given in to the pressure, never even thought twice about it. For three years he had been totally devoted to her and completely honest with her. Even about Cooper McKay—the only other woman he'd ever loved.

Cooper spotted Andrew sitting on the park bench exactly where he'd said he would be; his elbows rested on his knees and his hair just long enough to seep through the fingers buried in it. This was hard on him; she'd known it would be, and she couldn't imagine what she would do if she were in his shoes. She'd thought about him every night for the past week—after the second email had arrived, the one that asked the dreaded question.

"Hi," Cooper said shyly, noticing the red circles around Andrew's eyes before moving her focus to the water slapping against the brick wall. When he spotted her brown shoes, she watched him use his shirtsleeve to wipe the tears from his face, and it made her want to cry if for no other reason than for him to have someone to cry along with him. She stood a few feet from the bench and waited for Andrew to speak.

"Hey," he finally said, now staring at his own shoes—black like his belt, to match his shirt. "Have a seat," he gestured, sliding over to make room on the tattered bench.

As Cooper settled in, Andrew instantly second guessed asking her to meet him here—at *this* bench. Even though he hadn't explained the significance to her, something inside of him had convinced him that this is where he needed to be to make the most important decision in his life right now. This was a safe place.

"I brought the emails," she said, holding a manila envelope. "They're all here."

Andrew took the package, almost hesitantly, and began to pull back the seal. Cooper said nothing as he read the first email then the second and, a few tears later, the third. The emails were simple, each one to the point. All three had Meredith's email address and the date and time listed in the header. The first email introduced Meredith to Cooper, and below it, Cooper had included her reply.

"I can't imagine what was going through your head when you received this first email," Andrew said, glancing up at Cooper for the first time since she'd sat down beside him.

"At that point I didn't have any idea what Meredith wanted. All she had said was that she was engaged to you and that she needed me to help her with a favor. I thought maybe she was trying to throw you a surprise birthday party or something like that. Of course, I still couldn't imagine why she would need *my* help. I had no idea who she was."

Andrew flipped back to the second email, his hands trembling as he read the words again. This one hurt the most. It asked Cooper to happen upon Andrew, told her where she might be able to find him during the week Meredith would be in Florida. "Try the soccer field," it said, giving the date and times of his games. "Or you can run into him on his way to work, Andrew always arrives at the office around ten o'clock," it said.

Andrew turned to Cooper. "At least the email doesn't say, 'set up a meeting to view Gary Tyndall's place,'" he said, trying to find even a hint of humor in the situation. "Then I might get the idea that you were playing along."

Cooper didn't laugh as he had expected she would. She folded her arms and took a deep breath instead. Andrew tried to study her facial gestures, but she turned away gazing at a sailboat in the horizon. Judging from her reaction, he could tell she had taken offense to the comment.

"I want you to know right now, I never even once considered going along with this," she demanded. "I think this is ridiculous. It makes me sick to my stomach to think this woman would do this to you," she added. "I only told Meredith I would comply so that I could tell you what she is up to. I figured if I said no, she would just pick someone else." Cooper had come to the conclusion that Meredith was either lacking in self-confidence or just plain dumb. Whatever the case, she thought Andrew should know what he was getting himself into.

Andrew felt bad for insinuating that Cooper might have had something to do with the plot. "Thank you for coming to me with this," he said appreciatively. "You could have ignored it or just said no and left it at that. You didn't have to get involved, but you did. Thank you," he said again, meaning it.

"I felt it would be unethical not to," she said, her eyes following the path of the boat she had locked them on.

As the school-aged children who had been roaming the park loaded into two activity buses, Andrew and Cooper sat in silence. In an attempt to change the subject, Cooper questioned their being at the park during summer vacation.

"The elementary school started year-round school this past year," Andrew informed her.

"Really?" she said, as though she should have known about that. "I can't believe my mother didn't tell me. She is a schoolteacher at the middle school. Did I ever tell you that?"

"No," Andrew answered, nodding his head slightly. "You didn't."

"You look like you could use a walk," Cooper suggested. "Let's take a walk. Maybe we can clear your head," she said, softly touching his arm with her fingertips.

Andrew considered saying no, but at this point what did it matter? He pondered the offer for a short moment. It wasn't like she had asked him out for dinner, he decided. It was a walk, not a date or anything suggestive like that. But, nonetheless, he felt a little guilty at the thought of saying yes, and he found himself wondering if Meredith would get mad if she knew he was walking with Cooper McKay two weeks before their wedding day. What could she say though? He concluded that Meredith was the one who had some explaining to do, not him.

⤜❧⤏

Andrew and Cooper walked along the bricked sidewalk with nearly a foot of space separating them. They crossed under the old drawbridge and circled behind the Sheraton Hotel and Marina, where boats filled the docks and boaters were out in full force—tanning, drinking beer, and enjoying the company of friends. The conversation didn't flow like the river they were following, but Cooper could tell that Andrew felt more open now than he had at the park.

When the sidewalk ended, the two of them trekked across a grassy field and headed toward the rusty old train tracks that crossed over the Trent River. They tiptoed on the trestles and then let their feet dangle loosely above the murky water. In the distance, they could still see the boat slips and an assortment of sailboats and yachts of all sizes parked at the docks.

"I don't think I can marry her," Andrew revealed, slumped over and staring at his reflection in the water below.

Cooper knew one thing for sure—she hadn't come here to give Andrew advice on whether he should marry Meredith Hastings. Other than a few emails that had definitely rubbed her the wrong way, she didn't even know the woman. If Andrew had asked Meredith to marry him, then she must have some good qualities, Cooper had decided while flying above rain clouds in Oklahoma City. If their roles were reversed, however, she too would probably ask his opinion, most likely in a roundabout way just like he had done. She had already decided that the best thing to do would be to change the subject.

"I almost got married once," Cooper admitted.

Andrew looked up. "Really?" he asked. He said it as though the news totally shocked him, but after thinking about it for a moment, he wasn't sure why. Earlier today he had assumed she was married. Why not now, he wondered?

The expression on Cooper's face resembled the one Andrew had worn at the park, and like magnets her eyes appeared glued on the water below. This wasn't the subject she had thought about bringing up. Actually, she hadn't thought about any subject in particular and definitely not this one.

Andrew watched her jaw tighten, and it surprised him when a tear fell from her cheek and made a tiny ripple in the water. He wasn't sure why, but the river here was calm unlike it had been at the park. Must be something about the difference in water flow between the Neuse and Trent Rivers, he guessed. That wasn't important though. Why was Cooper crying?

"About a week after I called you from Texas, I called one of my ex-boyfriends from high school. His name is Chris Selzer. Do you know him?" she asked. Andrew shook his head side to side. "I needed someone to talk to, someone to lean on. I actually thought about calling you again, but I didn't want to intrude into your life. You were seeing someone and you barely even knew me anyway," she said raising her eyebrows. For the first time since that phone call to Andrew, Cooper wondered if Meredith had been the woman he was dating, but she went on without asking. "To make a long story short, Chris ended up moving to Fort Worth a few weeks later. He's a physical trainer, and he landed a transfer to a gym in Arlington, which isn't very far from where I live."

"That's good."

Cooper's cheekbones rose as she shook her head slowly. "It was the biggest mistake of my life," she admitted. "The reason I broke up with Chris in high school was because he was so aggressive. He is the most jealous person I have ever met, but like an idiot I fell back into his arms. He proposed a few months later, and I said yes." She paused. "I never told him about you because I knew he would get mad. Actually I never told him about any of the guys I dated after him." There had only been three, and she had lost interest in the other two a long time ago. Clay spent too much time washing and waxing his cars, and Jay had been afraid of commitment. "Then one day, he found out," she said with a sniffle.

"About me?" Andrew inquired.

"Yes. I kept a journal back then, until Chris tore it to shreds, that is. The date of the journal entry pushed him over the edge. You see the day I met you was also his birthday." Andrew listened intently as Cooper went on, forgetting for a moment about the current situation between Meredith and him. "He told me that if he ever caught me talking to you or even writing your name again, I would regret it. His tone frightened me, and then he said he would kill you if that happened."

Andrew's eyes nearly jumped out of their sockets; he couldn't believe what he was hearing. He had absolutely no idea any of this had happened. He'd always wondered if Cooper even remembered him or the night they spent getting to know one other.

"You probably don't want to hear about this right now, do you?" Cooper asked, remembering that Andrew was the one who had just found out that his fiancée had sent her here to try to hook up with him.

But Cooper's question, Andrew thought, was like asking a child if he wanted a lollipop. "Yes," he confirmed, "I want to know what happened."

"The next day, while Chris was at work, I decided to call you. I wanted to warn you just in case he decided to do something stupid," she said. Her face turned rosy red, and she paused for a moment as though she was trying to decide if she should continue. Andrew knew he hadn't received a call from her, and he began to worry about what she might say next. "Chris's training session got cancelled that afternoon. He caught me sitting on the bed with the cordless phone in one hand and the torn piece of paper you had written your number on in the other."

Andrew remembered writing down his number for Cooper. Before he left her apartment, she tore off a piece of paper from a notebook, wrote her number on one half, and he wrote his on the other. The next day, a Saturday, he traveled to Washington for a soccer tournament. He even invited Cooper to come along, but she already had other plans and wasn't able to be there on Sunday when the tournament sponsor handed him the *Most Valuable Player* trophy after his team placed first out of thirty. The entire weekend, on and off the field, he hadn't been able to keep his mind off Cooper. He vividly remembered the drive home—being more excited than the first and only time he visited Disney World. The minute his teammates dropped him off he dialed Cooper's number. Every day for the next week he took that piece of notebook paper out of his desk drawer and dialed it again, but not once did she ever answer. He left three messages, each one longer than the one before. With every ring his heart thumped hoping it would be the last before Cooper's voice chimed in, but it never did. After a few days of unreturned calls, Andrew decided to stop by her apartment. Her car was in the lot and he was certain he was knocking at the right door—the number on the parking space matched the one on the door, and he could vividly remember walking through that exact door the night they met, but knocking, like his phone call attempts, failed.

Cooper clinched the rusted outer shell of the tracks. "Chris snatched the paper from my hand and—"

Andrew felt the muscles in his body tense up as he pictured what might have happened next. He imagined Chris's thunderous and enraged voice, and then Cooper's, hushed and fearful. Had Chris hit her? Had he hurt her? Had that jerk left even one bruise on her fragile body? Andrew could barely sit still as he waited for her to sum up the courage to go on.

Cooper covered her face, wishing she could just lean forward, sink below the surface, and pretend none of this ever happened. This was the first time she had ever told this story to anyone, and she didn't know why she had chosen Andrew. Maybe it was because he was hurting now like she had been hurting then, like she had been hurting ever since Chris did what he did to her. Even her parents didn't know, partially because she was afraid to tell them but mainly because she was afraid of Chris—afraid of what he might do if anyone ever found out the truth.

9

Brooke led Mr. and Mrs. Avery into the conference room, provided them a cup of coffee, and informed them that Andrew should be arriving shortly. Anyway, she hoped he would. Every time she had tried his cell phone, though, it had gone straight to voicemail.

At her desk, Brooke dialed his number again. Nothing. The meeting would have to start without him, she finally concluded, when the attorney, who had graciously come on such short notice to assist with the closing, arrived. They stepped into the conference room together.

"Where is Andrew?" were the first words out of Mrs. Avery's mouth.

Brooke smirked, thinking: *Wait until I tell Andrew how badly Mrs. Avery wanted to see him again. Well, he was supposed to be here twenty minutes ago*, she wanted to reply, feeling foolish for having to cover for him. "He had something important come up, last minute," she said instead, giving the Averys the impression that she had spoken with him. "I am going to fill in for now," she informed them, "but he might pop in before we finish up."

Brooke wanted to leave the table open in case Andrew did show up. Because honestly, she had no idea where he was or what was going on. In the three years she'd been working for Andrew, he'd never missed an appointment.

∽✦∾

While the water softly slapped against the train trestles, Cooper McKay began spilling her heart. "Chris Selzer beat me to a pulp that afternoon," she admitted with tears streaming down her cheeks before catching in her necklace. "I was a sight—black and blue from head to toe, bleeding from the friction his knuckles had caused. He landed me a free stay in the hospital. Until this day I'm not sure which was worse: the physical pain I felt over the next few weeks or the psychological damage that still haunts me."

Andrew looked at the empty tracks, feeling a need to pinch his arm just to make sure a train hadn't barreled through the two of them. That is how he felt, like he had been slapped in the face by something larger than life. How could any man do this to a woman, he wanted to know, especially someone like Cooper. "What happened to him, I mean—did he get arrested?"

Cooper bowed her head. She'd been afraid that question would be one of the first to come if she ever decided to share this secret.

"He forced me to lie to the doctors—and the police. Out of fear and like an idiot, I claimed I had been mugged. Again, he threatened to kill you if I told anyone the truth. I thought it was best to just let it go," Cooper said as more tears lined her face.

At that moment, Andrew wrapped his arms around Cooper McKay, and for some reason he suddenly felt that it didn't matter if Meredith or the whole world was watching; Cooper needed someone to comfort her as badly, if not more so, than he did. He could feel her body as it continued to tremble violently as though the pain had been buried deep in her insides and was now working its way to the surface.

Like a lightning storm without thunder, sound did not accompany the falling tears. Though Andrew wasn't sure why, he felt the need to apologize for not being there when Chris hurt her.

When he said as much, Cooper shook her head. Sure, she could have used his help then, but she needed him now just as much. His arms, holding her against his chest, made her feel safe. Safe from Chris. Safe from bad dreams. Safe from two years-worth of lonely tears—enough to fill the river below if it ever went dry. She had been fearful of what might happen if she released the words she had just let out. Her injuries had been enough evidence of the damage Chris Selzer could cause when he got angry, and that is why it had taken this long to free herself from this bondage.

Andrew wasn't sure what to say, but he knew he was glad Cooper had chosen to confide in him. And if there was anything positive that could come out of this situation Meredith had brought on their relationship, this was it. "I'm glad you told me, Cooper." He paused, afraid to let her go. "Everything is going to be okay."

When Cooper heard those simple words, she realized why she had chosen to open her heart to Andrew Callaway. Andrew was unlike anyone she had ever known. The comfort of his voice set her at ease, and his gentle touch seemed to soothe the pain about which only she and God knew. If she'd known that telling Andrew this story would have lifted this much weight off her shoulders, she would have called him the day it happened. She would have spent this last twenty minutes on the phone—describing a beating that only took two—rather than waiting more than two years to sum up the courage.

"I didn't sleep one minute that night," Cooper said.

Andrew felt his nostrils flare and his jaw clench, and he wondered if Cooper noticed the cloud of righteous anger hovering on his face. He listened as she continued to describe in detail the painful incident. He wished there was some way he could have known. A way he could have been there to keep it from happening. In all honesty, he felt like she had taken a beating that was meant for him. His first reaction had been shock and shortly after that, sorrow, but now a bitter anger was setting in. If he could get his hands on Chris Selzer right now—

Andrew gritted his teeth and picked up a rock from between the trestles trying to harness his fury on its rough surface, almost rubbing his fingers raw. When Cooper looked the other way he hurled it violently into the river and then uttered the words he'd been saying over and over. "I'm so sorry this happened to you." What else was there to say? He couldn't imagine her flawless face bruised and battered. How, he wondered, could someone do that to a person as sweet as Cooper? "Did you leave him?" he finally asked.

Clinching her lips, Cooper shook her head in the direction Andrew hoped she wouldn't. "We stayed together for a while after it happened," she admitted, although embarrassed.

"Why didn't you leave him?"

"He promised never to do it again. He sent flowers and chocolates, and apologized over and over. But, mainly because I was stupid."

Andrew had to know: "Did it ever happen again?" he asked.

"That was the only time I had to be admitted to the hospital," Cooper answered, "but I don't really want to talk about it anymore if you don't mind."

He reached over and squeezed her hand, holding it just long enough to speak these words: "That's fine. I'm here if you need me—anytime."

Across town at Courts Plus, the local gym, Chris Selzer's face turned as red as a hot coal as he strained with every ounce of energy in his body to bench-press four hundred and five pounds. The bar bounced off his chest and a moment later the entire bench shook as the weight clanged on the rack above his head.

"Oh yeah," he grunted, sitting up to flex his biceps while

flashing an *'I know you want me'* smile at a group of college girls who had been drooling over his hard pecks and washboard abs since he'd taken off his shirt a little earlier. "If you ladies need a personal trainer, just ask one of the girls at the front desk for one of my cards—tell 'em Chris sent you. And let 'em know I said the first session is on me," he guaranteed with a wink.

Before Chris could catch the coeds' names, a rap song began screaming out of the speaker on his cell phone parked on the rubber floor beside the bench. While openly staring at the three girls in spandex as they headed for the aerobics room, he answered the call. "What's up, bro?"

The only reason his brother and workout partner Ricky wasn't at the gym with him today was because he had taken the day off to fish and drink beer. If the annual Big Man competition in Raleigh weren't coming up this month, Chris would have taken his brother up on the offer to spend the day on the water with him.

"You ought to be out here soaking in the rays and checking out these fine honeys," Ricky encouraged, his wife lounging only a few feet away at the front of a small bass boat. She overheard the comment but didn't bother to retaliate—mainly because her bulky, dark sunglasses were covering temporary tattoos from the last time she responded in a manner Ricky didn't approve. Meanness—it seemed to run in the family.

"Let me tell you about the honeys in here," Chris suggested, going on to explain in detail every curve on each of the three girls he'd just met. "And while they were checking me out," he added, "I bench pressed 405lbs."

"That's what I'm talking about," Ricky roared. "And you better get one of those hotties' digits."

Headed for the water fountain, the well-endowed blonde from the group emerged from the adjacent room, and Chris watched as she bent over to fill her water bottle. "I got my eye on the one I want as we speak," he smirked.

"You need to find you an old lady, brother. So we can take our women out for drinks and dirty dancing. And speaking of old ladies, remember that one who didn't like me because I was supposedly a bad influence on you—the one you stopped drinking for that time?"

"Cooper?"

"That's the one."

"What about her?"

"We parked the boat down at the Sheraton earlier, and that fine little thing walked past the docks with some guy. He looked like a lawyer or something."

"She's in New Bern?" Chris quizzed, his face turning even redder than it had earlier.

"It's either her or a twin sister that you kept hidden from me." At that comment, Ricky's wife lifted her head from the seat cushion. "I ain't talking to you," he yelled in her direction while pointing his finger as if to tell her she better not speak a word.

Chris furrowed his brow. "Who are you talking to?"

"Just my old lady."

"Did Cooper speak to you?"

"Nah. She didn't see me, bro. I was out on the boat with a bucket of beer. If I wasn't so plastered, I would have harassed the pretty boy she was with."

Chris's country boy accent had arrived as soon as his face turned red, and it became thicker as his anger grew heavier. "What did this guy look like?" he asked.

Ricky laughed. "I just told you. He looked like a pretty boy." He paused. "Come to think of it, I've seen him somewhere before."

"I bet it was *that* punk," Chris exclaimed.

"What punk?"

"Andrew Callaway."

"That's exactly who he is," Ricky confirmed as though a light bulb had just blinked on in his head. "The realtor guy—the one selling Gary Tyndall's mansion?"

"That's Andrew Callaway?" Chris said.

"Yes sir. What's he doing with your girl?"

"That's what I'd like to know." He paused as the three girls passed by and walked in the direction of the front counter. "I think the two of them had something going on while me and Cooper were dating."

"And you didn't rough him up?"

"I was in Texas, stupid," Chris spat out.

"Why didn't you call me? I would have stomped a mud hole in his rear end."

"Don't worry," Chris grinned. "When I found out, I hit her hard enough for him to feel it."

"Yeah, well he was feelin' her on the railroad tracks," Ricky teased.

"He better not be feelin' anything. I told Cooper to stay away from him."

"She ain't your property anymore, bro."

"Yeah, well, she sure as heck ain't going to be his either."

10

little less than three hours had passed since Andrew missed the three o'clock meeting with the Averys. He still hadn't found the courage to call Meredith and confront her about the situation Cooper had brought to his attention. Honestly, he didn't know how to bring it up or how to ask the questions that needed asking. He would figure all that out when he got home tonight he decided, as the sun beat down on his silver Land Rover, following the winding road that led through the Creekside Park sports complex.

Upon returning to the office earlier, he had found out that Brooke made sure the Averys paperwork was signed, dated, and filed in the appropriate places. He had also taken in an earful from her about not showing, and then she, while laughing hysterically, had gone on and on about how upset Mrs. Avery had been when she had to leave the office without a hug from Andrew. He seriously doubted a tear actually fell from her eye—as Brooke had seemed to enjoy describing in grave detail—and the only way he had been able to calm Brooke down was to offer her the rest of the afternoon off which had worked out well for both of them. If he would have spent any more time around her, he knew she would have been able to tell something was wrong, and he hadn't felt like getting into all that again today.

The windows in Andrew's SUV had been rolled down since he left the office, and now a mild wind—tugging at his antenna and blowing the hair on his left arm—had begun to cool the summer air making it a perfect evening for soccer. Dangling from the ignition, the keys rattled, and the entire car shook as he tapped the brakes upon reaching each of the half dozen or so cyclically placed yellow speed bumps on the way to the field making it impossible to reach the posted 15 M.P.H. limit.

From the gated entrance, it took several minutes to reach the fields, but, as always, Andrew had allowed for plenty of leeway before game time. Arriving forty-five minutes early gave him enough time to dress out and stretch his aging muscles as he liked to call them. Once parked, he threw a bright red bag over his shoulder and crunched across the gravel parking lot, headed for a small building that housed a locker room and public restrooms.

Just around the corner from the locker room door, the hands on the clock inside the snack bar were nearing six o'clock when Andrew strapped on his cleats and walked onto the field. This morning the schedule on his refrigerator had reminded him that his team was set to play the early game, and with a little more than half an hour until the first whistle would sound only a handful of people had begun to make their way out to the field.

Wedging his equipment bag beneath the team bench and then sprawling out on a sea of Bermuda grass, Andrew stretched as the parking lot slowly began to fill.

"How's it going, Andrew?" a man from the opposite side of the field shouted.

At the sound of his voice, Andrew lifted his back from the warm ground and spotted the other team's coach, sporting a purple jersey and a pair of silly looking eye goggles. The color of the uniform on his back, coupled with the name written across the chest, did very little for his team in the intimidation department, but through nine games, Sunshine Childcare Center remained perfect. Tonight's game would break a two-way tie for first place, and Andrew knew this was by far the biggest game of the season.

"Ready for a thriller?" Andrew asked, reaching for his toes.

The two of them chatted for only a moment.

A few of Andrew's teammates soon joined him on the field, and they spent the next few minutes talking strategy. Sunshine's players began to gather near their net to do the same.

When a thunderous voice echoed from the distance, Andrew, along with the rest of his teammates, turned. "Look at those pretty boys down there," Beast, Andrew's team's goalie, called out referring to the swarm of purple warming up at the other end of the field.

Throughout Andrew's life he had encountered many people with nicknames that made him ask why in the world they had been tagged with a particular name—such as Snookums and Baby Cakes—but Beast wasn't one of those people. The roster listed him at a generous 6'5" and 250lbs, and on the field his dark beard made him every bit as frightening as he really was. In his early forties the man had become a well-seasoned veteran who still seemed to possess the strength and agility of a twenty-one year old. Needless to say, he was one of those guys you loved having on your sideline. He'd been the one who saved the final goal in the Washington tournament where Andrew earned the first of the many MVP trophies that now lined almost an entire shelf in his office at home. Andrew had even tried to give that trophy to Beast, but he wouldn't take it.

"Glad to see you made it," Andrew said as the big guy joined them fashionably late.

"Have I ever missed a game?" he smirked, pulling a pair of cleats from his bag to replace the flip-flops on his feet. Supposedly, Beast's choice in footwear had become a pre-game ritual a long time back, but Andrew figured he really wore them just so people would ask why.

"Put some socks on," Barry, who had been the second player to sit down next to Andrew, said, "so you can stand in front of the goal while I whiz a few balls past your scary looking head."

"Good luck with that," Beast encouraged confidently. The team followed him and Barry toward the goal where they ran drills until the coach called them over to the sideline and announced the lineup.

When Andrew took the field with the rest of the starters, he noticed how full the bleachers on either side of the field had become. Before the whistle sounded, he spotted Brooke and her new friend. A few rows up he saw his mother sitting next to Marie. He waved in their direction. They waved back; the smile on his mother's face reminded him that he was supposed to take her to her doctor's appointment tomorrow. Both he and Barry had been trying to get her to go in for a check-up for the longest time, and last week she had finally agreed to go.

Meredith and her mother returned to their hotel room, and as soon as Sylvia grabbed a towel and headed for the pool, Meredith flipped open her laptop and connected to the Internet. When she logged into her email account, she found the email just like the anonymous caller said she would. The phone message had been left while Meredith and Sylvia were perusing the selection at Flowering Florida. Hoping this was a cruel joke, Meredith had opted not to share the information with her mother. The caller said she would find the contents interesting, but interesting was an understatement she realized, sitting Indian-style on the bed with her laptop resting on her knees.

As photos of Andrew and another woman popped on the screen one at a time, Meredith found herself fighting to catch her breath. She used the sleeves on her shirt to soak up the tears from her eyes as she screamed.

"Why? . . . Why? . . . Why?"

The sound of her voice echoed the walls as she scrolled through more than a dozen shots. Why would Andrew do this? She wondered, infuriated. If he were going to cheat on her, why would he take this woman to the spot he had taken her the night he proposed?

Maybe there was an explanation, she found herself praying. There had to be. But how could there be? The evidence was in black and white and right in front of her face. In one of the photos, Andrew was sitting next to this woman on the train tracks with his arms wrapped around her. In another he was holding her hand. Then there was the one of them going into Gary Tyndall's house together. Had Andrew taken her there hoping he wouldn't get caught at his own house? How long had this been going on? Had he taken her to other houses that he was selling?

Meredith brought her hand to her mouth. She couldn't take any more of this punishment. Quickly, she closed the screen, fighting to keep her mind from wandering even further, wanting to know what happened behind the closed antique wooden door in that last photo.

Ten minutes ticked off the game clock before either team scored a goal in what was already proving to be the most exciting soccer game of the season, leaving thirty-five minutes of game play in the first half. As the game progressed, thoughts of both Meredith and Cooper loomed in the back of Andrew's mind. However, his current off-the-field issues didn't keep him from dribbling through several defenders and scoring his team's first goal midway through the first half, tying the game at one a piece. Andrew always tried to play off how talented he was, but others knew he was only being humble. He was one of the best strikers, if not *the* best, in the entire league. Everyone on the field knew this which made it that much more difficult for him to find an open shot at the net.

Two trips down the field later, one of the other team's players ran into a wall named Beast, which forced an official's timeout. While some of the other players surrounded the injured man, Andrew jogged to the bench. In soccer, there are no timeouts, unlike most other sports, which is why a few of his teammates took advantage of the break in play to pour water down their throats and over their heads. In this league they'd always been extra cautious about injuries, so Andrew knew he had time to hustle over to the bench where he reached beneath for the cell phone in his bag. He found two missed calls. One from a number he didn't recognize, the other from one he did—Meredith's cell phone. After pressing a button, the display screen informed him that he had one new voicemail. Andrew was just about to listen to it when he heard the whistle blow. His eyes darted toward the ref then to his coach. Momentarily, he considered asking to be replaced for a few minutes, but when he looked across the field at the cloud of purple haze—remembering what was at stake here—he decided otherwise.

Each team scored one more goal before halftime causing Beast to stare at the scoreboard on the far side of the field and shake his head on the long walk back to the bench. Andrew, and everyone else, knew this one would most likely end up coming down to the wire. Knowing that the big fella always took responsibility for every goal scored against the team, regardless of whether a defender had made a mistake or the other team had just made a nice shot, he offered Beast a few words of encouragement.

A few random huddles formed along the sideline, but Andrew excused himself from the conversation he'd unwillingly gotten caught up in. Upon escaping his teammates, he headed straight for his cell phone and sat down while listening to Meredith's crackling voice in the message she'd left.

"Andrew," he heard her utter almost in a whisper. "The wedding . . . is . . . off." She sniffled, then came a short pause. Andrew's hand, holding the phone to his ear, began to shake as he waited for the words that would follow. "I will always love you, but I doubt I will ever be able to forgive you."

Andrew buried his face in his hands for the remainder of the fifteen minute halftime, and he barely heard the referee's whistle encouraging players to return to the field for another forty-five minutes of play. He wasn't sure if he could force himself to continue playing after hearing the words Meredith left for him. But he knew it would definitely be easier to keep from crying out there amongst twenty-one other sweaty men in live action than it was right here. He also knew he couldn't leave things like this, but now wasn't the time to return the call. She hadn't even said why, which bothered him. He wasn't stupid, though. He knew there were dots, he just wasn't quite sure how many or how to connect them. Yet.

He tossed the phone into his bag and began to stand. The moment his hands pushed away from the splintery bench, Andrew heard a voice from behind.

"Are you okay, Andrew?" she asked softly.

His ears perked up, but he couldn't put a finger on the voice. Andrew turned.

"Hey," he said wondering if she had heard the few sniffles he thought he had covered well enough for no one to notice. "I'm fine," he answered. "What are you doing here?"

"I needed to see you again," Cooper said.

Andrew, his mouth opened wide, was about to respond when Beast's voice carried across the entire field as though it had come through a megaphone, directing all eyes to Andrew and Cooper.

"You're almost a married man, Andrew Callaway, leave that pretty woman alone and get on the field with the rest of us sweaty old men."

Andrew's face turned fire engine red. "Can it wait?" he asked Cooper, turning his attention back to her. ". . . forty-five minutes?"

Cooper smirked. "Yeah, sure, go ahead," she insisted, motioning toward the field.

As Andrew jogged to his position, she watched his calf muscles flex as his cleats made impact with the ground. This was the first time she had seen him in shorts, and she found herself wondering if he frequented the tanning bed or if he was just one of those people God had decided to gift with a permanent tan. The forest green mesh shorts his team wore probably helped bring out his skin tone, she thought, following his every move on the field. The white shirt didn't play as a disadvantage either. Thankfully, though, his team's coach hadn't dressed Andrew and his teammates for the Barney reunion the other team must have made plans to attend after the game.

As Andrew weaved through his opponents hoping to score his second goal of the game, his mind was elsewhere. His eyes had been drifting to Cooper often, now standing on her tiptoes and covering her mouth with a nervous hand. When the ball had first come in his direction, he had noticed how excited she seemed, and on the final stretch of his twenty-five yard dash, Cooper McKay was basically doing jumping jacks on the sidelines. It sure was nice to have a personal cheerleader he thought, as his leg swung back to kick the ball. But what was she doing here? What did she need to talk to him about now? Did it have anything to do with Meredith's voicemail? He wondered. Knowing the answer was probably obvious.

Andrew missed the shot.

"That's okay, Andrew," Cooper encouraged, "you'll make it next time." She had watched the ball whiz past another player's head, appearing as if it was going to land in the net, but at the last second it curved to the left and hit the goalpost.

Andrew smiled in Cooper's direction, realizing there were

more butterflies in his stomach now than there had been when his team initially took the field although he wasn't sure why. It wasn't like he needed to impress Cooper. What he needed to do was figure out why everything in his life had changed so much since this time yesterday when he had been the happiest engaged man in the world.

✧

Whispers began to circulate amongst the players and in the bleachers. "Who is that?" people asked. "I've never seen her here before," some said. "Is she here with Andrew?" they questioned. "What about Meredith?" others wondered aloud. "Maybe she's a relative."

The soccer crowd consisted of regulars. Everyone knew which player was married to or dating the women at the field, and any time a new face appeared—especially one as pretty as Cooper's—it drew attention. Most of the players on Andrew's team were married, and some even attended church with him. Even most church going Christians couldn't help but take a second look at a woman as stunning as Cooper McKay.

Cooper pulled her hair into a ponytail and paced the chalk line in her New Balance tennis shoes, following the ball up and down the field as the sun slowly sank below the towering pine trees that surrounded the outer limits of the park. She was glad she had changed into a T-shirt before coming out to the game, and up until now she wished she had replaced her blue jeans with a pair of shorts. With the intense heat continuing to diminish, Cooper found herself crossing her fingers as though she had been rooting for Andrew's team all season. Then she suddenly found herself clearing her throat when she realized that Andrew, for the first time in this game, was coming out for a breather.

"I didn't realize soccer was this exciting," Cooper admitted when he joined her on the sideline.

"What did you expect? A bunch of old men hobbling from one goal to another?"

She snickered. "Yeah, pretty much, but your team is good."

"Not good enough," Andrew said pointing at the scoreboard that now showed his team trailing by a goal. "I've blown two shots that I should've made."

"I think you guys will pull it off," she said optimistically.

Andrew smiled. "Keep your fingers crossed," he suggested.

He felt kind of odd talking to Cooper here, like everyone was watching him. Even though Meredith had already called off their wedding, he still knew in his heart that he was definitely doing something wrong, yet he couldn't force himself to ignore Cooper or ask her to leave.

Cooper eyed the ground that she had begun massaging with the toe of her shoe. "So I guess you noticed that I keep crossing my fingers. It's an odd habit," she admitted with a smirk, feeling somewhat embarrassed by her intensity level. As soon as the thought entered her mind, she looked up and noticed Barry making progress toward the net.

"Go, go, go," she began to holler, her hands clasped together as she and Andrew moved down the sideline in unison. They watched Barry's leg fling through the air—which had instantaneously become silent—and with their mouths gaped they awaited the verdict.

Andrew dropped his hands when the goalie deflected the ball. Cooper uncrossed her fingers again.

A minute later, Andrew re-entered the game just in time to watch Beast sprawl out to make the save of the season. From the ground, Beast wore a large grin to go along with his dirty jersey, and Andrew smiled with him as he offered his hand.

When dusk began to set in, the pole lights—towering high above the field—flickered to life.

As the game wore on, both teams made some outstanding

plays. Barry scored the game-tying goal with just a few minutes remaining, and Cooper remained nervous. Curious onlookers had migrated over from the adjacent fields, joining Cooper and standing shoulder to shoulder from one end of the field to the other. When the scoreboard clock wound down to one minute, a bright glow took over the night sky and Cooper smiled, taking in the beauty of this atmosphere. There was nothing like the smell of popcorn and nachos or the sound of hollering fans— the same ones that had been getting onto their children the entire game for screaming and chasing each other up and down a nearby dirt mound, showering one another with dirt. Thankfully, she had been far enough away to miss the spray. A few others hadn't, and they were still picking particles from their hair.

In the final minute of the game, the purple team scored another goal, putting them ahead 4-3.

Then, Andrew's team began to play with an intensity that only the final moments of a close game could bring out in athletes. Cooper hung on like a hinge as she watched Barry and Andrew pass the ball back and forth several times, barely avoiding steals and collisions. She wanted them to score so badly. She could tell how much the game meant to the team, to Andrew.

With six seconds remaining on the clock, Andrew dribbled the ball through the legs of a defender, and the goal opened up as wide as the river behind his house. He could kick one-hundred out of one-hundred balls into that space. On the outside, there was no time for a smile, but on the inside he felt excitement begin to work its way through his body. He planted his left leg and swung back his right leg far enough to give him the power and distance he needed, but not so far that any of the defenders behind him could catch up and have a chance at changing the outcome.

❦

Cooper waited at a distance as Andrew emerged from the team huddle. "Good game," she offered. "I would slap you on the butt, but I'm not on your team," she added, laughing softly, hoping to lighten the mood.

Andrew forced a smile.

"You played very well," she told him.

He shook his head. "Until I blew the game."

He'd done everything right. It was a kick he'd made a thousand times, but somehow it had sailed inches over the goalpost.

The only positive thing about losing the game the way his team had is that Andrew and Cooper were able to slip into the parking lot without fifty questions from his teammates. He needed to let off some steam—a lot of steam—from the game—the voicemail—life at the time being.

After stuffing his bag into his vehicle, Andrew asked Cooper a question he wondered if he would later regret: "Would you like to walk down to the creek?"

11

A quarter mile walking trail that began at the soccer field parking lot and came to an end just past a cluster of softball fields brought Andrew and Cooper to a narrow clearing in the woods that Andrew promised would lead them to the creek. He held up a branch so Cooper could enter, and then he began to probe for spider webs and dangling limbs with one hand, using the other to position his cell phone, their only light source, as he led the way through the dark path. Behind him, Cooper took every step with caution as though walking on shards of glass, and he couldn't help but laugh every time she grabbed at his jersey, swearing something rubbed against her arm or leg. So far she had heard a rattlesnake, a bear, and a deer.

"What exactly do deer sound like?" Andrew inquired, holding a grin that Cooper was able to detect through the tone of his voice.

"Shut-up," she replied sarcastically. "Are we almost there?"

"Once we cross the suspension bridge, it's not much further."

Cooper furrowed her brow, and at the foot of the short wooden bridge that crossed over a small patch of swamp, she came to a staggering halt. For a moment, she thought, *maybe Andrew is just like every other man*, as he jumped up and down to test the durability of the lumber. There had to be snakes down there, she assumed, barely able to make out the outline of the muck. If she were to fall in accidentally, she knew luck would have it that a snake would bite her; with that thought in mind, she decided to take this opportunity not only to buy a little more time before crossing the bridge but to share her snakebite story with Andrew. It happened after Hurricane Floyd in 1998, she informed him. Floodwaters nearly three foot deep rose into her parent's house, and after they subsided, she had climbed into a pair of rubber work boots in the garage only to feel a thread of sharp pricks on the bottom of her left foot.

"What did you do?" Andrew asked.

"I jumped out of the boots—and a water moccasin slithered across the garage and hid beneath the water heater. My dad, who had been standing just as close as you are to me now, didn't even realize I had been bit. Eventually, he ran for his axe, killed the snake, and ultimately calmed down enough to take me to the hospital. The way he acted you would have thought he had been the one who'd been bitten."

"Your foot isn't green or anything like that now, is it?" Andrew teased.

"Why don't you stick your face down there next to it, and I'll give you an up close view," Cooper shot back. Then, playfully, she swung her leg in his direction. He flinched and reached for the handrails causing the bridge to sway back and forth like a Ferris wheel with a couple of teenagers stuck at the top. "Of course it's not green," she said.

A few more laughs was all it took to get Cooper to cross over the dilapidated structure, and though neither she nor Andrew ended up knee deep in mud, she felt both of them might be headed in that direction though not literally. With her feet once again on solid ground, Cooper's mind blinked to Meredith. *What type of woman was Meredith Hastings?* She wondered. *Was she good to Andrew? Had she only made a bad decision by sending the emails? Did she ever imagine it would lead to this?*

There were times since the emails had arrived when Cooper felt Meredith didn't deserve Andrew Callaway, and then there were times like this when Cooper didn't know if she could convince herself that *she* deserved Andrew any more than Meredith did. The two of them were engaged. They had spent years getting to know each other, falling in love and planning a future. The thought that she had come between them, whether willingly or not, frightened her. Sure, she hadn't agreed to Meredith's proposal, but she couldn't help but think that in a roundabout way what she was doing *was* helping make Meredith's worst nightmare a reality.

Andrew continued to follow the path, and Cooper followed only a short distance behind, her mind still churning as the trail forked through an even thicker wooded area before opening into a small grassy meadow.

"This is beautiful," she articulated.

The nightlight in the sky—as Cooper's mom had always referred to the moon when tucking her in bed at night—was casting a glow onto the creek making the thin ripples at the edge of the mysterious water visible as they slapped against a cluster of cypress trees. With a smile on her face, Cooper listened as an owl in the woods across the creek let out a welcoming hoot. Boy did she miss this. Two years of city life had erased even the memories of the sounds of a surreal Southern night—critters singing in perfect harmony and tree branches fighting in the wind. Nature at its finest, she reminisced.

"It's so peaceful out here," Cooper pointed out. "I could spend hours just taking all this in. It feels like we're on a remote island somewhere."

"I don't have anywhere to be," Andrew replied. Then he paused for a moment, just long enough to willingly collapse on a bed of boards making up the top of a desolate picnic table.

"Meredith called during the game," he said, once settled.

Cooper sat on the side of the bench closest to the creek and let her back lean against the table near Andrew's legs, waiting for the words that would follow the ones he'd just spoken. Would Andrew tell her that he had confronted Meredith about the emails? If so, would he say that he had forgiven her? Probably. Cooper imagined that Meredith most likely admitted to making a big mistake. Meredith probably even asked Andrew to find her and tell her that she was sorry for dragging another woman into this, which might have been why Andrew had been so quiet until they reached the bridge.

Gazing through towering treetops and into a starry night sky, Andrew, through watery eyes, couldn't see the expression of shock written all over Cooper's face as he released five words that hadn't even crossed her wandering mind: "She called off the wedding," he trailed off.

Other than the sound of chirping crickets and the monotonous hoots from the owl that had been spitting off like a caged dog, the air became eerily silent. Not sure what to say, Cooper sat as still as the ice sculpture Andrew had helped pick out for the wedding just a few days ago. How was she supposed to respond to Andrew's news? *Oh, I'm glad. What are you doing this weekend?* That wouldn't fly.

Andrew closed his eyes, still trying to figure out why Meredith, not him, had been the one to call off the wedding. He was the one who had a reason, not her.

"Meredith called it off?" Cooper double-checked, nearly as surprised as Andrew had been when he first listened to the message. "But, why?"

"I was hoping you might be able to help me out with the answer to that question. I thought that might be the reason you showed up at the game tonight. Do you know anything?" he probed. "Has she emailed you?"

"I'm sorry, Andrew, she hasn't. I haven't heard from Meredith since I've been in town."

Andrew lifted his head. "So that's not why you came tonight?"

He watched the back of Cooper's head as it shook from side to side.

"There is something else I wanted to talk to you about," she answered, "but it's not important right now." She paused briefly. "Meredith didn't give you a reason?" she inquired.

Andrew closed his eyes as he answered Cooper's question. "She just said, 'The wedding is off; I will always love you, but I doubt I will ever be able to forgive you.'" He paused for a short moment doubting he would ever be able to forget those words. "Forgive me for what? That is the part I can't figure out. I haven't done anything wrong," he barked.

Andrew and Cooper spent the next half hour talking in circles on a rectangular shaped picnic table. Neither of them could come up with a valid reason why Meredith would have called off the engagement without talking to one of them first. The conversation eventually turned to the soccer game and then to Vlade Divac. Andrew was amazed to discover that Cooper knew the name of a seven-foot Yugoslavian who played in the NBA. Other than Michael Jordan and maybe Shaquille O'Neal, it was rare to find a woman who could name any NBA player, current or retired.

"You're right," Andrew agreed, a mental picture of Beast in his mind. "Beast does favor Divac. The only difference is Beast is about as tall as that tree," Andrew said pointing to one pine and then to another taller pine, "and Divac is as tall as that one."

"And you and I are about as tall as those two," Cooper giggled, pointing at two of the shorter Cypress Trees still being slapped against by tiny waves in the creek. Then with a smile lingering across her beautiful face, she turned to Andrew. "I'm glad you brought me out here," Cooper uttered with a quick wink.

As a grounded fog settled in, Cooper joined Andrew on the table, her feet at one end, his at the other, and it seemed as though time began to stand still.

"Wow, what a view," Cooper pointed out. "How many of them do you think are up there?" she asked, referring to the stars he hadn't taken his eyes off since they arrived, other than when she'd just decided to climb aboard.

Andrew began to count out loud but stopped when he reached five. "A lot," he finally answered.

"I bet no one really knows."

"Only God."

"I wonder if He's named them all."

"Maybe there is a star for every person on Earth," Andrew suggested. "When you see a shooting star, that means that person made it into heaven."

Cooper pondered that thought for a moment. "I wonder where I am."

Andrew pointed to the sky. "You're over there near that lion-shaped thing."

"Is that you," she motioned, "right beside me?"

Andrew rolled his neck to face her. "I'm brighter than that," he laughed. "I'm probably the North Star; where's that one?" he teased.

Cooper and Andrew spent nearly an hour taking in and talking about the stars before Andrew stretched his aching muscles and began skipping stones across the surface of the steaming creek. The rising heat gave it the appearance of a gigantic hot tub, and Andrew, as his attempts to land a pebble on the opposite shore failed, thought seriously about plunging in.

At the picnic table, Cooper grinned. After ten tries Andrew hadn't even come close, and she was seriously thinking about going over there and making him look bad. Watching him brought back childhood memories of the times she'd spent at the river with her father, and she began to tell Andrew about the time her dad had devoted an entire day, when she was nine, to teach her how to skip pebbles.

"So that makes you an expert, huh?" Andrew teased.

"Nope, but it does make me better than you," she shot back.

Andrew shook his head and tossed a rock in her direction. "Nice catch," he admitted. "Now let's see what you got," he antagonized, offering a handful of stones as she met him at the shore.

"No thanks, I won't need all those."

Andrew stepped back and watched Cooper's arm swing back, and then nearly touching the ground with her fingers, she released the rock like a sidearm pitcher in baseball.

The pebble skipped once.

Andrew furrowed his brow.

Twice.

Andrew raised his brow another centimeter.

Three bounces.

Another centimeter.

Then when the rock sank below the surface, he watched Cooper kick the ground, and he couldn't help but laugh at how mad she seemed to get.

She reached out her hand, "Okay, I might need one more."

Andrew handed her two, and she dropped one back into his hand. He had to admit that he liked the competitiveness—and the optimism.

Then came the wind-up, the release . . .

One bounce.

Andrew didn't raise an eyebrow this time.

Two bounces.

Okay, raised them a little.

Three bounces.

A little more. Actually, a lot more. Even he hadn't been able to get two consecutive rocks to skip three times. If she could get the fourth bounce, he knew the rock would make it to the other side, and he would look like an idiot.

With his thumbnail in his mouth, Andrew waited impatiently, and as soon as the pebble bounced the fourth time and reached land on the other side, the owl let out a hoot.

Andrew screamed at him: "Oh, shut up, of course you're on her side!"

Cooper smirked, folded her hands behind her back and hopped about an inch off the ground.

Andrew chuckled, "What was that?"

"My victory dance."

"You didn't win."

"I won." She paused for a short moment and looked Andrew square in the eye. "You lost."

"Beginner's luck," Andrew assured, handing her another stone. "You can't do it again."

Andrew watched eagerly, and not only did Cooper land it on the other side once again, but if it was daytime he could probably swim over there and find it within a few feet of the first one she had skipped across the creek. Even Tiger Woods would be happy with two lies like the ones Cooper had just landed. As he stood silently in amazement, she smirked and wiped her hands clean.

"You were right, beginner's luck," she said sarcastically. "I'll give you two chances to match me, and if you don't land at least one pebble, I, the WIN-NER," she sounded out slowly, "get a prize."

"What kind of prize?"

Cooper, rummaging her mind, squinted her right eye and

shifted her lips to that side of her face. "How about dinner?"

Andrew thought for a moment: *Technically, I am a single man now*, he concluded. That sure did sound funny, though, after being engaged and in a serious relationship for three years. Then, the word, like a freight train, hit him again: *Single*. He really was *single*—unless he called Meredith tonight and talked her out of her decision. That, he had thought about—might even be doing so at this very moment if Cooper hadn't shown up at his game which reminded him—why *had* she shown up at his game? He had forgotten to bring that subject up again. Oh well, Andrew decided, maybe he would mention it later. All he knew now, and all he wanted to know, is that he was at the creek with Cooper making plans for dinner; and for the most part, Meredith, who he thought trusted him one-hundred percent, was not bombarding his every thought.

"Deal," Andrew finally agreed, rearing back to throw the first pebble.

Cooper watched it skip twice before it sank to the bottom of the murky creek. She smiled. "Last chance," she reminded him before he threw the next pebble. "If you make it, I'll pay."

Andrew chuckled at her offer. It would be nice if he could actually get at least one pebble to land on the other side of this stupid creek, he thought, but if this one did make it, he would still pay for dinner. He just wouldn't look like as much of a loser when he pulled out the cash and handed it to the waitress.

Cooper watched closely as the pebble made impact and shot into the air, skipping once, then twice. When it took a third hop, she furrowed her brow. This one might actually make it she realized. Out of all the practices she watched Andrew throw earlier, he had only been able to make that happen a few times. Her eyes grew when the pebble touched the water a fourth and final time, and she couldn't help but raise her hands and cheer when it reached the other side of the creek.

"Yay! You made one. Your little pebble is over there with my two pebbles now," she teased.

Andrew shook his head and then joined Cooper as she sat on the grassy area near the water. "You know I'm not going to let you pay, right?"

"I figured you might say that," she answered with a smile. "A few years after my dad taught me how to skip pebbles, he taught me that a gentleman wouldn't let a woman pay for dinner unless they had been dating for a while."

"Are you labeling me?" Andrew asked.

"Are you admitting you're not a gentleman?"

"I might be."

"You might be a gentleman or you might be saying that you're not a gentleman?"

"I guess you'll have to be the judge of that."

"Well, Mr. I may or may not be a gentleman, since I told you the story about my dad teaching me how to beat you in a pebble skipping contest, it's your turn to tell me about something you did when you were a kid," Cooper requested.

Andrew wiped his hands on his shorts, brushing away the grit from the rocks. "Do you want to hear a funny one or a humiliating one?"

Cooper smirked a little. "Humiliating, of course."

Andrew racked his brain for a good story. "Actually, I think I have one that covers both," he said with a smile as he thought about the night he and his friends still laughed about until this day. "When I was about ten years old, my brother, a couple of our buddies, and me snuck out of the house one summer around midnight. We wandered down to the river—about a mile walk—and went skinny-dipping. At the time, it was the most daring thing any of us had ever done. We had to be extremely quiet because we were swimming behind someone else's house. When we'd been in the water for about an hour, we started to get cold," Andrew snickered, remembering how embarrassing what happened next had been. "Before we could get to the shore where we left our shorts, Old Lady Pike came running at us with a broom, yelling, 'I got your britches, my dears, and the police are on the way.'"

Erupting with laughter, Cooper fell back in the grass, and Andrew kept a smile on his face as he continued to reminisce. "She had been sitting on her back porch the entire time watching us, waiting for us to get out of the river. I've never been so embarrassed in all my life," he exclaimed.

"What did you do?" Cooper asked while her eyes watered from laughing so hard.

The animation in Andrew's voice grew even higher as he answered the question that he must have been asked a hundred times. "We high tailed it back to the house."

"Naked?"

"We had no other choice," he exclaimed.

"Did she really call the police?"

Andrew shook his head from side to side. "We huddled up by the front window for an hour watching for the cops, but they never did show up. It turned out Old Lady Pike was just pulling our chain." He paused. "That was the last time we ever went near her house though."

"Did she know who you were?"

"Oh yeah, like I said, she watched us for an hour. She waited that entire time just so she could spook us when we walked out butt naked." Cooper watched Andrew's face turn red as he visualized the gray haired, humped-back woman who'd, for as long as he could remember, always walked with a cane. "Even now, when I see that woman, I cringe. She always smiles at me, wearing that 'I've seen you naked' grin."

"That must have been exciting, though."

"What?" he asked wondering to which part of the story she was referring.

"Skinny-dipping—it's always sounded so daring to me."

Andrew furrowed his brow. "You've never been?"

"Nope, I've never tried it."

"How did you make it through your teenage years without skinny-dipping at least once? Your friends never tried to talk you into it?"

"I don't think they ever did it either, well, not the girls anyway. A few guys did mention it on several occasions, but I never felt comfortable enough with them."

Andrew, wanting to take hold of the innocent hand stretched out next to his, suddenly found himself studying Cooper's small fingers. She was so gorgeous, every inch of her, but he knew touching her hand would only lead to other things, and he shouldn't even be sitting this close to another woman right now, especially one with whom he was talking about skinny-dipping.

"What's it like?" Cooper blurted out, the smirk on her face describing the thoughts running through her mind.

At that moment, Andrew felt his insides buckle. "What?" he mumbled, knowing exactly *what*.

"Skinny-dipping," she replied without hesitation.

Since crossing the parking lot three hours ago, Andrew and Cooper hadn't seen or even heard another human being. The glow from the lights at the fields had faded nearly thirty minutes ago, and now Cooper presumed she and Andrew were the only people remaining in the park. Otherwise, she wouldn't have even considered suggesting such a frivolous act. This, Cooper figured, was about as alone as two people could get on a creek and now was as good a time as any to try skinny-dipping.

Andrew, unlike John in high school and Robbie in college—both had asked her to go skinny-dipping in the river behind her parent's house—hadn't even brought up the subject, well, not directly anyway. He *had* told the story that surfaced the idea, but she was the one who had put it out there as an option. The reason she had declined those other guys wasn't because she didn't want to give it a shot back then too, but because those guys were only interested in seeing her naked and hoping it would lead to something else. With Andrew, it felt different. Cooper doubted very seriously if Andrew Callaway, who had just found out today that he wouldn't be getting married next weekend, would try to put the moves on her whether naked or fully clothed.

"I can't describe the feeling," Andrew said trying to push the same thoughts Cooper was having to the back of his mind, but that seemed to be a lost cause. "You'd have to try it yourself to find out."

Then, Cooper asked the question that was on both of their minds: "You want to?"

At those words, Andrew felt his body cringe, just as it had when he'd run into Old Lady Pike at the grocery store a few weeks ago, but this cringing felt different like he was doing something wrong, but at the same time it felt so right. "Right now?" he double-checked, glancing at Cooper, then at the creek—already in way over his head. "Here?"

"Why not?" she questioned, reaching for her nose and then pinching it with two fingers while continuing to talk in a nasal tone. "You need a bath anyway. You're dirty from the game, and I've been meaning to tell you—you kind of stink," she teased.

"It's been so long, I'm not sure if I remember how," Andrew said with a smirk.

"If you don't feel comfortable, that's fine," Cooper said, almost unable to believe that she was the one egging this on.

Andrew stood and slowly pulled his shirt over his head, then tossed it onto her lap. "Your turn," he said as though it was a game of truth or dare.

Feeling her heart begin to pound, Cooper put her hand to her chest. All of a sudden the playful banter had become real. "Okay," she agreed, hesitantly. "But face that way. And when we get our clothes off we have to jump in at the same time," she instructed.

Andrew, twisting his body to face the other direction, willingly conformed to her request. "I'll see you in the water," he clarified.

"You'll see the part of me that's above the water," she said, feeling her hands begin to tremble.

"Are you nervous?" Andrew asked. Though he doubted he would admit to being somewhat terrified, he knew *he* was, which Cooper could probably tell by the crackling sound in every word that had come out of his mouth since she posed the question of the night.

"No," Cooper answered trying to convince herself that the reason she was having a difficult time unsnapping a pair of jeans that she had unbuttoned a hundred times was because the temperature had dropped a few degrees. "I hope no one wanders out here," she added, studying every shadow within sight.

The trees filtered the moonlight except on the creek's silky surface where reflections slowly danced. "They couldn't see us anyway," Andrew assured as Cooper's last article of clothing fell to the ground.

"Okay, I'm ready," she said. "Let's jump at the same time—and when I come up out of that water, I better not see you standing up here fully dressed pointing and laughing at me."

"I can't believe you would even imagine I would be capable of such a thing."

Cooper began the count: "One. Two. Three," and then two completely naked shadows darted toward the creek making a simultaneous splash that convinced a few critters to scamper through the woods.

Cooper emerged from the water first and instantly began searching for Andrew. A moment later, she watched his head pop up about ten yards out.

"So how is skinny-dipping?" he asked, wiping the water from his eyes.

"Refreshing," Cooper admitted, folding her arms beneath the surface to cover her bare chest with more than just water.

"Yeah, that is how I was going to describe it earlier, but I figured it would be better if you experienced it for yourself," Andrew revealed, barely able to touch bottom.

Andrew Callaway and Cooper McKay spent the next hour of their lives wading in the creek, naked and at a distance comfortable for both of them. While Cooper was impressed that Andrew had enough respect for her to resist the temptation of moving in a little closer, she had known all along in the back of her mind that he would. The thought had to cross his mind, though, she knew because she too had been fighting the electrifying urge she'd first felt when he spoke the words *skinny-dipping*. The feeling had only intensified when she removed her clothes and then, neck deep in the creek, spotted his on the shore just a few feet from where she had dropped her own.

12

The next morning Andrew pushed open the glass door at Greg's Garage and Body Shop before stepping up to an empty elevated counter. Eager to hand over the keys to his Land Rover, he instantly spotted Greg through an opening that led into a garage filled with grease and auto parts stacked from floor to ceiling.

Greg—his name stitched on his button-up blue work shirt to prove it—had looked up from beneath one of three racks as soon as the bell jingled. With a lit cigarette nestled in the corner of his mouth and a dingy orange rag hanging from his torn shirt pocket, he waved in Andrew's direction and then pushed a button that began the process to lower the car he had been working on all morning. When the wheels touched the ground, Andrew watched Greg reach into his pocket and wipe the fresh oil from his fingers.

"Andrew," he called out making his way to the lobby furnished with red plastic chairs and a week's worth of the local newspaper. "It's been a while; what brings you in today?"

"I wish it was a while longer," Andrew answered honestly. "Wait until you see what I have for you."

With an interested smirk on his face, Greg held up a finger gesturing for Andrew to hold on for a minute so he could hand a key to a customer waiting in one of the red chairs. He took a check from the man and then followed Andrew to the parking lot where both of them stood in total silence, their arms crossed as if they were analyzing a work of art in a museum.

"Who would do something like this?" Greg finally dared to ask. "You must have really pissed someone off," he added before Andrew had the chance to reply.

"I have a couple people in mind," Andrew trailed off, unwilling to offer the names he and Cooper had tossed back and forth last night—Eric Hastings and Chris Selzer. Both had a motive, but neither he nor Cooper had been able to decide which of the two might be responsible for the free paint job.

As Greg began to examine the damage, Brooke pulled into the parking lot at eight o'clock sharp, just like Andrew had asked. Grinning from ear to ear, she stepped out of her car. "You didn't tell me it was pink. It's . . ." She paused for one more look, "pretty!"

"It isn't funny," Andrew declared.

"How did this happen?"

So far this morning Andrew had already been through this story with Barry and Marie, his mother, and one of his neighbors who had been walking past his driveway when he was leaving. Now, he started the story for Brooke making sure to once again leave out the part about he and Cooper skinny-dipping at the creek: "After my game last night, I went down to the creek with a friend, and when we made it back to the parking lot," he said, thinking: *with wet hair and dripping bodies*, "we found a surprise. And that's it—," he added, pointing at his SUV, "my silver Land Rover . . . spray-painted pink."

"Did you call the Sheriff?"

"Yes. Ronnie came out and took a look at it, even snapped a few pictures for the file he said he was going to start when he got back to the station last night. The three of us surveyed the area but didn't find anything suspicious. There were no kids loitering near the park and no parked cars or empty paint cans. And you can't really pick out a footprint in a gravel parking lot where a hundred people have walked all over. So, basically, there is absolutely no evidence to go on."

The wheels in Brooke's mind began to churn; she remembered Andrew having the early game because she and Roger had picked up take-out afterward, made it to his place, and finished eating well before nine o'clock. There was no way that she and a hundred other people would have missed the Pink Panther if the incident had taken place during the game.

"What time did you say this happened?" she asked.

I didn't say, Andrew thought to himself. "I found it around eleven."

Brooke noticed that this time Andrew chose to use the word "I" instead of "we". "What were you doing down at the creek so late?" she probed.

"Just hanging out," he answered nonchalantly.

"Uh-huh, I see," Brooke gestured. "And who did you say you were with?"

I didn't, Andrew thought again, gritting his teeth. He glanced at his shoes and kicked a rock across the parking lot. "Okay, Sheriff Ronnie Ringer," he shot back sarcastically. "Am I going to be in trouble for being at the park after hours, or are you going to let that slide since my truck got vandalized?"

Brooke threw up her hands and stepped back. "If you don't want to tell me that's fine. Who you were with and what you were doing is between you and Meredith."

Brooke and Andrew barely spoke on the drive to Andrew's house to pick up the dilapidated old truck his father had passed down to him. She considered continuing her cross-examination to find out just why Andrew had been at the creek with another woman so late last night, but after the way he'd snapped back at the garage, she decided it might be best if she left it alone for now. Anyway, she figured that Andrew, in time, would tell her what was *really* going on.

An hour later, Brooke poked her head in Andrew's office, confident the question that had been racking her mind all morning had just been answered. "There is someone here to see you," she informed him.

"Okay. I'll be there in just a minute." Before Brooke pulled the door to, Andrew asked, "Who is it?"

"I'm not sure, Candice is at the front desk; I was just passing through and she asked if I'd tell you on my way back here."

Andrew dropped his pen on a stack of papers and scooted his chair out from beneath his desk. On his way to the lobby, he made a pit stop at the restroom, and when he turned on the water at the sink, he heard the stall door behind him creak open. Startled, Andrew turned.

"I didn't realize there was anyone in here," he said as a man he had never before seen rolled up his sleeves and made his way to the sink next to his. Andrew offered a half smile and studied the stranger for a moment. "Are you Chris?" he finally asked.

"Yes, sir," the man answered politely, and Andrew couldn't help but notice that the button-up shirt and tie he was wearing didn't quite seem like comfortable clothing for this fellow. "And you're Andrew Callaway . . ."

"All day, every day," Andrew responded, and when he noticed the guy seemed at a loss for words, he made another comment to keep the conversation flowing. "I've heard a lot about you."

"I've seen your picture in the paper and in magazines," Chris replied, not sure how else to respond. "Just out of curiosity," he asked, "how do you know who I am?"

Andrew stared at Chris's shirt and grinned. "Consider this your first lesson in real estate," he offered. "Learn to read name tags," he said with a wink, pointing at the name Chris Taylor on an oval piece of plastic. "I see Brooke made one for you." He paused for a moment. "She says you are interested in getting into real estate after college."

"Yes, sir, that's why I'm here," he answered, drying his hands.

"You're her cousin, right?"

Last week, Andrew had agreed to let Chris visit the office for the remainder of this week and all of next. The kid was on summer break and wanted to get some first-hand experience in the real estate environment. When Brooke said she would teach him the ropes and promised not to pawn him off on Andrew, he said yes without reluctance, but a week ago he hadn't had a problem with the name Chris. Oh well, he decided, it wasn't Brooke's cousin's fault that his mother had given him the same name as a jerk like Chris Selzer.

"Yes, sir," Chris confirmed.

"Well, Brooke knows just as much about this business as I do. It'll do you some good to listen to her advice."

"Thanks, I will."

Andrew shook the young man's hand and tossed a paper towel into the trashcan before heading to the lobby where he found Cooper being eaten by the gigantic leather chair near the window in the far corner.

"Surprise," she said.

"Good morning," Andrew replied, trying not to stare at her tanned legs crossed at the knees. Come to think of it, he had never really noticed *any* woman's knees before, but for some reason, he couldn't help but notice how her knees complimented her legs.

"Hey," she replied, standing to greet him. "Thank you again for following me home last night," she said appreciatively. "I had a hard time falling asleep after what happened, and I know I would have been scared to death if I would have had to walk to that door alone."

Brooke, standing near the front desk pretending to offer some type of instructions to her cousin, raised her eyebrows at Cooper's comment.

"My pleasure," Andrew replied softly, catching a glimpse of Brooke out of the corner of his eye. "Let's step outside," he encouraged. "I could use the fresh air."

Outside, parked cars lined the street next to the busy sidewalk, so Andrew and Cooper moved to the nearby grass—still damp from the dew that had fallen the night before—to make way for pedestrians.

"Did you call Meredith last night?" was the first question out of Cooper's mouth.

"I did," Andrew replied. "But she didn't answer any of my calls. I left a couple messages asking for clarification, but she hasn't called back yet." The conversation came to a brief halt while Andrew took a moment to acknowledge the mailman, who shook his hand and then made his way toward the front door. Then, Andrew turned back to Cooper and changed the subject. "So, what is on your agenda for the day?" he asked.

He listened as Cooper rambled off a list of errands: pay the electric bill for Mom; pick up milk at the grocery store; buy stamps. "But the real reason I came down here," she admitted, "wasn't just to swing by City Hall to drop off the electric bill; I was wondering if you might want to have that dinner tonight?" she asked with a smile, lifting her body off the ground with her tiptoes like an excited school girl.

Andrew took a moment to gather his thoughts, contemplating whether he should decline. Having Cooper around had been nice given the current situation, but what about Meredith? Even though she was the one who'd called off the wedding, if there was any chance they could somehow work things out, the time he was spending with Cooper wasn't going to help their odds. On the other hand, Meredith hadn't returned his phone calls nor his crying pleas, and she was the one who had sent Cooper his way in the first place. This was all Meredith's fault. Whatever happened, he could blame it on her: the episode at the creek last night; the dinner he had promised Cooper. "Yes," he finally agreed. "Tonight would be fine."

"Great," Cooper exclaimed. "I hope it was okay to stop by your office like this."

Andrew gave her a wink. "I'm the boss, so I can pretty much do whatever I want around here. Just don't tell Brooke that," he said with a smile.

"Well then, boss, where would you like to have dinner?"

"Let's see," he began, arms crossed and scratching his chin, thinking of whom they might run across if they went out. "How about you come over to my place and I'll cook?" he suggested.

"Sounds fabulous," Cooper responded, trying to remember the last time a man had offered to cook dinner for her. "Tell Brooke I said it was nice meeting her."

"Don't you mean Candice?"

"It was nice meeting her too, but I only spoke to her for a short moment when I first came in. Then Brooke walked me to the waiting area; we talked for a few minutes before you came out. She sure is nice," Cooper complimented as Andrew's face turned firecracker red. "She said she recognized me from the game last night and even invited me to come sit with her and her boyfriend if I get a chance to come to another game before I leave town."

Boyfriend? Picture Boy? That was quick, Andrew thought, wondering what all Cooper and Brooke had talked about as he went over the directions to his house with Cooper.

When he finished and she walked away, Andrew stood at the front door for a moment preparing his thoughts for Brooke who eyed him as he strolled into the office with his hands in his pockets. "My office," he said with his lips nearly closed.

Brooke sent Chris on an errand, and then as she headed to see Andrew, she felt like she was on her way to the principal's office. "I'm not in trouble, am I?" she asked, shutting Andrew's door behind her.

"What did you say to her?"

"Who?" Brooke replied, playing dumb.

"You know who," he said sternly. "Cooper. Or better yet, what did you convince her to tell you?"

"Nothing, really. She just said the two of you had a good time at the creek last night."

"I guess you're happy now that you know who the other person was."

Brooke shrugged her shoulders. "I already had a good idea. I saw the two of you talking at the game last night." When she paused for a moment, Andrew could tell what question was about to pop out of her mouth. "Is everything okay with you and Meredith?" she asked.

"Cooper and I are *just* friends," he clarified.

"Okay," Brooke conceded, taking a step toward the door where she stood for a moment watching Andrew run his fingers through his hair. She could tell, once again, that it was time to back off; when Andrew was ready to talk to her about Meredith, he would. Until then, she would just have to make assumptions as to what was going on between two of her best friends in the entire world. At this point, all she knew was that something was wrong. Extremely wrong, and she had even begun to wonder if ten days from now she would be singing at Andrew and Meredith's wedding. The singing part she would get over, but the thought of the two of them not getting married brought her to tears as she rushed into the bathroom and shut the stall door behind her.

Andrew, his head supported by a stack of papers on his desk, wished he had wings like the fly that had been buzzing around his office all morning, so he could fly away from all of his problems and clear his head for just a few minutes.

If Andrew Callaway *could* be a fly, he would land on the wall at the restaurant he and Barry had eaten lunch at yesterday and listen in on the conversation at the booth next to the one on which he had left a two-dollar tip for Lucy Lamm.

"What can I get you guys today?" Lucy asked the two guys who walked in just moments ago with grins on their faces.

"I'll take a cheese steak," the man wearing a camouflage hat answered.

"And can you cook that pink?" the other asked, laughing as though he had just shared the funniest joke he'd ever heard.

Lucy furrowed her brow. "We can cook it medium-rare if you would like."

"That's okay," the first man answered. "He's just messing around. It's an inside joke of sorts."

Confused, Lucy walked away and placed the order with the cooks as the two men at the table continued to chuckle.

"That mess was so funny last night," one of them joked.

"I would've loved to see his face when he saw that pretty pink on his ride."

"I told you we should have waited for him. That would have been the perfect place for me to give him the beating he has coming."

"He probably parked his car there for the night."

"Why would he leave his car in a deserted parking lot all night?"

"He probably went home with his new girlfriend after he was finished with her in the back seat."

"That isn't funny. That jerk is going to pay for what he is doing."

13

Still frustrated with Brooke, Andrew left his office and ended up at Dr. Mark Haywood, Jr.'s office after picking up his mother at her house. She'd been a patient of his since her hair turned gray which must have been ten years ago Andrew figured, if his math was correct. Before that, his mother had been a patient of his father's, Dr. Mark Haywood, Sr., who'd pulled her from her mother's womb.

In New Bern, passing the baton from one family member to the next was a tradition that had been going on for centuries. Like the Haywood's, Andrew too hoped to one day be able to pass down his agency to his son or daughter, but as far as today went, he hoped his mother's visit would turn out well. She had been taking her medication regularly and making sure to get plenty of rest—both prescribed by Dr. Haywood the last time she came in for a check-up. As far as Andrew could tell—though he had to admit the medical field was out of his realm of expertise—his mother's condition had improved drastically over the past year, and it had been more than two years since she had the heart attack that scared everyone to death.

"Do you want me to go in with you, Mom?" Andrew asked after signing her in at the front desk. "Or would you rather I stay out here in the waiting room?"

Andrew watched his mother's rosy cheeks light up. Filling the chair next to his, she gazed at him with her gorgeous green eyes. "I used to ask you that same question when you were a little boy." Wanting to remember those times, she paused for a moment to recollect on the days when the extra fifty pounds she carried into the doctor's office was in the form of a little boy. "You would always say, 'Mom, what do I look like, a little kid?' I would tell you that you were a big boy, but that big boys needed their mothers, too. Then I would say, 'Even your daddy likes me to go in with him when he sees the doctor.'"

"So you're saying you want me to go in with you?"

"No, I'm a big girl," she answered, and then she watched Andrew tilt his head slightly, almost like a dog trying to decipher the human language. "You only thought you were a big boy," she confirmed.

A few moments later the nurse called Rosemary's name, and Andrew found himself alone in the waiting room with a copy of the most recent Sports Illustrated magazine in his hand. The cover showcased Kobe Bryant, and the story inside highlighted the best game of his career—an 81 point performance. How one player could score two-thirds of his team's points in a single basketball game was beyond Andrew. In all the years he had been playing soccer he had only done that once, and the final score to the game was 6-4 not 122-104.

When Andrew finished reading about Bryant, he skimmed over the next twenty pages, mainly taking in the pictures and reading the captions below. He was about to pick out another magazine when he heard his name being called.

"Mr. Callaway."

Andrew turned. "Yes," he answered making his way toward the doctor.

"Can we borrow you for a few minutes?" he asked.

"Sure," he said, a little confused by the request.

He'd brought his mother here a handful of times but never once had Dr. Haywood asked him to come to the back where the two of them, after walking down a short hallway and making one right turn, joined his mother. She was sitting in the corner of a small examining room and for some reason, she wouldn't look him in the eye. Instead, she only stared at the out-of-date carpet, reminding him of a time when the roles had been reversed. He was the one in a chair in the corner, but instead of being in the doctor's office he'd been in the principal's office after pushing a kid off the merry-go-round for calling him Andrew Cowaway.

"I'm a little concerned about your mother," Dr. Haywood said in a calm voice as both he and Andrew took a seat. "It seems she hasn't been taking her medication regularly."

Andrew immediately chimed in, "Mom, you told me you had been . . ."

"I try to, Andrew, but sometimes I forget."

A fifteen-minute discussion with his mother and Dr. Haywood had revealed to Andrew that the word *sometimes* meant half a bottle of blood thinner pills were sitting in her medicine cabinet untouched, which equaled bad news. Not only had his mother been forgetting to take her pills, but she was also putting herself at risk for another heart attack. When he helped her into the truck, he made sure to remind her of that.

"Mom, if you want to move in with me, I can help you remember to take your medicine," he offered. "Plus I can keep an eye on you," he said, looking over his shoulder, the elongated gearshift in reverse.

Maybe that would be best, he thought. When Cooper left town, he would need somebody to keep him company. Otherwise, he would probably go crazy thinking about Meredith and what he could have done to avoid this whole situation. Besides, his mother had always been there for him. The things he had been doing for her—mowing her lawn once a week, taking out the garbage on Tuesdays, and cooking a meal for her every once in a while—was nothing compared to all of the dirty diapers she'd changed and the countless times she'd sat at his bedside when he was sick.

"I can't do that," she replied.

"Why not? We lived together for a while when I moved back after college and that worked out alright."

"You're not a woman so you might not understand this, but Meredith wouldn't appreciate coming home from her honeymoon to move in with her new husband *and* her mother-in-law."

"Mom," Andrew said in a serious tone, "I'm not sure if Meredith gets an opinion on this one."

"She is going to be your wife, which means she gets an opinion on everything," his mother explained.

Glancing back and forth from the road to his mother, Andrew spent the ride to her house explaining why Meredith would most likely not be moving in with him following a honeymoon since it looked like there wouldn't be a honeymoon. While his dad's old Chevy idled beneath a basketball goal he'd shot a million hoops on, Andrew listened as his mother offered her two cents: "You should call Meredith again. You need to work things out, Andrew. I know it is hard to understand why she would do something like this, but she is probably just scared. Maybe even having second thoughts. People have second thoughts, Andrew. Before your father and I got married, I had second thoughts. And look how our marriage turned out; we were married forty-one years before he passed away. On top of all that, there is a good chance that there is more to this story. If you ask me, I think both of you are missing a few pieces of this puzzle." Rosemary reached across the truck and kissed her son on the cheek. "I'll say a few extra prayers for you, Andrew," she promised.

Andrew walked her to the door and made sure she locked it before climbing back into the truck. Then he stared aimlessly into the backyard where he could vividly remember playing near the rusted tin shed, climbing the magnolia trees and wrestling in freshly fallen leaves. There was one day in particular that he had never forgotten. It seemed like yesterday—the day his brother climbed into their tree house and opened the family Bible to John 3:16. That day had changed Andrew's life. Since then, prayer had always been important to him, and he knew in the middle of a week filled with bad news, he needed God now more than ever. Not only had Meredith called off the wedding, but now he was going to be worried about his mother's health every second of every day. If anything could get him through all of this, it was prayer.

He knew he needed to call Barry, too, before his mother made the call for him. He needed to fill him in on everything that had happened since lunch yesterday: the talk with Cooper on the train tracks; the phone call at the soccer game from Meredith; and even what happened at the creek last night—the true story not the abbreviated one.

He dialed the number, and before his conversation with his big brother ended, Barry pretty much offered the same advice their mother had: "Call Meredith," he said, "and figure this out."

Sitting in the two-tone Chevy between two white lines in the grocery store parking lot, Andrew heard Meredith's voice for the first time in two days. He nearly let the phone drop from his ear as nothing more than the sound of his breath crossed the line. After a moment, he cleared his throat and began to speak.

"Hey, it's me," he uttered, more nervous than he'd ever been while talking to her—more nervous than the day at the blood drive and the night he'd asked her to marry him combined.

"Hey, Andrew. How are you?" she asked sounding much nicer than he had imagined she would.

If there was one thing Andrew wanted to avoid in this conversation, it was small talk. He felt it would be best to jump right to the heart of the matter, and so he did: "Why are you doing this to me?" he asked, demanding a better explanation than what she had provided in the voicemail yesterday.

"Doing what to you, Andrew?" Meredith suddenly shouted loudly and clearly. "You are the one who did this to me. As soon as I get on a plane to Florida to plan *our wedding*," she emphasized, "you're running around with some other woman."

"What?" he asked, offended by the accusation under the circumstances. Meredith hadn't mentioned anything about Cooper yesterday. At least that was whom he assumed the words *another woman* referenced.

"Don't even try to deny it. I have pictures of the two of you—on the railroad tracks, going into Gary's house, and even on the park bench where you asked me to marry you. And now you're calling me to ask why *I* don't want to marry *you*!"

Andrew cut Meredith off and, his voice growing louder, rolled up the window as he fought to defend his position. "What do you mean you have pictures? What did you do hire a private investigator or something? Was that part of your master plan? Send Cooper here to see if I would cheat on you and then have someone take pictures for evidence?"

"What are you talking about, Andrew? I didn't send anyone for you to cheat on me with. Why would I do something so stupid?"

"I have copies of emails—sent from your email address, Meredith. Emails you sent to Cooper asking her to do this for you."

"Who is Cooper?" Meredith asked, pacing an empty hotel room.

"She is the woman in the pictures you say you have."

"But *who* is she, Andrew?"

"I've told you about Cooper. She is the woman I met at the video store before you and I started dating."

"Why would I email her, Andrew? That is ridiculous."

"You tell me."

"I don't know what you're talking about, Andrew. I don't even think you know what you are talking about, and this is the absolute worst lie I have ever heard in my entire life. If you'd called to admit that you cheated on me, then maybe I would want to talk to you about this, but for you to call with some elaborate lie about me sending some woman for you to cheat on me with, that is absurd."

Andrew stared in the rearview mirror, watching his nostrils flare as words began to fly out of his mouth. "Absurd? You're absurd. If you didn't have something to do with this, then how did you get pictures of me with Cooper? Did they just happen to show up in the mail in Florida?"

"No." Meredith paused for a moment wondering for the first time if Andrew's story had some relevance. "Someone sent them to my email."

"Who?"

"I don't know who."

"Oh, you don't know who! How convenient." Andrew paused to catch his breath. "Who's lying now?" he asked.

"Not me."

"Well, your story doesn't add up."

"And neither does your story. So if you decide to tell me the truth then call back and I might listen. But until you're willing to admit what you've done, don't call me," Meredith instructed, throwing her phone across the room at the same time Andrew slid down the vinyl seat, a grip on his cell phone so tight that it felt like it might explode into little pieces at any moment.

After the call ended, he seriously considered letting the weight of his body carry him into the floorboard so that he could roll into a little ball and cry until someone knocked on his window to make sure he was okay. But then Andrew's phone began to ring.

"What?" he rumbled assuming it was Meredith calling back to yell at him some more.

"I'm sorry, is this a bad time?" Cooper inquired.

Andrew felt dumb for not taking the time to check the caller ID.

He straightened his body and tried to change his tone. "No . . . no, it's not," he replied, clearing his throat.

"Are you sure?"

"Well, it was, but it's not now," he said.

"Is everything okay?"

"Yeah, it's just that," Andrew paused for a moment still trying to shake off the madness that had been running through his veins. "I thought you were Meredith; I just got off the phone with her, and it didn't go so well."

"Do you want to talk about it?"

"Right now I just want to forget about it."

Andrew got out of the truck and headed toward the store.

"If you think having dinner tonight is a bad idea, I would understand," Cooper assured.

"Actually, I'm about to pick up the ingredients now."

Inside the store, Andrew continued the conversation with Cooper as he pushed a shopping cart in and out of the narrow aisles.

"What are we having for dinner?" she asked.

"It's a surprise."

"What if I don't like surprises?" she said with a grin on her face.

"Then I guess you won't like what we're having for dinner," Andrew said laughing a little.

Cooper noticed that his voice had finally returned to normal.

"The reason I called in the first place was to see if you might want to watch a movie after we eat."

"A movie sounds nice."

"Since you're cooking, I'll pick up the movie."

Reaching for the top shelf on aisle three, Andrew couldn't help but smile. Cooper. Dinner. A movie. This brought back memories—good memories. Scratch that, great memories. He could vividly remember every word that had flowed from her lips the evening they met. She was moving into a new apartment that day and had come to the video store in search of a movie to watch with the friends who'd helped her move in. He and Cooper had stumbled into a wonderful conversation—sparked by the movie *Message In A Bottle*—which led to an invitation to have dinner with her and her four friends. She fixed filet mignon, and after eating, her couple-friends nestled up on the couch and love seat leaving Andrew and Cooper on the floor eating popcorn while watching Kevin Costner and Robin Wright Penn fall in love on her nineteen-inch television.

Andrew closed his eyes for a moment, breathing in the memories of that night as the rest of the world moved on around him. He realized that even after all this time he hadn't forgotten the smile Cooper seemed to have patented, the light blue tank top she wore so well, and the way she had laughed when he accidentally spilled an entire can of Mountain Dew on the carpet she'd spent hours steam cleaning. Although he hadn't kissed Cooper McKay that night or even held her hand, he could still remember the feeling of finding out that love at first sight did truly exist.

"Do you have something in mind?" he asked.

"It's a surprise," she teased.

"What if I don't like surprises?" he asked.

"Then I guess I'll be watching a movie by myself."

Meredith left the pieces of her broken phone scattered across the hotel room floor and began to search for her mother. Maybe she could help make sense of the story Andrew had fed her, she thought, as the elevator carried her to ground level. She remembered her mother saying, "I'll be at the pool if you decide to quit pouting." Those were the words her mother had left her with as she slammed the door shut.

What else did her mother expect her to do? After receiving an anonymous tip about an anonymous email containing pictures of Andrew—the man she was supposed to marry next weekend—with another woman, she had called off the whole ordeal, and now she was stuck in Florida with nothing to do. At this point she hadn't even summoned up the courage to call her bridesmaids to let them know there wasn't going to be a wedding. Maybe she would do that tomorrow—or maybe the next day—or maybe she would just tell them when she picked them up at the airport next week. The airfare had already been paid for so there was no sense in telling them not to come. She figured that they, like her mother had chosen to do, could make a vacation out of her upcoming wedding gone sour.

Outside, Meredith's bare feet danced across the sun-scorched cement as she headed for the black metal gate separating the swimming pool from the beach. She opened the latch but didn't find her mother in the water or in the row of hotel-provided lounge chairs where the two of them spent the better part of yesterday. She checked the sauna but had no luck there or in the gym on the third floor.

Where in the world could her mother be? Meredith wondered. Probably off gallivanting with some man she met at the pool, just like she had done yesterday. Why did she do that? And better yet, why had her mother been trying to set her up with random men ever since she'd informed her of her decision to call off the wedding? Why hadn't she taken her out for a quart of Ben &

Jerry's ice cream and a sappy movie instead of trying to get her to rate guys in Speedos?

Meredith retrieved her flip-flops from the hotel room and took a stroll down the beach. She came across two of the men who had spent time with her mother since they'd arrived in Tampa on Tuesday. It didn't surprise her that neither of them had seen her mother today, nor when one of the men—even though both were over fifty—offered to take her, not her mother, out for dinner tonight. She declined, of course, and then headed back to the pool. Hopefully, swimming laps would help get her mind off Andrew.

Once through the gate, Meredith made a dash for an open lounge chair in one of the corners on the beach side of the pool and made sure to mark it with her white tank top and blue gym shorts before diving into the deep end hoping to drown her worries down near the drain at the bottom. And again today, she thought about sliding her engagement ring between the square holes, but she just couldn't force herself to let it go. The sensible side of her convinced the other side that she would rather keep the diamond on her finger a little longer even though it would leave a tan line similar to the one that circled her back before this trip. A few hours in the sun had made that one vanish, but she guessed that really didn't matter now that she wouldn't be wearing the wedding dress she'd picked out two weekends after Andrew proposed.

After one lap of trying to dodge kids in dinosaur floats, which only frustrated Meredith further, she toweled off and then laid on her stomach in the lounge chair. Instinctively, she un-strapped her top, and as the Tampa sun slowly began to suck away the beads of water her towel had left behind, she thought back to the argument she'd had with Andrew earlier. Why would he make up the story about Cooper and the emails? She wondered. As far as she knew, Andrew had never lied to her. He had always been honest about everything, even Cooper. As soon as he'd mentioned the part about meeting Cooper in the video store, she had remembered exactly who Cooper McKay was—the only other woman Andrew had ever loved; he'd told her that early on in their relationship.

With these thoughts rummaging through her mind, Meredith began to analyze the predicament, asking herself question after question, one leading to the next: Who could have sent the pictures of Andrew with Cooper? Why had they chosen to remain anonymous? Did that mean it was someone she didn't know? Or someone she knew well? Someone that didn't want to get in the middle of this? Or someone that did? She had to admit, as she continued to rack her brain, this did sound like a set up. Maybe someone really had emailed Cooper. Maybe Andrew was telling the truth, but even if he was, that didn't explain the pictures. Regardless of how this all came about, Andrew, in some form or fashion was guilty. That was clear from the pictures. But who else was guilty? If there *were* emails, had the person who sent the photographs also been the one who sent the emails?

No one else had access to her email account. Or did they? She began to rack her brain suddenly remembering giving access to at least one person that needed it to help with some wedding details when she'd been tied up at the bank one day with no access to email.

No way, though. There was no way her mother could have done this—could she?

Meredith found herself contemplating that thought. She had to admit her mother did seem to have motive. But her own mother? Would she do that to her only daughter? Meredith wanted to believe otherwise, but her mind immediately shot back to the conversation she'd had with her mother at the pier. Then there was also the talk they'd had yesterday just before she received the call about the emails: "Mom, do you really think Andrew would cheat on me?" she remembered asking, her nose buried in a white rose at Flowering Florida. The moment they'd walked through the door of that place she had become so excited that she nearly passed out. Extravagant bouquets filled the main building and an enormous greenhouse sheltered fields of flowers that reminded her of what paradise might look like.

"When presented with the option," her mother had responded, "all men do."

"Not all men," Meredith combated.

"Most of them," she assured Meredith.

"I wonder what Andrew is doing right now."

"Quit thinking about Andrew and enjoy your vacation with your mother. Even if Andrew ends up making a stupid decision, you'll always have me." Sylvia smiled and wrapped her arm around her daughter as they walked.

Lifting herself from the lounge chair, Meredith fastened her bikini top and pulled the white tank top over her shoulders. As she headed for the room, she honed in on two of the comments her mother had made: "When presented with the option, all men do," and "Even if Andrew ends up making a stupid decision, you'll always have me."

Those words played over and over in her mind as the shades of red blanketing her face became darker. *Why had she not picked up on this earlier*, she wondered? In a way, she wanted nothing more than to find out that her mother hadn't had anything to do with this, but on the other hand she wanted to find out that all of it was true. That Andrew's story hadn't been merely an excuse. She needed answers, and she needed them quickly.

14

"Bye, Mom."

Cooper's voice reached her mother at the back of the house as the screen door clanged against the frame. "Have a good time, sweetie," she heard her call out. "I love you."

"Love you, too," Cooper replied over her shoulder, skipping down the steps and then all the way to the car.

She reached for the lever to adjust the seat and then angled the mirrors to provide for the three inches she had on her mother, thanks to the height from the branches on her father's side of the tree. *Her father*—she needed to buy him a gift for his birthday, she remembered as she opted for the scenic route on the way to the video store.

Once there, a mountain of memories made their way to the forefront of Cooper's mind as she stepped into the video store that she'd last walked out of with Andrew Callaway. It was hard to believe three years had passed since that night. Though not much had changed inside the store, she found herself scanning the new release section, but coming across very few titles she hadn't already seen. She wished she could say that is how many dates she had been on, but truth be told, living alone without a stack of movies as high as Ebert's and Ropert's on her coffee table made for lonely nights and weekends—no dogs, no cats, not even a fish. Maybe when she got back home she would get a pet.

Two trips around the store picking up every genre from romance to action brought Cooper to the register with a case whose cover featured a couple cuddled near a warm fire on a sandy beach wrapped in a blanket and surrounded by the ocean. She wondered if Andrew would remember this movie, and she couldn't help but allow her mind to flash back to a feeling she'd felt when they watched it together for the first time; she remembered wishing she was Robin Wright Penn and Andrew was Kevin Costner. Of course, she had neglected to share this with Andrew or anyone else for that matter, but the thought of cuddling up with him near a warm fire was sensual.

She was still thinking about the first time she'd watched this movie with Andrew when she made the turn onto the road that would lead her to his house. From memory, she knew that miles of winding road mirrored the waterfront, but she nearly screamed at the sight of an oncoming truck as she watched it veer out of its lane and swerve onto her side of the road. Immediately, she yanked the wheel hard and to the right and felt the tires beneath her dig into the gravel that lined the road opposite the Trent River. Her car fishtailed two or three times before sliding to a stop throwing a cloud of dust into a patch of trees she could probably reach out and touch if she rolled down her window.

In the rearview mirror, she watched a yellow truck with oversized tires straighten out and speed into the distance. "Jerk!" Cooper reeled off wishing the driver could hear her, wondering why he hadn't stopped to check on her. For all he knew she could be unconscious and bleeding from the head. Thankfully, she wasn't . . . just a little shaken up, that's all. And it took a few minutes for her heartbeat to find a familiar rhythm.

Cooper's hands continued to shake as she gathered the items

that had been flung from her purse and had somehow made it into the back seat. She brushed a few strands of loose hair from her face and decided to guide the car back onto the asphalt, thinking: *Where do people like that idiot learn to drive?*

❧

An hour earlier, a cloud of dust rising toward the trees before falling onto the freshly cut lawn had followed Andrew and his old Chevy down his driveway. Looking through the window clouded by time, Andrew let out a smile as he took notice of the hard work he'd put in Tuesday afternoon; the perfectly edged grass along the drive and the neatly shaved matching holly bushes beneath dark blue shutters hugging the house on either side of the front porch looked nice. Almost professional, he thought, thankful he had picked up his father's knack for working in the yard.

He could still remember the summer he turned seven; from then on his dad had given him a fifty-cent piece every time he helped mow the lawn. It wasn't much then or now, but to Andrew it meant the world. With the exception of the first coin which he used to buy his mom an imitation rose at the gas station near the home he grew up in, Andrew still had every shiny half-dollar he ever earned tucked away in his sock drawer.

Inside, Andrew put away the groceries and darted past the answering machine. In his haste to make it to the upstairs bathroom, he didn't take time to notice the flashing green light; his mind was set on freshening up.

The warm water felt good to his face, and his mouth felt a lot fresher after a few quick swipes with a brush traced with Colgate. Then he scurried from room to room rounding up every picture of Meredith in the house. The plan had been to take them down last night, but after getting home so late he didn't get around to it.

He closed the closet door knowing they'd be safe in there for now.

Wanting this dinner to be more meaningful than if he had taken Cooper out to a fancy restaurant, Andrew took his time setting the table. Anyone with a credit card could take a woman out on the town, he figured, hoping Cooper would appreciate the thought he'd put into the evening he'd spent the whole day thinking about.

❧

Tired from stirring, Andrew poured a cold glass of sweet tea, and just as he was about to head into the living room to watch television, the blinking light on the machine caught his eye. Initially, his mind went straight to Meredith. *Had she left a message?* he wondered, touching the button to find out. The first voice wasn't hers; it was his mother's. Worried about Andrew, she'd called to check on him and to see if he had called Meredith. Then came Barry's message—nearly the same as his mother's. If Andrew didn't know better, he would think his family had put him on suicide watch.

If the third message ended up being from Marie, a cousin, or an aunt or uncle, Andrew decided he would walk upstairs to his bedroom, get his pistol from the drawer with the coins, and fire shots into the machine until no one other than himself would ever know it even existed, but as the low and muzzled voice began to seep through the speaker, he found himself leaning in close only wishing it had been a relative. Andrew's heart began to speed up as he deciphered three of the most frightening words he'd ever heard.

I'm watching you . . .

❧

In her mother's Honda Accord, Cooper coasted up Andrew's driveway, thinking that if she didn't know better she might mistake Andrew Callaway, the realtor, for a landscape artist. For some reason with that thought in mind, she drew a mental picture of him working in the yard with cut off sleeves, a pair of work gloves, and a shovel—the type of man she'd always told her mom she wanted to marry. Someone she could spend Saturdays with outdoors, her tending to the flower garden while he mowed the lawn. When her husband needed a break, she could bring out a cold pitcher of iced tea, and they could sit together on a porch swing beneath a wrap-around porch—just like Andrew's. Maybe thinking of Andrew Callaway as that man was taking their current status a bit far, Cooper considered, but she could seriously see herself with Andrew—and some nice flowers would complement his holly bushes well, she thought, guiding the gearshift into park.

Letting the engine continue to run so the air conditioner would keep her cool, Cooper used the visor mirror to touch up her makeup.

At the sound of the doorbell, Andrew shut off the television and picked himself up from the couch. Sitting near the front window, he'd spotted Cooper's car coming up the drive, and he had been a little worried at how long it had taken her to get to the deadbolted door. The message he'd received earlier had sparked him to double check the locks on all the doors, as well as the windows, in the house.

He left the remote on the coffee table, and when he twisted the doorknob, breathing became difficult. If a word in the English language could describe how beautiful Cooper McKay, standing on his front porch with a smile on her face and a purse to match her outfit, looked, it had been left out of the dictionary on his bookshelf. Glowing. Luminous. Angelic. Those came close but didn't quite do her justice.

"Hey," she offered, wondering if Andrew had forgotten how to speak.

Stuck in the doorframe, Andrew smiled back. "Hey," he uttered, still in awe.

She couldn't help but wonder if he held a staring contest with all of his guests or just her. "Are you going to invite me in," she said, "or should I just stay out here for a while?"

Her silky brown hair fell effortlessly on the shoulders of the simple button up white blouse covering her evenly tanned skin, and black capris complimented her long legs. Andrew couldn't help but think how her figure resembled the models from the magazines Meredith often left laying around his house—not too much, not too little.

"Did you have any trouble finding the place?" he asked, giving way to the ground he'd been guarding, watching Cooper step into his house for the very first time.

"Not until I pulled into your driveway; I thought I might run out of gas before I made it to the house," she teased, studying the inside of the place.

Andrew grinned. "There is always a price to pay for living away from the crowd."

Her eyes still wandering, Cooper wondered if Andrew or Meredith had been the one who'd picked out the area rug covering the portion of the hard wood flooring in the living room between the sofa and entertainment center. "Your home is gorgeous," she complimented.

"Thanks, I'll give you a tour if you'd like," he offered. "You might not guess it, but I'm actually pretty good at showing houses."

"Really?"

Andrew led Cooper into the hallway. The first thing she noticed were the holes in the wall where pictures once hung. Pictures of Meredith, she assumed, wondering when Andrew had taken those down. Last night when he got home? This morning? Maybe just before she got here this evening? It didn't matter really, she guessed, but she found herself wondering if he had taken down the photos so she wouldn't see them or because he didn't want to look at them anymore. Maybe both, she concluded, following him through the first door on the left where an overwhelming amount of books filled a built-in bookshelf.

"My brother and I built those shelves, so you might not want to get too close," Andrew teased as Cooper reached for a book.

She chuckled, and took her chances anyway. "*Real Estate Law for Dummies*, huh? Is this a good one?" she asked, leaning against the corner of his desk with the book held open.

"I only made it to . . . ," Andrew stepped closer and flipped to a page in the middle of the book, ". . . right there," he said, locating a creased corner. "It got kind of boring, or maybe it was confusing; I can't really remember which," he added with a smile.

"Real estate law can get pretty tricky."

"Does the firm you work for handle real estate?"

"Yeah, but I deal with it more in my classes." Cooper watched Andrew furrow his brow, and she realized he had no idea she had been accepted to law school. "I just finished my first semester of law school," she decided to tell him. "I'm studying to be a real estate lawyer," she smiled.

Andrew's eyes perked up. "Really?"

"Yep. It looks like you and I will be in the same business—well, kind of."

"Congratulations," he offered sincerely.

As the tour moved on, the conversation turned back to the house and its décor; the final stops ended up being Andrew's bedroom and then a quick peak into the bathroom. He kept the place nearly spotless, Cooper noted, especially for a man. The bedroom didn't have clothes strewn all over the floor; his office didn't have dust on the shelves; and the bathroom looked as clean as her own, and as tidy as she kept her bathroom, that meant something.

"Does—or I guess I should say, *did*, Meredith live with you?" she asked hoping Andrew wouldn't take the question as an intrusive one.

Andrew wondered why Cooper wanted to know, but he didn't mind telling her. As far as he was concerned, a man and a woman shouldn't live under the same roof before marriage. Kind of took away the importance of actually saying 'I do,' he had always thought. "No," he answered without hesitation, "she has her own place."

"Do you have a maid?"

Andrew wrinkled his brow. "I can't even afford a dog."

Cooper giggled. "Then who dusts your lamp shades?"

Oh, that is why she asked about Meredith, Andrew realized—because he kept a clean house. "I do."

"I'm impressed."

"Are you one of those women who are under the impression that a man can't clean house?"

"Not unless he's—you know—"

"Gay," Andrew said for her.

Cooper nodded. "Should I be worried?" she teased, openly analyzing Andrew's habits: "You're cute, well dressed, and your house looks like Martha Stewart's," she reeled off with a mischievous grin covering her face. "I guess the true test will be dinner. If you're a good cook, then . . . ."

Laughing, Andrew cut her off. "In the direction you're headed, you'll be lucky if you even get a chance to taste dinner."

Forbidden to enter the kitchen—one of the only two rooms Andrew didn't show Cooper during the walk-through—she once again found herself consumed by the shelves in his office. The book in her hand offered detailed instructions on how to write rental property contracts in order to guarantee renters would follow the specified guidelines. She set it on the desk and plucked another, noticing that there seemed to be more books on real estate in this one room than the library at her college.

When she'd asked Andrew about coming in here—while he added a few more touches to their top-secret dinner—he'd said that she could borrow any of the books she thought might be helpful to her studies. So far she had a couple stacked on the desk, but now after taking a moment to examine the trophies on one of the higher shelves, she wished she hadn't come back in here at all as she stared at the inscribed date on the trophy in her hand.

Cooper felt her face tighten trying to fight the tears—Andrew had received the MVP honor at the soccer tournament the weekend they met—the same day her grandmother had passed away.

Andrew put away the flour and a few other ingredients and went to look for Cooper. When he turned the corner into the hallway, he found her sitting on the floor just outside his office. She'd heard him coming and pretended to be reading one of the books in her lap as she cleared her throat.

"Did you find some that interest you?"

"Yes," she answered. "I figured I would wait here until you finished." She looked up. "Would you like to get some fresh air?" she asked.

"Sure," Andrew replied.

Cooper followed him outside to a set of lawn chairs thirty yards off the river where a pair of squirrels put on a show for the two of them as the water wrinkled at the shoreline. Andrew often came out here for no other reason than to watch the squirrels sling their bodies amongst the group of oak trees to their right, and he figured Cooper would enjoy watching their circus acts as much as he did, if not more, since she hadn't met these characters before.

"How do they do that?" she asked rhetorically as the squirrels, performing stunts she had never seen before, ran up and down the trees and danced in the dirt that mirrored the drooping branches. "And what do you feed these things—chocolate?"

Andrew shrugged his shoulders. "Sweet tea," he replied. "Would you like some?"

"Yeah and make sure to get me the special blend that they get," she requested laughingly.

Andrew headed to the refrigerator to pluck ice cubes from plastic trays, and Cooper couldn't help but think back to the thoughts she'd had in the driveway. Sweet tea with Andrew Callaway—she wondered if it would always feel this way—feel this good. If it were possible for things to work out so they could be together, would they still have evenings like this one once the new wore off? Would Andrew cook dinner for her once he found out he didn't have to?

Brought up in a traditional southern home, Cooper had been raised, in her mother's words, "like all women should be raised." Unlike the modern day woman, she knew how to cook and clean and do all the things to make a husband appreciate his wife. When she married, she knew she wanted to be with someone like Andrew, a man with strong morals and values who would respect her not take advantage of her like Chris had.

Enjoying the cool breeze blowing off the river, Cooper opened her eyes when she heard the sound of ice jingling in glasses filled with homemade sweet tea. She stood, taking her glass from Andrew so he could sit down without spilling tea all over himself.

"Thank you," she said.

"Oh, that one's not for you," he joked, "It's for the squirrels."

Cooper pretended she was going to take the glass to the squirrels but then leaned back again.

"I used to try to mimic them all the time," Andrew said, referring to the squirrels. "I would climb any tree with branches just to see how far up I could go." He chuckled, took a sip from his glass, and Cooper could sense another funny story coming on. "One time, I was out in the woods with some friends, and I began climbing the tallest tree I could find. When I was almost to the top, I heard the branch beneath my feet snap, and I tumbled at least twenty feet and landed on my head. They said that when I hit the ground I looked like an arrow sticking out of a target, but then I toppled over."

Cooper decided to hold in the laughter building in her stomach until she found out if Andrew ended up in the hospital. "Were you hurt badly?" she asked.

"No, I got lucky, and all I have to show for it is this." Andrew pointed to a small scar on his right arm, and then Cooper burst out in laughter. "It's not funny," he explained with a fake frown. "Until this day I don't know how I didn't die; God must have been looking out for me."

Cooper continued to laugh. "You get yourself into the most awkward situations."

Like skinny-dipping with you and inviting you to my house for dinner the following night? Andrew considered replying but didn't. "I could have been paralyzed," he explained instead, a line that worked on most people but not on Cooper.

She continued to grin from ear to ear as though she had an image of his head buried in the dirt. "But you're not, that's why it's so humorous," she responded, taking a sip of tea.

"I'll give you a chance to work all that laughter out while I check on our food." Grinning, he paused. "I might just add something extra to yours."

The sun began to drop beneath the trees across the river, painting the sky a pinkish-purple, and Cooper figured that must be the mosquitoes' alarm clock. At first they began to circle her like the seagulls hovering above the river, preying on small fish, and then after she swiped at a few of them on her arms, she decided to make her way up to the deck and unfold a chair for her and Andrew.

Even though dinner would be ready soon, Andrew lit the citronella candles surrounding the deck so they could enjoy a few more minutes outdoors without having to worry about getting bit.

"So, what movie did you pick out?"

Cooper decided to ruin the surprise. "*Message in a Bottle*," she replied. "Have you seen it?" she quizzed, hoping he would remember but doubting he would. Most guys didn't pay attention to that sort of thing.

She watched Andrew put his index finger to his chin. "I'm not sure," he said, pretending to ponder the question as he unconsciously crunched on a piece of ice like it was bubblegum. "I think I watched it with some woman that picked me up at the video store this one time, but I can't seem to recall her name—" he trailed off.

Impressed, Cooper grinned. "I wondered if you would remember." Even though he passed the test, she couldn't let him get away with the title he'd given her: "Some woman?" she asked, pouting just a little. "That's what I am to you?"

"That's it," he responded with a wink. "Just some woman that hit on me at the video store," he teased.

"If I'm not mistaken," Cooper rifled back, "you are the one who initiated the conversation."

"After you smiled at me."

"You were the one checking me out from across the store."

"You looked back."

"You walked my way."

"You met me in the middle."

Both paused for a moment, thinking back to that day.

"You were almost standing on top of me," Cooper said. "What was I supposed to do?"

"You could have walked away."

"You probably would have followed me."

"Are you saying I'm a stalker?"

"No, because you didn't find me when I left town."

The air suddenly became silent, Andrew recalling the many times he tried to find Cooper, and Cooper wishing she hadn't said what she'd just said. If he had found her, he thought, things might have turned out differently. Maybe Cooper would have been the woman he asked to marry him. Who knows, by now they might even be married, and instead of sitting on the deck thinking about what might have been, he would take hold of her hand, lead her to the bedroom, and as the cool breeze blew in off the river, the curtains would sway and the wind would crawl across their naked bodies.

"I guess I missed my chance," he uttered, staring at the wrist he was screwing his watch around.

Cooper reached across the space between their chairs and rested her hand on his. "I'm here now, aren't I?"

Andrew smiled, wishing he had the guts to wrap his arms around her and kiss her soft lips until he forgot that Meredith even existed, but he couldn't—Meredith was still there. Still in the back of his mind, still in the pictures in the closet—and he couldn't help but feel like what he was doing was in some way, maybe many ways, wrong.

15

Cooper washed her hands for dinner and then met Andrew in the living room. Taking her hand, he led her into a small room overlooking the river they had sat near earlier. He took in the expression on her face as her silhouette danced about the wall.

On a small square table sat a single candle, illuminating a crystal vase holding a red rose hugged by baby's breath, which drew Cooper's eye. Two wooden chairs faced one another, and on matching placemats, Andrew had prepared a plate for each of them. Though she wasn't sure the bottle of red wine mirrored by two wine glasses would go with pancakes, her favorite food in the whole world, Cooper had already decided this was the most romantic dinner she'd ever had. Not only had Andrew remembered the movie they watched, but he remembered pancakes with whipped cream and blueberry topping, her favorites. This, she could get used to.

She offered her arms to Andrew, and at the moment "Wow" was the only word in her vocabulary. Hamburgers and French fries on paper plates is what she had expected, and to be honest, she would have been completely satisfied if that is what he'd fixed, but this was more, much more. It was thoughtful, breathtaking, and intimate.

"Thank you," she whispered into Andrew's ear, then softly

kissed his cheek.

With her lips pressed against his skin, Andrew wished this moment could last forever or at least a while longer so she wouldn't find out about the mistake he'd made.

Stepping back, Cooper held his eye. "Never in my life have I had a dinner this fabulous even before I sat down to eat." It didn't matter that the pancakes looked a little overcooked; if Andrew didn't bring it up, neither would she.

Sitting in front of plates piled with crispy pancakes, the words that Andrew Callaway spoke next meant more to Cooper than anything he had ever said to her.

"Is it okay if I say a quick prayer before we eat?" he asked.

For as long as she could remember, her father had always asked a blessing over the meal when her family sat down at the table, but this was the first time she had ever heard a man, with whom she had a romantic interest, make such a profound statement. Even men who normally prayed before a meal were too ashamed to bring up the subject on a dinner date. In those situations, she always made sure to say a silent prayer, but even then she didn't close her eyes like she probably should.

Andrew Callaway, Cooper reminded herself, wasn't like most men. The way he'd brought up praying made her comfortable; it made her feel like they had sat at this very table and eaten a hundred meals together. In a way, Andrew reminded her of her father, and she liked that about him.

"That would be great," Cooper agreed, closing her eyes.

"These are the best burned pancakes I've ever tasted," Cooper admitted not long after Andrew finished praying.

She had spent the last few minutes talking him out of ordering out. Although now as she took the first bite of her second pancake, she thought pizza might not have been such a bad idea after all. As long as she chewed slowly and kept the food as far away from her tongue as possible, the pancakes didn't taste all *that* bad, but not particularly good either. *Edible*, she decided, might be the best word to describe them.

Andrew hadn't burned the pancakes enough to scrape off the top layer with a fork, but the edges were crisp and the pile of remnants on his plate continued to grow as he ate. Trying not to laugh or cry, he couldn't decide which brought on more suffering: eating these terrible pancakes or watching the expressions on Cooper's face during every bite—which reminded him of a baby being forced to eat a jar of something it didn't like.

"They are probably the only burned pancakes you've ever tasted," Andrew responded, wishing he hadn't used all of the mix at once.

Tonight was the first time he'd tried out the stovetop grill that Barry and Marie had given him for his birthday, but just because it would hold enough pancakes to feed a small army didn't mean he had to cook them all at once. What had he been thinking? "Who burns pancakes?" he asked rhetorically.

"Let's be optimistic about this," Cooper insisted. "You tried your best, and that is what really matters. At least now we know you're not gay."

A somewhat full stomach, Andrew scooted his plate to the middle of the table and balanced his chair on two legs, stretching his belly to make a little more room for the fourth pancake. He waited for Cooper to throw in the towel or in this case a napkin, which would crown him the official burned pancake eating contest champion.

To make Andrew feel better about burning dinner, Cooper had made a bet that she could eat as many burned pancakes as he could. But no matter how bad she wanted to scarf down number four, it wasn't going to happen. Not tonight, maybe next time—

and next time *she* would make the pancakes, and they would have to rename the contest.

"Okay," she finally uttered smiling from ear to ear, "I give up. I can't eat the last one," she said, rising from the table and picking up both her and Andrew's plate.

In response, Andrew dropped his chair on all fours, let out a victory chant, and then jumped up quickly. "I'll get those," he insisted.

"You're the cook," Cooper responded. "The least I can do is clear the table," she added while guarding the plates.

With syrup in one hand and butter in the other, Andrew followed Cooper into the kitchen. He closed the refrigerator door and then stepped out onto the deck to relight the citronella candles so they could sit outside and enjoy the sound of high tide making its way toward the grass in his backyard.

"Well, now that we've determined I'm no chef," Andrew admitted, sitting in the same spot he had earlier, "What about you? Are you a good cook?" he asked.

Cooper shrugged. "If you asked my mother that question she would say *yes*. She taught me how to cook, and I've always considered her an excellent cook, so I guess that at least makes me decent. My mom is one of those people who when you walk into her house around dinnertime you think the entire neighborhood has been invited."

"Do you think you'll be that way when you have a family?"

"I've always said I won't be, but I probably will. It runs in the family. Every year for Thanksgiving we used to go to my grandparents, and the night before the big day I would help Mom and Grandma in the kitchen. I was in charge of dessert until I got old enough to help with the turkey and dressing and all the good stuff," Cooper informed Andrew. "My grandmother taught me how to make all kinds of pies—pumpkin, pecan, chocolate, lemon—I made them all, year after year."

Cooper found herself thinking back to the times she had spent in her grandmother's kitchen—Thanksgiving hadn't been the same since she passed away, and she hadn't made a pie since. "I used to get so anxious about eating Thanksgiving dinner," she said. "At the table, we would go around from person to person and tell what we were thankful for that particular year. That was so much fun to me. The night before Thanksgiving, my grandma would let me eat one slice of pie and that meant as much to me as opening a present on Christmas Eve." Cooper paused again, and this time Andrew could see the sadness in her eyes. "I wish you could have met her. She would have liked you," Cooper said confidently.

"If she was anything like you, I'm sure I would have," Andrew declared.

"She was great," Cooper said simply.

"What did you all do after Thanksgiving dinner?"

Cooper glared at him as if there was only one option: "Watched football," she proclaimed.

"Really?"

"I told you I'm a sports fanatic. I got it from my dad and grandpa. Once we stuffed our faces to the point our stomachs were about to explode, kind of like the way you looked when you leaned back in your chair at the table," she said laughing, "we would watch the games. My grandma loved football, too. She and Grandpa debated every call the referees made. Watching the two of them was more entertaining than listening to the commentators."

"Were your grandparents really close?"

"Extremely. After Grandma passed away, it took my granddad a long time to get used to not having her around, and he never returned to his old self. He piddled in the yard, rode his bike, worked in the shop, and tended to all the animals they had. Keeping busy was the only way he knew how to live without

Grandma. Late at night he'd sit in his old beat up rocking chair for hours, doing absolutely nothing—the television screen blank, the radio silent, not a noise in the entire house. Those were the times he missed her the most." Andrew continued to listen as Cooper carried on about her grandparents. "The week after my grandmother passed away, I cooked every day. There was already plenty of food from what other people brought over, but that was the only way I knew how to deal with what happened. Her kitchen reminded me of her, and even though she was gone, I felt like she was still there when I was alone in the kitchen. I couldn't sit around the living room with everyone else and listen to stories about her . . . I missed her too much." Missing her was an understatement, Cooper thought to herself; she hadn't slept the same since her grandmother passed away, and she couldn't count the times she'd gone to her grandparent's house and unconsciously expected her grandmother to be sitting in her old wooden rocker where her feet had made permanent imprints on the red shag carpet. "When I was a little girl, I helped her with everything; nothing was ever too important for me to be a part of. She let me cook, wash the dishes, clean the house, wash clothes— in her eyes, I was a grown up, and she made me feel like one." Andrew watched her lip curl just a little. "Back then those things seemed like fun, not chores. She had a way of making everything fun. She's the reason I like to clean tables," Cooper said smiling.

Andrew found himself wishing he'd had the chance to know his own grandparents, but they'd all died when he was young, and the only positive thing about that was that he didn't have to deal with the hard times that Cooper had. She went on to tell him about losing her grandfather within a year of her grandmother's passing, and Andrew had to admit he had no idea how that must have felt.

"Are your grandparents living?"

Andrew took a sip of wine. He'd poured a glass for him and Cooper when they first came out here to sit beneath the moon, now shining like a flashlight across the surface of the river. If he told her the story about his grandmother, he knew he would need another glass—or maybe two.

"They all died when I was younger," he answered softly, licking his bottom lip and setting the glass on the small table separating him and Cooper.

"I'm sorry."

"My mother's parents both died before I was born, and my father's dad died when I was three. My parents said he was around quite a bit before he passed away, but I don't have any memories of him."

Cooper couldn't help but wonder why Andrew hadn't mentioned his grandmother on his father's side. "What about your . . ." she trailed off deciding at the last moment that it was none of her business. If Andrew wanted to talk about his grandmother, he would have brought it up on his own. Now she felt bad about starting a question she should have kept to herself in the first place.

As she watched Andrew run his thumb around the brim of his glass, she wondered what he was thinking. The look in his eyes made it evident that something terrible had happened, something that seemed to bother him a great deal.

Staring aimlessly into the glass he'd picked up nearly as soon as he set it down, Andrew said nothing, his grip so firm that Cooper could see the muscles in his forearm tightening. She reached across the table and touched his arm hoping to bring him some comfort. "I'm sorry. I shouldn't have asked."

Before she could say another word, Andrew chimed in. "She died the day I was born," he uttered, staring at the wood beneath his feet, rubbing the grain with his shoe.

16

*H*is grandmother died the same day he was born?

Had Cooper heard Andrew right? What were the odds? One in a million? It was almost too much to comprehend. Death and life in the same day; how would someone handle the degree of emotions that would accompany such a freak occurrence? Sure, babies were born and people died every day but not in the same family. Cooper could honestly say tonight is the first time she'd ever heard of this happening, not just to someone she knew personally but to anyone. Trying to fathom how difficult that day must have been on Andrew's family, especially his father, seemed impossible.

"I'm so sorry," she said.

Even though there was no way she could have known how or when his grandmother died, Cooper felt horrible about forcing it out of him. She wished she had just kept her mouth shut. "I had no idea . . . ," she added.

Andrew recognized the expression on Cooper's face, the same expression that had been on Meredith's when he told her this story three months into their relationship.

"It's okay," he assured Cooper. "I just don't talk about it very much, that's why it's so hard on me."

"We can talk about something else if you'd like."

Andrew went on as though he hadn't even heard Cooper. "He always said it was one of the greatest days of his life," he started, his eyes still fixed on the wine glass, his grip loosening slightly. "My dad that is," he clarified, "but I think he just said that to keep from hurting my feelings although it wouldn't have." Cooper held Andrew's eye as he continued, "She died early that morning and I was born later that evening. Dad was in the hospital sitting with my grandmother on her deathbed when my mother called to tell him she was having contractions. They only had one car so he had to drive all the way home to pick her up." For the hundredth time, Andrew wondered what that twenty-mile drive must have been like. Cooper watched the skin on his cheek stretch outward as his tongue circled inside his mouth. "And when he got back to the hospital he found out his mother had died," Andrew said trying not to choke up like he had when he told Meredith. At this point in the story, he remembered Meredith taking hold of his hand and rubbing his shoulder as he talked. "How can a person deal with something like that?" Andrew asked rhetorically. "I can't imagine experiencing those two extremes in one day. I can't even begin to fathom the emotions that must have swept through my father during those hours at the hospital."

Andrew set the empty glass in his hand on the table.

When he began talking again, Cooper tilted the bottle and poured him another. "I know how much I love my mom, and when she dies, I feel like a part of me will die with her. How Dad could hold himself together during a time like that is beyond my comprehension."

Feeling a tear about to roll down her cheek, Cooper turned her head and cleared her throat.

Andrew spoke slowly, "He watched as my mother screamed and cried giving birth to their son. A life he created came into his world only hours after he'd lost the very woman who'd brought *him* into this world."

Cooper reached for her own glass this time, thinking this had to be the saddest story she'd ever heard. She hadn't been able to keep a lid on her tears, now streaming down both sides of her face just as steady as the river's tide.

Andrew's eyes, too, were watered up; she'd watched him reach up to wipe away the pain.

"My biggest regret is that I never asked my dad about that day. I wish I could have known what he was thinking, what he was feeling. I wonder if he was able to hold me in his arms without crying." He paused to take a breath. "How could he celebrate my birthday every year? While I was running around with bb guns and Tonka trucks, he had to be thinking about his mother. He never let me know it bothered him, he always treated my birthday just like Barry's even though it was different."

Cooper wiped the tears from her cheek and Andrew picked up his second glass of wine. "This is going to sound uncanny," she said, pausing for a moment to contemplate whether to continue the thought. "Hard times bring families closer," she began, ignoring the puzzled expression on Andrew's face. "I'm sure what happened that day made your dad love and cherish you that much more . . ." Focusing on how to say what she wanted to say next, she paused for a moment more. "God gave him you, Andrew . . . a wonderful son . . . to help him through the tragedy of losing his mother."

A single tear slid down Andrew's recently dried face and then disappeared beneath the collar of his shirt. He had never thought of his birth in that way. Maybe it had been a blessing, in an odd sort of way, he considered for the first time in his life.

Two hours after popping the corkscrew, Andrew finished his second glass of wine. He and Cooper talked about their parents and grandparents as the sound of night settled in. The conversation became lighter as time progressed and eventually laughter took the place of tears. In the kitchen, Andrew watched Cooper work a dishrag down the mouth of a thin wine glass with a light pink shade of lipstick on the rim. Her lips looked so perfect that he almost wanted to keep the glass for decoration, just to remember them when she wasn't close enough to stare at. He couldn't believe he'd agreed to let her wash dishes in his home, but she had been so adamant. He'd said no three times and then she put her hands into the dishwater anyway and told him, in her sweet southern vernacular, to shut up and rinse.

Pressed against the counter beside her, Andrew realized this was the life he wanted. He imagined coming home every day to a smile like hers and after dinner watching the sunset from the back porch with his arms wrapped around her. When it got cold outside, they could pull a blanket from the closet and cuddle up near the fireplace or watch television in their pajamas. The only problem with that life, Andrew realized, is that he already had it— with Meredith. He and Meredith did all of these things together. She made him feel special every day. She did everything that Cooper had done for him tonight. To be honest the only difference between Cooper and Meredith, besides the fact that Meredith had made it clear she wanted nothing more to do with him, was a name.

"Are you always this amazing?" Andrew asked trying to shake off the comparison.

Keeping her focus on the soapy water, Cooper smirked. "Are you asking if I'll do the dishes every time I come over?"

Andrew couldn't help but laugh at her comment. "Well, I *have* always despised washing dishes," he joked.

She handed him a plate to rinse, and he felt her elbow graze his arm. For a moment he held the plate in midair, wondering if the simple touch that made the hair on his arm stand up had even registered on her *that felt kind of nice* Richter scale.

Peering out the small window in front of the sink, Cooper, also, wondered if the touch of her skin had done for Andrew what his had done for her. What kind of thoughts were running through his head, she found herself pondering, and wanting to turn to him, gaze into his beautiful brown eyes and find out if something else might spark from an accidental bump. But she also knew she didn't want to push things and so she continued to stare at the outline of flickered out citronella candles and empty lawn chairs as she caressed a fork below dirty dishwater.

Tonight had been the best time she'd had in a long time, maybe the best time she'd had since she last spent an evening with Andrew Callaway. Oh, she remembered, that had actually been less than twenty-four hours ago, but before that, she reminded herself, it had been a while.

The thing she liked most about being with Andrew is that she felt safe with him by her side. Andrew Callaway was a man, a real man, leaps and bounds of a man above Chris Selzer. Along with muscles and good looks, Andrew possessed both charm and intelligence, and he had feelings, too. He wasn't afraid to show his emotions. Heck, he'd already cried in front of her. In the years she and Chris were together, Chris had never cried in front of her. He'd only made her cry . . . just like he'd done yesterday.

Oh crap, Cooper thought. She still hadn't told Andrew about Chris's visit—the reason she showed up at his game yesterday. With the episode at the creek and then finding his truck painted in the parking lot, she hadn't gotten around to telling him.

Andrew stacked the last dish in the drainer and handed Cooper a towel to dry her hands. Inside the house drops of water continued to fall from the neatly stacked dishes, and outside a drizzly rain began to wet the freshly cut lawn.

"Chris came by my house yesterday," Cooper admitted abruptly, working the towel in and out of her fingers.

Andrew froze for a moment. *Chris? What did he want? And*

why hadn't she told him this last night when Chris's name had come up?

"Oh," Andrew responded, his face showing a hint of redness. "What for?"

"Are you mad at me?" Cooper immediately asked.

Andrew shook his head side to side. To be honest, he wasn't sure if he was mad, but if mad was the feeling his body was fighting right now, he was mad at Chris not at her.

"That was the reason I came to your game last night," she told him. "I planned on telling you, but then one thing led to another and after we found your truck like that I didn't want you to go after Chris. I think he probably did it, but I thought it would be better to tell you once you had a chance to calm down a little."

Andrew took a deep breath. "Cooper, I'm not Chris. I'm not going to hunt someone down and beat them up because they did something juvenile." He paused for a moment, wanting to do exactly what he just said he wouldn't do but knowing it wouldn't be in his best interest. Going after Chris would only add fuel to the fire.

He continued. "So, are you saying that you think Chris is the one responsible for the paint job?"

"I can't be certain, but the reason he came over is because his brother saw you and I together down by the docks at the Sheraton yesterday."

Andrew furrowed his brow. "So . . . ?"

"So Chris is Chris—he's stupid, he's immature. And he said that he didn't want you and me together."

"What you and I do is none of his business," Andrew said sharply.

A frightened look on her face, Cooper took a step backward, and instantly Andrew wished he hadn't raised his voice. He could tell the tone he took startled her, and her reaction reminded him of an abused dog, hit so many times it was afraid to let anyone pet it.

He knew Chris was to blame for that.

"I know, Andrew. I told him that," she said in an almost pleading voice.

"What did he say?" Andrew asked, his voice suddenly much calmer.

She hesitated before answering. "He said that he better not catch us together."

Andrew walked to the answering machine, and as the message he'd played over and over earlier played out once again, Cooper held her hand over her gaped mouth.

"Is that Chris's voice?" he asked.

For a moment, she said nothing.

"I can't tell," she finally answered.

Andrew played the message two more times, but Cooper couldn't be certain that the muffled voice was Chris's.

"Have you called the police?" she asked.

"Not yet."

"Sheriff Ringer said to call if anything else weird happened, and that's pretty weird, Andrew," she proclaimed.

"All Ringer is going to do is listen to the message all night, and then when he can't figure out what to do with it, he'll drop it in the file along with the report from last night."

"At least then he knows a threat has been made. Maybe he can find out where the call came from," she suggested.

"I checked the caller ID and dialed *69, but the number was blocked," Andrew said. "I doubt if Ringer will be able to find out where the call originated from either, but if it will make you feel better, I'll give him a call," he said. "Has anything else weird happened to you that I should mention when I call?"

In her mind, Cooper swept through the last twenty-four hours of her life.

"Anything at all—?" Andrew added.

"I did get run off the road by a big truck on my way here, but—"

Andrew chimed in. "What kind of truck?" he asked, squinting his eyes just a little.

Cooper thought back to the quick glimpse in her rearview mirror. "It was yellow—"

Andrew filled in the rest: "And it had big tires and was lifted way up off the ground?"

Cooper wrinkled her brow. "How did you know?"

"Eric drives a truck just like that."

"Meredith's brother?"

Andrew shook his head and then listened intently as Cooper went over the rest of the story, exactly as it happened from the moment she first noticed the truck in her lane until the moment she pulled back onto the asphalt. When he asked, she told Andrew that she didn't get a look at the driver, and she didn't notice if there were guns in the back window or a toolbox in the bed. It had all happened so fast.

Andrew set the phone back on the receiver and then explained Sheriff Ringer's half of the conversation to Cooper. There wasn't much going on down at the station, he'd said, so he would be right over.

Other than Andrew's, the only call Ronnie had received all night was about a few kids who'd decided to build a bonfire and throw a party out in the middle of one of Harry Johnson's cornfields. The five holding cells with the exception of the one named after Sammy, the town junkie, were empty. Sammy, who he'd brought in earlier this evening for public drunkenness, would probably sleep another three hours before he realized he was alone.

Attempting to lighten the mood, Cooper flipped the dishtowel in her hand in the direction of Andrew's leg. In one motion, he jumped back and grabbed hold of the opposite end; tugging slightly, he pulled her body toward his.

"What was that for?" he asked, close enough to catch a drift of the mint she'd popped in her mouth after dinner.

"Fun," she said, laughing like a playful kid.

He wanted to pull the towel just a smidgen more, bring her close enough to feel her body pressed against his. He wanted to follow the impulse drawing his lips toward her lips; instead, he released the towel and slid his hands into his pockets fiddling with the change he'd gotten back at the grocery store.

"Wait until the Sheriff gets here," he teased, "I'm going to have you arrested."

Ten minutes after the call came in, Sheriff Ronnie Ringer's patrol car whizzed down Andrew Callaway's driveway, blue light swiveling and siren singing. The porch light was on to greet him. Andrew and Cooper, peeking out the front window, watched Ronnie jump out of the driver's seat and jog toward the porch with his hand on his hip. If they didn't know better, they'd have thought someone called in a burglary.

Grinning from ear to ear, Andrew turned to Cooper. "That man is way too into his job," he said while letting the curtain fall so he could answer the doorbell.

She had thought the same thing last night when Ronnie pulled a shovel from his trunk and dug up at least ten footprints from the gravel parking lot. But, figuring it was better for him to collect too much evidence, she hadn't said anything. Either that or he needed to fill a few potholes in the police station parking lot. Maybe he knew what he was doing though, she thought, since he didn't seem to have a problem keeping the crime rate in New Bern way below that of the surrounding counties.

Ronnie took his hat off and stayed at the house for a good hour. He spent most of his time bent over the answering machine listening to the message over and over trying to decipher the voice. In a small notebook, he wrote down the words and then took notes as Andrew and Cooper answered a string of formulaic questions. Before leaving, he took a walk around what he called '*the premises*' and when he didn't come up with anything else, he shook Andrew's hand and said, "I'm going to add this to our file when I get back to the station."

The house to themselves again, Andrew and Cooper decided to put in the movie before it got too late for two adults to stay up on a Thursday night. Still rattled by the words from the message and at how seriously Ronnie had taken the threat, Cooper asked Andrew if he would mind double-checking the front door. Ronnie suggested it would be a good idea to keep windows and doors locked even during the day. Andrew also made sure the curtains were closed all the way; the thought of someone peeking in through a crack unnerved him just as much as it did Cooper.

She waited on the couch for him to secure the house, and when he sat down next to her, a bowl of popcorn separated the two of them. She felt her heart begin to race a little faster, and she wasn't sure if the patter picked up when he turned off the inside lights or when the weight of his body on the cushion beneath her made her torso, and the popcorn bowl, shift in his direction.

Since the previews were outdated, Andrew reached for the remote and fast-forwarded to the opening scene. As the story unfolded and the smell of fresh buttered popcorn faded, Cooper couldn't help but glance toward the dark holes that led to the kitchen and the hallway, wondering if someone really was watching them. She knew the chance of someone getting into the house without them knowing it was slim. Regardless, she considered asking Andrew to turn the lights back on, but instead she inched a little closer to him and tried to move such thoughts to the back of her mind.

About the same time when Andrew noticed that Cooper had moved the popcorn bowl to the coffee table, he also realized the gap between them had all but disappeared. Though he wasn't quite sure how they had gotten six inches closer, he wasn't going to complain about it. Reaching for his watered-down sweet tea, he considered putting his arm around her when he sat back, but he didn't, not immediately anyway. Upon leaning back, he was pleasantly surprised to feel her head nestle up against his shoulder. After freshening up earlier, she'd drawn her hair into a ponytail, and when he glanced down, he watched her alluring smile lift her soft cheeks.

"Is this okay?" she asked, her breath brushing against his ear as she whispered.

Andrew felt the tiny hairs on the back of his neck stand up, almost like a cat being approached by a dog. A sharp, tingling sensation quickly traveled up his spine and the only answer he considered was yes, which is what he replied as he repositioned his arm so it wouldn't remain wedged between the left side of her body and the back of the couch. He placed it around her shoulder, and then she scooted in a little closer.

Outside, clouds covered the moon, and as the light drizzle turned into a heavy rain pounding the ground on the other side of the window next to the couch, Kevin Costner sailed into the sea, and Cooper McKay fell asleep to the subtle beat of Andrew Callaway's heart. Andrew, already familiar with the ending to the movie, chose to watch her sleep; there were some things he hadn't figured out yet, though—like how tonight would end. Would he let Cooper follow him up the stairs to his bedroom? Would he be able to hold her so tight that she would forget about Chris? Would she be able to hold him so tight that he would forget about Meredith?

The desires, the urges, the chemistry—it was all there; it had been building the entire evening, but there was so much more involved, so many variables. Andrew didn't want to regret anything with Cooper. He didn't want to look back on this night and say, *I wish I hadn't done that.*

17

Feeling disoriented, Cooper lifted her head and began to rub her eyes.

What time is it? She wondered, keeping her hand in front of her face to shield the brightness beaming into the room through the curtains.

"Good morning, sleepy head," Andrew offered from above, watching her yawn turn into a smile.

It took a moment for Cooper to digest Andrew's words, but then when she realized what he'd said, she nearly jumped off the couch.

"Good what?" she asked scanning the dark room for a clock.

"I'm just kidding," Andrew, after witnessing her reaction, quickly verified.

Cooper sighed. "My mother would kill me if I didn't show up until morning," she said, continuing to search for the time.

Andrew pointed to a clock on the wall behind them, and Cooper squinted to find out that it was almost midnight. "I feel like I've been sleeping for hours," she said.

"I hope you didn't miss curfew," he teased.

Thinking of the days when she lived at home, Cooper snickered. "My mom probably is waiting up for me. If she knows

I'm coming home, she can't fall asleep until I get there, or so she says. So I think I will call it a night."

As the two of them headed for the front door, Andrew nearly collapsed on the coffee table as he took his first step. He hadn't realized that his leg had fallen asleep, and so he walked the rest of the way drunkenly searching for props along the way.

Cooper laughed as she watched him use every piece of furniture between the coffee table and the doorknob to keep his balance. "You may need a cane, old man," she suggested.

Instead of a cane, Andrew pulled an umbrella from a basket near the door and escorted her to her car.

As the rain beat on the hood, Andrew settled for a hug, and then Cooper lowered herself into the cloth seat and thanked him for dinner. Smiling, Andrew closed the car door and took two steps backward. He felt his feet sink into the soggy gravel, and he treaded lightly as he watched her car reverse down the narrow drive. Even though the umbrella had kept his hair dry, the wind was blowing the rain onto the rest of his body. He could feel his pant legs becoming heavy, and his arms were dripping like the leaves in the trees; nevertheless, everything seemed perfect. The night would end on a good note; he would go inside, jump into the shower, and then fall into bed with a smile on his face. But . . .

As soon as Andrew looked at the ground beside him, he changed his mind. Footprints, about the size of his own, led to where Cooper's car had been parked—to where her back door would have been if the car were still sitting in front of him. Neither he nor Cooper had gone near that door; he knew that for certain. Also the rain, he realized, would have washed away old prints.

At that moment, the natural surround sound of frogs croaking a harmonious melody and rocks jumping like jacks, as raindrops pounded them into the gravel path, seemed to turn to silence. The glow of the pole light—the one that had been shining through the window when Cooper awoke in Andrew's arms—helped Andrew's investigative eyes follow a trail of prints across the front yard leading in from the road.

Reality suddenly set in.

Andrew's heart began to pound fiercely, and before he even realized that his instincts had taken over, the umbrella fell to the ground and rested in one of the footprints.

18

istracted by a distant blur, Cooper took her eyes off the rearview mirror. She touched the brake with her foot, and holding it there, inched her face closer to the foggy windshield. The wipers continued to sling rain from the glass, and as the image coming toward her became clear, she wondered why Andrew was sprinting down the center of the driveway headed straight for her car?

Maybe she left her purse in the house? She considered, but then she looked in the passenger seat and saw the movie casing wedged between the opened zipper. It must be something else.

But what else could there be?

Wanting to keep the inside of her mother's car as dry as possible, Cooper cracked the window and waited for Andrew. Breathing heavily, he passed by the open window and flung open the back door. In high school, he had probably run a hundred track meets but never had he run the forty-yard dash as fast as he had tonight. There was a huge difference, however, in winning a plaque and saving a life. That is how he'd felt when he spotted the footprints-Cooper's life was in danger, and he honestly felt that if she made it out of the driveway he might not ever see her again.

Belted in, Cooper twisted her neck as far as she could to get a glimpse of Andrew. The enraged look on his face frightened her, and she still couldn't figure out why he'd sprinted past her door and opened the other door. As her mouth opened to ask the question, her eyes nearly left their sockets when a dark figure lunged from her back seat through the opened door.

Along with whoever had been hiding in the floorboard of her back seat, she watched Andrew tumble forcefully into the wet grass, and she screamed louder than she ever had.

In a state of panic, Cooper couldn't get the door to open, and honestly, she wasn't sure if she should get out or stay in the car, but her instinct was to get out.

Andrew couldn't see the face in front of him—maybe because it was so dark or maybe because the two fists attached to the body pinning him to the ground were swinging at his head as fast as a lawnmower blade. Even though he'd expected someone to be in the back seat, in a way he hadn't. This was the kind of thing that happened in the movies, not in real life. You always thought there was someone in your car or in your house or following you through a dark parking lot, but there never really was. This time, though, had proven different. This was as real as real could possibly be.

Finally, Cooper found the handle and nearly yanked it off the door. "Andrew," she yelled out, springing from the car, wanting to do something, anything to help.

She could see fists flying, but she was afraid to move any closer to the dark shadows. The person on top seemed to be getting the better of the other, but no matter how hard she focused, she couldn't tell which body belonged to Andrew.

Like a boxer trapped in the corner of the ring, Andrew, wedged between the attacker's body and a spongy ground, continued to cover his face with his arms. He had only been able to get off three or four punches of his own so far, and he wasn't sure how many of those he'd actually landed. The other guy had landed a handful on him, mainly on his upper torso, and Andrew knew he had to get him off soon or he might not have any strength left to do so. Bravely, he opened his guard and took one punch to either side of the face just so he could get his arms into his attacker's chest. Quickly, he dug his fingers into the guy's shirt and pushed him up far enough to free his right leg.

Cooper watched the body on top suddenly fly through the air and collide with a nearby pine tree. Then she watched that person get up and run toward the road. Knowing now that Andrew was the one who'd been on bottom, Cooper breathed a prayer as she dropped to the ground beside him. Her knees dug into the muddy grass, and she gently touched his leg with her fingertips. He was breathing heavy, and she knew he had to be hurting.

Holding his ribs, Andrew watched the silhouette of the person who'd been in the backseat reach the end of the driveway and disappear onto the road. As soon as he knew that Cooper was safe, he used his battered arms to scoot his body to the same pine tree he'd kicked the other guy against.

"Andrew, are you okay?" were the first words that rolled off Cooper's trembling lips.

Before he could speak, they heard an engine start out on the road, and both of them turned to look. A set of headlights cut on, but the vehicle was way too far away to make out a license plate number in the dark. Andrew wanted to jump into Cooper's car and chase the guy down, but at this point he didn't feel like moving. Plus he didn't want to wreck her mother's car—that always happened in the movies, too.

Instead, Andrew put his hand on top of Cooper's and tried to smile.

One of his eyes felt swollen, and he could taste blood in his mouth. "I'll be fine," he mumbled.

❧

Safely inside, Cooper began to draw a bath for Andrew just after she called her mom to let her know she'd be home later than expected without citing the real reason.

In Andrew's bathroom, she fetched a Carolina blue washcloth from his linen closet and found herself wishing someone had been there to mix Epsom salt in a warm tub of water when Chris beat her like a rag doll and left her bleeding and bruised. She couldn't help but think he was to blame for this attack, too. Although she couldn't be certain; it had happened so fast that she hadn't been able to get a good look at the person hiding in her backseat.

Andrew hesitated for a moment before stripping down to his boxers, but he knew Cooper was right—the sooner the gash on his cheek and the cuts on his arms and chest got attended to the better they would look tomorrow and even a year from now for that matter. It wasn't like he was taking a real bath where he would be totally revealed although he'd already been close to totally revealed in front of Cooper—well, kind of anyway, at the creek.

Letting go of the thought of indecency, he sunk below the water, and Cooper watched every muscle in his body tense up. He probably wanted to cry, she figured, knowing she would if she were the one soaking in murky water with him on the dry side of the tub. She couldn't help but wonder how dirty the bath would be if she hadn't gotten him to rinse off beneath the showerhead to rid most of the muck he'd brought in from mud wrestling in the front yard. That was part of a joke she'd made earlier hoping to get Andrew to laugh, but when he'd started to chuckle, he pulled his hands to his side and nearly began to cry because the pain was so sharp.

The sting of hydrogen peroxide, Andrew decided, didn't seem as painful as long as he gazed into his personal nurse's brown eyes each time she dabbed his face with the rag in her hand. He hated that this had happened to him, but if he had to look and feel this way, at least he had Cooper here to take care of him. As he thought about how beautiful, actually how sexy, Cooper looked every time she dipped the washcloth into the bucket of water sitting next to her, it made him want to pull her into the tub with him. On second thought that might not work out too well, he decided, since his ribs were bruised and the water looked more like a soggy mud pie than a romantic hot spring. Plus Cooper might not be all that attracted to him right now. On his way into the bathroom, he had taken a glance into the mirror and even he didn't like what he saw; along with the gash beneath his right eye, it looked like the left one might soon turn black, he recalled, as the water began to cover his chest.

"So you don't think Eric was the one in my backseat?" Cooper asked.

Andrew shook his head slowly.

It hurt to move, and it hurt even more to talk. "Eric," he whispered, agonizing in pain, "isn't that strong, and he is a little chubbier than that guy."

It all happened so fast, though, that Andrew knew he wouldn't be able to make the guy out if he walked into the bathroom this very moment. Not unless he could look for a shoe print on his stomach or bruises where his fingers dug into his chest.

"I wish one of us would have gotten a better look at him," Cooper said. "But if you are sure it wasn't Eric, it had to be Chris . . ."

Ronnie Ringer made it to the house before Andrew was able to get out of the tub and put on a pair of gym shorts. While he waited in the living room, he could hear Cooper opening and closing the kitchen cabinets; looking for a glass, he assumed, to pour the tea in which she had been nice enough to offer before showing him to the couch. His investigative mind was always at work even when it didn't have to be; he could tell by Cooper's actions that she wasn't very familiar with this house. This might even be her first time at Andrew's, he concluded, but then Ronnie reminded himself that Andrew's personal life was none of his business. To solve this case, he didn't need to figure out why Andrew and Cooper had been spending time together like everyone else in town had been asking, he just needed to find out who attacked Andrew tonight.

When Cooper came back into the living room, Ronnie took a sip of tea and began asking questions about Chris Selzer. Considering the circumstances, Cooper decided to tell him about everything that Chris had done to her in the past. When she finished, Ronnie wore a look almost as frightening as Clint Eastwood in Dirty Harry.

"I won't put up with this in my town," he assured her. "I'm going to pay Mr. Selzer a visit before the night is over," he guaranteed, looking up as he heard Andrew coming down the stairs.

Ronnie stood to shake his hand. Then he took a look at the marks on Andrew's body and said it would probably be best if they took some pictures for evidence. The camera Ronnie kept in his patrol car must have been fifteen years old, Andrew figured, as he posed for instant Polaroid shots. Jokingly, Ronnie promised he wouldn't post them on the Internet, and then in a more serious tone he said he would add them to the file.

It was getting late and Andrew had promised Cooper he would take her home; while Ronnie detained her mother's car as part of the crime scene, Andrew started the old Chevy and pushed through the mud on the other side of the driveway to get around the yellow tape Ronnie had strung up like Christmas lights.

When Andrew made it back to his house, Ronnie's patrol car was gone. He locked the deadbolt and minutes later climbed into bed. Just when he was about to silence his cell phone, it rang. Before looking at the caller ID he expected to discover Cooper's number, but it wasn't. It was a blocked number which meant it was probably either Ronnie or another threat. When he answered, the voice sent him into a momentary state of shock.

"Hey, Andrew, sorry to call so late, but I really need to talk to you," Meredith said softly.

The bedroom pitch black, Andrew sat up and rested his back on the headboard. It was obvious that Meredith had been crying. "Is everything okay?" he asked instinctively.

Of course everything wasn't okay, he reminded himself. The woman on the other end of the line, Meredith, *his* Meredith, had broken off their engagement less than forty-eight hours ago. After three wonderful years together, their relationship had come to an abrupt ending less than two weeks before *The Big Day*.

"I found out how all of this happened," she said.

Andrew took a deep breath, not sure he wanted to know, but he asked anyway.

"Mom confessed everything to me tonight," Meredith replied. "I spent all day yesterday and part of this morning trying to track her down. She was hiding from me because she was afraid I would find out it was her after I got the pictures. Andrew, she is the one who sent the emails to Cooper." She paused for a moment, ashamed of her own family. "And Eric is the one who took the photos. They had this all planned out. Neither of them wants us to be together."

"Why?" Andrew asked. "What have I ever done to either one of them, except had a few petty little arguments?"

"Andrew, I don't know, but it's not up to them. We need to talk about what they've done *and* what you've done. I need to know everything that has happened between you and Cooper . . ."

Andrew ran his left hand through his hair. "I'm not sure if tonight is a good time to talk about this, Meredith."

For a moment, a lull took over the conversation.

"Why not?" she finally asked.

"Someone attacked me tonight."

Meredith chimed in. "Are you okay?" she asked searching for the breath she had lost the instant that statement had exited Andrew's mouth.

"I'll be fine," he assured her. "I just have to figure out who did this." He paused for a moment to let her calm down. "Do you think your mother and Eric have anything to do with it?" he asked.

Meredith leaned back in the driver's seat of her rental car. As soon as she had finished yelling at her mother, she'd left the hotel and was now in the parking lot of the next hotel she had come across, planning to check in after she and Andrew made some sense of the worst thing that had ever happened in her life. She'd taken her mother's phone since she'd decided it was her mom's fault that her phone was scattered all over their hotel room in the first place. She didn't feel bad about stealing the phone, but she did kind of feel guilty about slapping her mom in the face. Growing up, Meredith's mom had slapped her in the face more times than she could count, but today was the first time she'd ever returned the favor. Her mother deserved it, but at the same time she didn't want to turn out like her mom. A while back, Meredith had made a vow with herself and with Andrew that when they had kids she would never slap them, but now, she didn't know if they would ever make it that far.

"At this point, I would say anything is possible," Meredith responded. "But I seriously doubt if they would want to bring harm to you, Andrew. What they've done was stupid, but I don't think they're cruel enough to have someone physically attack you."

He wanted to believe Meredith, but he knew he had to figure this out on his own before he could move forward in any direction. Without going into detail, he told her that the attack had happened in his driveway and that Sheriff Ringer was doing an investigation. Meredith begged him to stay on the phone a little longer, but he couldn't. Every time he spoke he felt a sharp pain in his ribs, and now, on top of that, a headache was settling in. He needed sleep, and he had a gut feeling that if they talked about all of this tonight it wouldn't turn out well. He needed to get through tomorrow, figure some things out.

Andrew was surprised when Meredith agreed to call him back tomorrow evening, but then again he realized that she probably needed some time to process all of this as well. When he set the phone back on the nightstand, he wrestled with the idea of calling Cooper. He even picked the phone back up several times and began dialing her number, but instead of calling her, he decided to finish off the bottle of wine they'd started at dinner and he fell asleep half watching the second run of *The Tonight Show*.

19

$\mathcal{E}$ight o'clock came quickly. Standing at the sink, Andrew let out a blast of joy when he discovered that the discoloration, around the eye he thought for sure would have turned black by now, barely resembled anything more than lack of sleep, which brought another thought to mind: Why did people call it a black eye when the skin actually turned more of a purplish color?

Growing up, he'd had two or three black eyes from blows to the head during soccer matches. One time, the entire white part of his eye turned bloodshot red, and another time he could remember having a single red dot that looked like a laser pointer was shining in the white of his eye for about five days straight.

Black or purple, the thought of his skin changing color didn't sound like good news. For a kid, a black eye was cool. Almost as cool as sporting a cast after breaking a leg and then having all the kids at school sign their names to it, but for an adult—especially a businessman—not much good could come from a black eye. A real estate agent could lose sales over something like that.

Andrew ran water over his face and started to consider the same what-if's that had run through his mind as he lay in bed last night: *What if* he and Meredith ended up getting married next weekend? *What if* his eye turned black later today? The possibility of either seemed slim, but logically both could still happen. After his conversation with Meredith last night, he could actually imagine going through with it—*if* he could be certain Meredith had nothing to do with the set-up and *if* she would agree to forgive him for spending time with Cooper. And, *if* she did choose to do so, he would have to remember to say a special prayer to thank God for keeping his eye from turning black or purple. Because *if* it did—the wedding photos—Andrew could hear Meredith now telling stories about the pictures in the album: "Oh, my husband decided to get into a fist fight over another woman the week before we married." That would be a hoot. He knew Meredith wouldn't actually put him through that kind of torture; she had more class than that, but, nonetheless, it would be embarrassing to explain. Between the two of them, surely they would be able to come up with a way to minimize the awkwardness of the situation.

Andrew finished cleaning out the gash beneath his eye—the way Cooper had shown him while he relaxed in the tub last night. After showering, he packed his beach gear. One more day with Cooper McKay couldn't hurt, he had decided. So far nothing physical had happened between them; he hadn't slept with her or even kissed her, but he had promised her a day at the beach which he knew would give him one more thing to explain to Meredith— *if* they ended up deciding to work things out. That was a chance he was willing to take since Meredith hadn't actually mentioned working things out, only talking about them. At the moment, he had to admit that the idea of a wedding taking place, after all that had happened in the last two days, was pretty farfetched.

The screen door at Cooper's parent's house opened, and Andrew got out of the truck and smiled at Cooper. In a pair of cotton shorts and a tank top, her arms crossed and a good morning grin on her face, she made her way to the base of the concrete steps. As soon as Andrew's first flip-flop found grass, he looked for the mud puddles he and Cooper had dodged when he'd dropped her off last night. It seemed the morning sun, alone in a cloudless blue sky, had already toasted the yard. Thankfully, his ribs took to walking much better than expected after some rest last night.

"Great morning for the beach," Cooper announced enthusiastically.

She held her hand to her forehead just above her eyes, and Andrew couldn't imagine having to walk up to her now only to bow out on his offer. Taking Cooper to the beach was the right thing to do. He wouldn't let anything happen between the two of them, and if he found out Meredith had absolutely nothing to do with the set-up, he would tell her about this trip just like he would tell her about skinny-dipping at Creekside Park and dinner with Cooper at his house.

Unlike last night, Andrew followed Cooper through the front door. Her father, a muscular man with a handshake to match, offered his hand, and then Cooper's mother hugged Andrew's neck like she had known him all her life. For some reason, Andrew wasn't surprised. He could see Cooper doing the exact thing to a man her daughter might bring home thirty years from now. The resemblance between Cooper and her mother, he couldn't help but notice, was unreal. Their eyes, their hair, the sound of their voices, even their mannerisms were all the same—identical, almost.

The glass of tea Cooper's mother brought out from the kitchen for Andrew seemed to go by quicker than a beer in the hand of a thirsty alcoholic. The stuff was good. Scratch that, addicting. If making sweet tea like this was another trait Cooper had inherited from her mother, he might have to forget about patching up things with Meredith and keep Cooper around.

Thoughts like that were the reason Andrew was glad no one could read his mind. Seriously, though, he could easily go through a twelve pack of these liquid treats in one night.

With Cooper's dad now sitting next to him, Andrew felt a little awkward when Cooper invited him back to her room. Of course, she wasn't inviting him in the *do you want to come up to my place for coffee* sort of way, but he had to admit, even at the age of twenty-eight, he did feel like he needed to be on his best behavior, keep his hands to himself, his eyes above the neck.

Before politely excusing himself from the couch, Andrew glanced to his left and then to his right. He determined that neither set of eyes seemed to be judging him. In Cooper's bedroom, he sat at her desk while she stuffed a white T-shirt and a beach towel into an old worn out book bag. He couldn't help but notice her laptop sitting near the edge, and he summoned the courage to ask the question that had been on his mind since she'd handed him the printed emails at the park.

"Will you show me the actual emails that Meredith sent to your email account?" he requested, wondering if she'd think he didn't trust her.

"Sure." It only made sense to Cooper that Andrew would want to see the actual evidence first hand. If their roles were reversed she sure as heck would have asked. Anyone could have easily typed up in a Word document something that resembled an email.

Andrew watched as Cooper opened a web browser and typed in her password. If his request had bothered her in any way, her reaction hadn't shown it. A couple of clicks later, the emails were right in front of his face. Each email was definitely from Meredith's account, and everything matched exactly what Cooper had printed out and brought to him. He knew this for sure because he had read them enough to memorize every word.

Without any further discussion on the matter, Andrew said, "Thanks." Cooper shut off her laptop, and then they headed back through the living room. The two of them took a moment to say bye to her parents before walking out the front door.

The straw basket in Andrew's hand had been sitting next to the door when he first walked into the house, and as he lifted it into the bed of the truck, he looked in Cooper's direction.

"What is this?" he asked.

"Lunch."

"I haven't even had breakfast yet," Andrew replied grinning.

When Cooper had quietly asked him in her bedroom about his injuries, he'd fudged just a little on how much they hurt after a night's rest. He didn't want her thinking he was a wimp or anything, and he definitely didn't want her feeling like she had to carry things all day. He was relieved to get out of her parent's house without either of them asking about his face. Last night when Cooper was cleaning his wounds, she'd told Andrew that she'd mention his injuries to her parents, nonchalantly, as something that had happened at the soccer game. Thankfully, that had worked out well.

Behind the wheel, Andrew headed him and Cooper in the direction of Atlantic Beach about forty miles east of New Bern. Before they reached the first stoplight on Highway 70, Cooper asked about the air conditioner. He knew the question would come sooner or later, and even though this wasn't his normal vehicle, he felt kind of embarrassed that for forty-five minutes they would have to rely solely on rolled down windows as their only source of air. Last night when he'd taken her home she probably hadn't noticed since it had been a little cooler, and they'd had so much on their minds. He apologized for the lack of modern amenities, and then thought that maybe he should have taken Cooper up on her offer to drive her mother's car—still parked at his house this morning minus the crime scene tape. Then she wouldn't have had to pull up her hair as soon as she buckled in and then listen to him laugh as she struggled with two hands to roll down the stiff window as fast as she possibly could without throwing her shoulder out. He wouldn't have felt right driving her mother's car, even though it would have only been from his house to her parent's house, nor would he be okay with making her drive it to the beach. That wouldn't be very gentlemanlike, he'd decided, which is exactly why he had courteously declined, suggesting they could get the car when they got back from the beach. As they talked about the air conditioner, though, he quickly realized, just as he'd expected, that Cooper wasn't the type of girl who was bothered about her hair blowing in the wind a little, or a lot.

"What did you pack for lunch?" Andrew asked, lowering the volume of the radio as a cool breeze blew across the truck.

"Ham sandwiches, apples, and Doritos," Cooper replied. "Did you bring the sodas you promised to pick up on the way over this morning?"

"Of course. The cooler is buried back there," he said, pointing to the truck bed, "beneath half of your belongings."

"Ha. Ha. What did you get?"

"I grabbed a couple of six packs."

"I thought you said you didn't drink beer?"

"I don't, but I drink Mountain Dew and Pepsi," he said grinning. "They come in six packs, twelve packs, twenty-four packs—they have a variety of options," he added, as Cooper thought about smacking him on the arm sticking out of his sleeveless T-shirt. "I also grabbed a Snickers bar for each of us."

Cooper perked up. "Snickers are my favorite," she said excitedly.

A little later, Andrew slowed for another stoplight. "So, what makes you think I like ham sandwiches?" he asked.

"You like apples and Doritos, too, don't you?" she suggested.

Andrew recognized a hint of confidence in her tone. "You got lucky this time."

"No, I'm just smart," Cooper replied with a smirk. "I may have taken a peek in your refrigerator and your cabinets as I was putting away the dishes last night," she admitted.

"Oh, so you were snooping."

"Snooping . . . or putting away your dishes; just depends on how you look at it."

Andrew smiled. "I guess I'll let you off the hook this time but only because you helped with the dishes."

Without realizing her own dramatization, Cooper cocked her head and raised an eyebrow. "Helped?"

Thirty minutes after backing out of the driveway, the old truck struggled to climb the high-rise bridge connecting Morehead City and Atlantic Beach. At the top, nearly the entire island became visible. One left turn and a few more miles brought Andrew and Cooper to Fort Macon State Park where a rectangular blue sign read: Public Beach Access. Several hundred cars had already packed the lot, and a beach patrolman, standing at the gate, motioned for Andrew and a long line of other drivers to continue down the road. As Andrew knew from previous visits to this beach, the guard would only allow one vehicle to enter as another exited. Knowing also that the island road dead-ended a mile up and that everyone would be turning around to come back for a second try, he scratched his head. After rounding the first curve, instead of following the crowd, Andrew pulled the truck into the grass on the right side of the road and made a quick U-turn.

Cooper shifted in her seat. "What are you doing?" she contested.

Andrew smiled mischievously while turning the loose steering wheel around and around nearly three times before ending up in the opposite lane headed back for the gate.

"You can't do that," Cooper alleged, laughing as she watched the disgruntled faces of the people in the vehicles that had been behind them.

"It's not illegal."

"Then why did you wait until we were out of the guard's sight?"

"Well, maybe it is, but they're doing it, too," Andrew argued, glancing in his rearview mirror.

Three other cars followed suit, Cooper found out as she rotated in the toasty vinyl seat to look through the back glass. "I still say you're a cheater, Andrew Callaway," she let him know. "It will be funny if the Park Ranger arrests you."

"He has more important things to do . . . and if he did arrest me, you would have to sit in jail with me because you wouldn't have a way home."

Thankfully, the guard didn't notice how quickly they made it back, and after being waved in, Andrew drove through a short and narrow path overlapped by shady cedar trees. In the parking lot, Cooper helped him unload the truck before heading up a set of stairs toward a small building, where they stopped at the restrooms before passing a concession stand full of junk food and cold beverages. They followed a wooden boardwalk that spanned across mountain-like sand dunes, eventually opening into a canapé that accommodated beach goers with a picnic area and grills. As the ocean's rolling waves came into view, Cooper followed Andrew down a ramp that led to a wide-open beach. On the radio, she'd heard that today's forecast called for near triple-digit highs, and as soon as Andrew took off his flip-flops and began plowing through the sand, she watched in amusement as he began to perform the peepee dance. The early morning sun had already scorched the beach, and he recognized the burning sensation on his bare feet about a step and a half too late.

Cooper held her hand over her mouth laughing at him harder than he had laughed at her in the truck. "What are you doing?" she asked, watching as he tried to get back into his flip-flops.

"I didn't think the sand would be so hot this early," Andrew declared, turning to let out a wince as Cooper scouted the beach for a spot to camp out for the day. His feet quickly reached normal temperature again, and he found himself gingerly rubbing his side as Cooper pointed to a clearing a hundred yards or so away where the crowds dwindled just a little. "Let's go down there," she suggested.

"That's a *mile* away," Andrew complained somewhat seriously but coming across as jokingly.

Cooper curled her lip and looked at his feet. "What's wrong?" she asked, speaking to him like she would a toddler, "You can't handle the walk? Is the sand too hot for your little feet?" she said sarcastically.

"Oh, I can but I figure you'll probably ask for a piggyback ride about halfway there," he teased.

"I can manage the walk, but if you're offering, I'll take the ride," she agreed, knowing she really wouldn't because she had seen the pain in his face when he'd started his dance in the sand. He was hurting, but he didn't want her to know how badly. Kind of sweet, she thought.

The two began to zigzag through chairs and blankets filled with sunbathers and families alike. On the last twenty yards of the trek, Cooper was suddenly surprised by Andrew's strength. Out of nowhere he'd come up beside her, and the next thing she knew she was on his back; he had the cooler in one hand and the straw basket and a small bag weighing down the other.

"This backpack sure is heavy," she complained, but Andrew could hear the smile in her voice.

He shook his head and marched on, panting slightly by the time she climbed off.

"Good boy," she said, patting his back.

Andrew set the cooler down and took off his shirt as Cooper stretched her towel across the sand. Figuring Andrew had worked hard enough just to get to this point, she spread his out too, with only an inch of sand separating the towels.

Sitting Indian-style, she reached for her bag. "I brought a book in case you become boring," she kidded, pulling a thick novel from her bag.

"I brought you in case I get bored," Andrew countered, unable to keep a straight face.

Cooper attempted to shoot an evil stare in his direction, but as soon as his eyes met hers, she turned away and laughed. He always seemed to find a smart comment to combat the ones she threw at him. She liked that about him. She'd liked that ever since the day at the video store when he'd jokingly said: "Why would I be by myself in a video store if I didn't like watching movies by myself?" But it wasn't just the silly comments that made him so easy to like; the laughter that followed is what made them worthwhile . . . the feeling she felt every time they debated over something that had absolutely no relevance: Six packs of Mountain Dews; hot sand; piggyback rides. This man, this unbelievable Andrew Callaway, made her feel at ease like no other man ever had. With him, she felt almost like she was hanging out with one of her girlfriends or her mother. She could be herself; she could even say something stupid and not worry about him judging her.

As Andrew settled on his towel, Cooper, a smile on her face, drew her knees toward her chest and stared out over the ocean—the water almost as calm as a river. She wondered what path the day would take as she watched a young boy fly a kite before her attention moved to a middle-aged woman collecting sea shells and then to an elderly gentleman casting a line near a large group of boulders that reached from the sandy shore into the dark blue waters of the Atlantic. Minutes later the man reeled in a good-sized fish, and from afar it seemed that Cooper enjoyed the catch as much as he did.

A few minutes later, Cooper pulled a bottle of sunscreen from her bag.

"Want some?" she asked Andrew who was lying on his stomach with his chin rested in his hands.

"Is it forty-five SPF?"

Cooper studied the label. "Thirty-five," she answered. "My mom was kind enough to put some on me earlier because I like to let it soak in before I get to the beach."

"Good. Last time I came out this early in the morning and stayed all day I ended up looking like charcoal." Even the memory was painful. "That was sweet of your mother," Andrew added, almost as an afterthought.

"Did you put sunscreen on that day?"

"Yes, but it was only an eight. That's why I asked."

Cooper shook her head—yet another reason why men couldn't function without women. "We won't let that happen today," she promised in a motherly tone. "Want me to put some on your back?"

Would that be outside the boundaries? Andrew wondered. "Sure, that would be nice," he finally agreed, knowing that a few days ago it would have been, but now for some reason, he saw everything related to Cooper as gray area.

Lining her palm with lotion, Andrew watched Cooper squeeze the bottle and then cross the line in the sand, scooting up close to him on his towel. At the touch of her fingertips, he felt his eyelids relax, and his arms became weightless. Every worry consuming his mind drifted away like a bottle stuck in the current below the sounds of the ocean. Diligently, she worked her fingers around his shoulders and down his back, tenderly massaging the oil onto his already tanned skin. She felt his muscles tighten then relax as she pressed firmly, rasping his skin. She, too, closed her eyes imagining the two of them on the beach alone as she continued to caress his neck.

As the waves crashed in the background, what had begun as a friendly application of sunscreen turned into a five-minute massage, Cooper kneading every nook and cranny from Andrew's waist up; he appreciated how she was cognizant of the scratches and scrapes on his back—most likely from pinecones—and he couldn't help but wonder if feeling like those were her fault was one of the reasons she'd given him the extra attention. Regardless, it felt nice.

"Do you want me to get your face and stomach, too?" she asked when she finished his back.

Whether or not Andrew *wanted* to flip over and let Cooper run her hands over the rest of his body wasn't the question running through his mind as he lay with his face in the blanket, paralyzed by her touch. "I don't think I can move," he insisted. "If your offer still stands when I wake up, I might take you up on it," he added.

Cooper put away the bottle.

"Thank you," Andrew murmured into the towel beneath his face.

"My pleasure," she replied sweetly.

The pleasure was all mine, Andrew wanted to say, realizing that boundaries had definitely been tested. He couldn't remember the last time he'd been on the receiving end of a good massage and never had he been given one quite like that. The only thing keeping him from rolling onto Cooper's towel—other than promising himself he would make wise decisions today—was the multitude of people sharing the sandy bed beneath them.

Thirty minutes later, Cooper woke up on a makeshift pillow that Andrew had created for her out of his T-shirt. If she could force herself to open her eyes, which would require adjusting to what at the moment seemed like an unbearable sun, she could check the time and find out if she needed to flip over. Trying to convince herself of just that, Cooper reached blindly for her watch. She remembered dropping it into her bag prior to dozing off, but as soon as her hand swept through the humid air, she came across another object—something stiff, yet—

What was it? And why was it on her towel? Cooper wondered, her eyelids opening faster than her mind could process the feeling of a human foot attached to a pair of legs standing between her and Andrew—who at the moment looked as though he was dreaming. In one motion, Cooper jumped off her towel and let out a squeal.

20

ndrew sprang into action. What was going on? Was Cooper okay? Had the football being thrown back and forth by a group of teenagers who'd been playing behind them hit her? Maybe a swimmer was being attacked by a shark? These thoughts darted through Andrew's mind, but when he realized that none of them had anything to do with the ear piercing tone that had awakened him, he found himself sizing up a pair of legs.

Why was this person here? Andrew wondered as Cooper said, "You scared me," in the midst of catching her breath.

As soon as Andrew realized that Cooper was okay, he smiled at the little boy who had scared the crap out of both of them. What was he doing here? Andrew wondered, looking around to see if anyone might be on the way over to get him.

"Where is your mother?" Cooper probed as the youngster, openly amused by the disturbance he'd brought about, giggled before lying in the sand between her and Andrew's towels.

Who did he belong to? Cooper wondered. Was he lost?

"Ova dare," he said.

Cooper sighed. At least he could talk, she thought, as her eyes followed the direction in which the boy's finger was pointing.

When she spotted the woman she assumed to be his mother, about thirty yards down the beach, she turned to Andrew with a look of disgust covering her face. Andrew shook his head in agreement. Even a good mother could lose her son, but it seemed as though this woman didn't have her priorities straight. With a towel draped over her face, it appeared as though she was sleeping in her 1980's style lawn chair. Toys, along with at least eight empty beer bottles, filled the sand at her feet. Andrew had never understood how a parent could drink that much beer in front of a child and expect him to grow up to be a normal kid. Not to mention, alcohol wasn't allowed at this beach.

Cooper wasn't sure what they should do with the little guy; she felt bad for him. Sure, she and Andrew could walk him back over to his mother, and everything would be okay, or at least as okay as being raised by a mother so busy trying to find a buzz that she'd managed to lose her son could be. If she'd neglected him today, though, how many times had she let this happen in the past? How many times would it happen in the future?

"Does she know where you are?" Cooper asked, knowing the answer already.

He shrugged his shoulders.

"Can we keep him?" Andrew asked jokingly, yet after seeing the condition of his mother, somewhat wishing the request could be serious.

Cooper playfully rolled her eyes. "He's not a puppy."

Andrew laughed. "How old are you?" he inquired.

The boy began to use his fingers to count his age. "Tree," he finally called out, holding up that many fingers.

"You're three," Andrew said excitedly. "You're a big boy."

Cooper laughed out loud as the little fellow stretched his arms toward the sky and mimicked Andrew. "Ina big-oy."

"Yes, you are. My name is Andrew, what is your name?"

"Josh," he answered clearly.

"Josh, would you like to help me build a sandcastle?"

The boy's eyes widened, and Cooper wondered if that was a good idea. She was about to mention that to Andrew, but then she found herself wondering if anyone had ever taken the time to build a sandcastle with Josh. She doubted if his mother ever had. The boy could probably use some attention, she decided.

"Uh, hu," Josh answered, shaking his head up and down just as fast as a three year old possibly could.

Taking hold of Josh's hand, Andrew led him toward the water.

Pretending to read her book as Andrew's and Josh's sandcastle took form, Cooper smiled as Andrew and the little boy—covered from head to toe in the mushy sand he'd been wallowing in—chatted like best friends. Andrew found out that this was Josh's first sandcastle, and he made the most of the opportunity by teaching him how to mix the right amount of sand and water to create perfect layers. The three-year-old told Andrew he didn't have a dad, which could mean a number of things, but that was about as much information as Andrew could get out of him on that subject. Who knew where the dad was or if he even existed? For all Andrew knew he could be a good dad working hard to provide for his family while they enjoyed a day at the beach. At least that is what he wanted to think. The boy did seem happy, though, especially when he and Andrew completed the castle; it stood a few inches taller than Josh. His favorite part was the water, streaming from a trench connected to the ocean and running beneath bridges and into a tunnel below the castle.

When Andrew looked in Cooper's direction, she clapped her hands silently and smiled. Nearly an hour had gone by since the little boy first appeared. His mother, Cooper noticed after filtering through the multitudes of people who'd crammed their beach gear between her and the woman she had been trying not to judge, still hadn't moved. For a moment, she became a little worried, the thought that the woman might be dead crossing her mind, but after staring for a few seconds she realized her beer gut was moving up and down.

Scores of other children now packed the shoreline, some digging in the sand, some playing with hermit crabs, and others splashing in the shallow water. Josh's attention span amazed Cooper; she couldn't believe that a three-year-old would play with an adult for this long when there were other children around to play with. Actually, as she watched Josh hustle to and from the water, trying his best to guard the finished castle, it seemed as though he didn't even notice the other kids. When the water would draw near, he would toss aside the bucket he'd pulled from beneath his mother's chair a while back and sacrifice his body for the sake of the castle. Having made it through only one chapter in the last hour and a half, Cooper closed her book and decided to join Andrew and Josh. Josh demanded her attention as he went over the entire castle building process. When he asked her to lay in the wet sand with him, after she and Andrew spent twenty minutes helping him build a wall nearly a foot high and five feet long, she assured him that the fort was secure. Josh sighed and Cooper watched him lift his sandy body from the shore and walk toward Andrew. Andrew rose to his knees and Cooper watched Josh, at eye level with Andrew, wrap his arms around him. With a big grin, the little fellow uttered seven words that she knew she would never forget: "I luff you—ewe-r my bess fiend."

In that moment, Cooper realized that Andrew Callaway would be a great father one day. The entire time she'd been watching Andrew and Josh play together that thought had been running through the back of her mind. As a tear slid down her cheek, Cooper found herself praying that she would one day be the mother of a man's children who had as much love and patience for a child as Andrew had shown this little boy whom he didn't even know. She realized that it would be weird to wish to be the mother of Andrew's children at this point in their relationship, whatever the definition that word encompassed in their particular circumstance, but what woman in her right mind wouldn't?

A moment later, a large dog walked by and scared Josh to tears. Instinctively, Andrew picked up Josh and held him in his arms while Cooper walked back to the cooler for some snacks that she promised would help solve the problem; with two cold Pepsis in her hands and a bag of Doritos wedged between her fingers as she made her way back to the castle, Cooper noticed that Josh's mother's chair was now empty. Frantically, she studied the beach and finally found the woman, making a b-line toward the man holding her son.

"What are you doing to my child?" Cooper heard the woman, gripping a fresh Coors Light, shout.

Even though her boorish tone shocked Andrew, he remained calm. "We just finished building a sandcastle," he answered, letting Josh down.

He was surprised she had taken the time to open a new beer while her son was missing.

Without reply, she snatched her son's arm violently whipping him to her side. "You don't know this man; he is a stranger," she yelled into Josh's face before popping the back of his head harshly.

The two sodas and the chips hit the sand, and Cooper forced her way into the confrontation. "Excuse me," she demanded, "that is no way to treat your child."

"Who are you to tell me how to treat my child? You're not his parents," she said, angrily pointing her beer can at Cooper and then at Andrew.

"I guarantee you he'd be better off if we were," Cooper combated without even thinking twice about her choice of words.

Andrew, surprised by Cooper's tone, watched her become animated. For some reason, her comment, even under the current predicament, made him feel good inside.

Cooper continued. "If you weren't over there sleeping, neglecting your child, he wouldn't have wandered over here to us. You're so busy drinking your beer that you forgot you had a three-year-old to take care of."

It didn't surprise Cooper when the ill-tempered woman threw her can to the ground. "I don't have to listen to this—heck, I'm old enough to be your mother," she said rigidly, staring Cooper in the eye.

"You're not fit to be anyone's mother," Cooper told her.

Without another word, the lady stomped away, dragging along her crying son. Her back turned to Cooper and Andrew, she held up her middle finger.

Consumed by the altercation, Andrew and Cooper hadn't noticed the crowd of bystanders who had gathered to watch. People were whispering and pointing telling others their version of what happened. Andrew ignored the stares, but Cooper instantly felt bad for criticizing the lady. She couldn't help but wonder what others might say about the way she'd handled the situation.

"Thank you for taking up for me," Andrew said, putting his arm around her.

"It makes me sick to see what's happening to that little boy; he's done nothing to deserve that kind of life, yet he's stuck with it. He was so happy building that sandcastle with you, but she just had to come over here and yank him up like a dog taking a crap in someone else's yard."

Amused by her analogy, Andrew began to laugh. "Interesting choice of words," he said.

Not sure whether to laugh or cry, Copper smirked. "I shouldn't have said that she wasn't fit to be a parent, especially not in front of the boy." She paused. "I don't even know her."

"Yeah, but it's pretty obvious what kind of life she leads," Andrew replied. "And he doesn't deserve that type of abuse; he's an innocent kid."

"It was nice of you to build a sandcastle with him," Cooper said, touching her finger to his stomach. "I could tell he really enjoyed your company. And I think you enjoyed his just as much," she smiled. "So much that I had to come down here because you had forgotten all about me."

"You were reading the entire time," he said in defense.

Cooper grinned. "That's what you thought."

Andrew rinsed the soda cans off in ankle deep water, and holding one of the Pepsis away from his body popped open the top.

"What are you doing?" Cooper asked.

"I'm afraid this thing might explode . . . I saw how hard you slung these things into the ground," he laughed.

On a red and white checkered table cloth that Cooper found in her mother's linen closet earlier this morning, she set out the ham sandwiches and freshly diced apples while Andrew ripped open the bag of Doritos. Over lunch, they laughed and giggled, and then without waiting the fifteen minutes their mothers had taught them to, they waded out into the ocean. Cooper burrowed her toes beneath the cool, soft sand and watched Andrew slip below the surface. In the murky water, he swam around like a fish searching to see if he could find anything exciting on the ocean floor. He could only see a yard or so ahead, but he finally stumbled upon something—Cooper's feet. How could he pass up a perfect chance to startle her? He couldn't. Cooper's knees buckled, and she lowered her arms into the water trying to keep her balance. Seconds later, she saw Andrew's head surface, and as he attempted to wipe the water from his face, she leapt onto his shoulders forcing him back under. Beneath the water, she connected her legs around his waist and latched on tightly. Floating loosely in the ocean's current, Andrew twisted his body, finally slinging it around to face hers. As the two emerged from the ocean's grasp, their bodies remained intertwined. The saltwater slid smoothly down their torsos and without any plans of this happening, each became lost in the other's stare. Andrew slid his hands below her backside and pulled her closer locking his fingers as she crossed her legs around his thighs. Cooper draped her arms over his shoulders causing their bodies to become flush.

As they meshed, a sudden friction created a sharp and steady sensation filling their inner confines. Cooper caught a glimpse of Andrew's muscular chest peaking just above the ocean's surface, and her eyes slowly drifted downward. Resting buoyantly in each other's arms, their bodies began to shiver in the warm water—unconsciously, both had been anticipating this moment the entire week—the entire time they'd known each other.

For a short moment, Andrew's eyes, too, shifted downward to Cooper's top pressed against his chest. Eventually, they climbed upward; he met her gaze and for a moment they were motionless, enveloped in one another's embrace. Cooper brushed the hair from her face as Andrew tilted his head, and the world around them became void as he softly kissed her tender lips.

21

"Hey, Andrew, it's me, Meredith. I'm in New Bern . . ."

Those words, on Andrew's voicemail, sent a chill down his spine as he felt the old Chevy begin to struggle toward the top of the high-rise. On the way over he'd wondered if the bulky piece of metal might conk out and send him and Cooper sliding back down the bridge like an out of control sled on an iced-packed mountain. But it hadn't, and now, out of the corner of his eye, Andrew caught himself peeking at Cooper. Her attention seemed to be focused on something in the water outside the passenger window while he pushed the phone tight against his ear hoping to muzzle Meredith's voice as the message played out: "I couldn't get a plane ticket, so I drove back. I went by your house, but you're not there. I'm at Union Point Park now—at *our* bench—will you meet me here as soon as you get this message?"

Andrew glanced at his watch, four o'clock, which meant Meredith had to have driven overnight. She must have left Tampa not long after he got off the phone with her, he concluded, after quickly figuring up the driving hours in his head. Part of him wanted to race back to New Bern, drop off Cooper, and get to that park as fast as he possibly could, but the other part, the part that had let him kiss Cooper McKay in the Atlantic Ocean while salt water tried but failed to ooze between their bodies, was telling him that he had screwed up any chance he had of reconciling his relationship with Meredith.

Since the wheels on the truck had touched the foot of the bridge, Cooper had been watching a couple of teenagers on jet skis down below. She was wondering if Josh was okay. She and Andrew had watched his mother snatch up her lawn chair and cooler in one arm, Josh in the other, and stomp toward the boardwalk. Josh seemed content, though. He'd even waved over his mother's shoulder as the distance between them grew further. A moment later, Andrew and Cooper were able to flag down a Park Ranger who was driving a four-wheeler and alert the officer about the woman's condition.

"That was Meredith, huh?" Cooper asked, pretending to be more interested in what was on the other side of the window than on the content of Meredith's message—the same thing she'd been doing while Meredith's concerned voice made it to her side of the truck, loud and clear—especially before Andrew nearly shoved the phone into his ear. Snooping had never really been her thing, though, and she hoped Andrew wouldn't think that she had been eavesdropping.

"Yes," he answered honestly.

No need to lie, he figured. Lies would only make this situation even more complicated than it had already become. Throw in a few more twists to this plot and Hollywood could make a movie out of it. If that didn't work, everyone involved could appear on one of those daytime talk shows and embarrass themselves and the town of New Bern.

"Are you going?" Cooper openly asked.

Knowing the answer that needed to be said, Andrew stared aimlessly at the red stoplight beyond the bottom of the bridge. "I talked to Meredith on the phone last night. I don't think she is the one who sent the emails . . ."

Then who did? Cooper wanted to ask, her brow furrowing as the question crossed her mind. *You saw the emails this morning, remember? And why did you kiss me?*

Instead of jumping to conclusions, Cooper waited to see if Andrew would reveal that bit of information.

"I think it was her mother, and yes," he finally answered, "I have to go."

As Andrew went into further detail about his conversation with Meredith last night, Cooper seemed to take the news well. If it bothered her as much as he thought it might, she kept her emotions well hidden. She didn't raise her voice, nor curse or call him names, like he figured most people in this situation would have. For the most part, she just listened as he rambled on and on about the woman he loved more than anything in this world— more than her, Cooper knew. So when Andrew said, "Will you go with me?" she nearly fainted.

22

Why on earth had she not gotten into her mother's car? Cooper contemplated. That was the only reason they'd veered off Highway 70 and headed back to Andrew's house in the first place. When he'd asked about her going with him to talk to Meredith, she'd said she didn't think it was a good idea, and they'd barely spoken after that. But then, at the last minute—only a few steps from her way out of this whole mess—she'd changed her mind. The car had been sitting right there in Andrew's driveway only fifteen yards from where Greg had parked Andrew's freshly painted, shiny silver Land Rover. She even had the keys in her hand. But instead, she surprised Andrew and herself when she opened the passenger side door and sat down as he plucked a note from beneath the windshield wiper. What was she going to say when she saw Meredith anyway? Would her being there actually do any good? And, more importantly, what would Meredith say? Would she yell and scream at her? Would she try to attack her? If the roles were reversed, Cooper wasn't sure if she might not choose to opt for one of the above. Maybe even both. Whatever the case, she would endure it. If she could help Andrew out, she would. It wasn't like she had been an innocent bystander in all of this. She could have called him sooner like her mother had advised. Hopefully, Cooper thought, as Andrew started the engine, he would be as good of a mediator as he was a kisser.

Thinking about the note from Greg, Andrew reminded himself to think positively. This would all work out. Somehow, someway, it would turn out for the best. His vehicle being finished early had to be a good sign although he still wasn't sure who this new guy was.

Andrew ran Greg's scribbled handwriting back through the monitor in his head:

"I owed you a favor for getting me a good deal on the new garage. And this new guy I hired is awesome. He said he knows you and he came in early this morning just to help me finish up your vehicle so we could surprise you with it this afternoon."

Surprised, Andrew definitely had been. Even under the circumstances, he'd taken a moment to scratch his head and think about who this new guy might be. Whoever it ended up being, he would have to make sure to say thank you. Probably an old friend from high school; a few of the guys from his shop class had turned out to be mechanics. Most of them floated from one garage to another. Trading mechanics in New Bern was like trading baseball cards when he was a kid. When one guy wasn't producing, you let him go and picked up another from the kid next door. But two months later you'd find the first player back in one of your collector's books. Whoever it was, they'd done Andrew a big favor. If he had to drive that old truck five miles further, he felt like it might actually conk out on him, although he'd felt that way every single time he'd cranked the engine since his dad passed it down to him.

The note secure on the dash, Andrew sped down the dusty driveway, throwing rocks into the background and making the very first dings in the new paint job. Driving fifteen miles an hour over the posted thirty-five mph speed limit, he barely touched the brakes before turning onto Brices Creek Road. As they closed in on the city limit, he slowed realizing that if he continued to speed he risked being stopped by Ringer or one of his deputies. Although he knew he could probably talk his way out of a ticket, blue lights would slow him up, and he would be angry if he missed Meredith who hadn't answered her cell phone either time he'd tried to call her.

When Andrew pressed the brake pedal this time, a sharp, grinding noise erupted. The sound seemed to be coming from beneath the passenger wheel, but he couldn't pinpoint the source. Cooper tensed up and looked in his direction, asking with her eyes what that noise meant. The brakes still seemed to do their job, Andrew recognized, but he had never heard the noise before, and he wondered why it had come out of nowhere. There hadn't been any trouble with the brake pads or the rotors before he dropped off the vehicle at the garage, and since Greg hadn't worked on the brakes, he didn't understand how anything done at the shop could have caused this problem.

"That's just the brakes talking a little," Andrew assured Cooper. "Nothing to be worried about."

As long as they worked, which they did, Andrew decided to ignore the noise and continue toward their destination. When they reached the stoplight to turn onto the only major highway that ran through town—major meaning four lanes and very few stoplights—the brakes only squealed a little, and both Andrew and Cooper seemed to relax. Sixty seconds later, he merged the SUV onto the first exit they came to, and with only one mile of road, a stoplight, and the drawbridge standing between Andrew and Cooper and Union Point Park, the two seemed to tense up even more than they had when the brakes had screamed at them. As they descended the exit, Andrew peered ahead at the stoplight in the distance. At the bottom of the ramp, it was shining red, but he knew from experience that at this rate of speed it would turn green by the time they reached it. Just beyond the intersection, the drawbridge would lead them across the Trent River. Andrew found himself tapping the brake twice on the way down just to make sure it would work if need be. To his delight, the stoplight turned green as they closed in on the intersection, and again he pushed the accelerator. He looked across Cooper through the passenger window and surveyed the waters of the Neuse River, which before meeting up with the Trent mirrored the road he was now driving. He didn't see any boats in the horizon, so there should be no cause for the bridge keeper to open the drawbridge, which at this point was the only thing that could possibly delay his arrival.

Just another minute, he thought.

We're almost there, Cooper thought. *God be with us all.*

Also to the right, spanning the river Andrew was now giving the once over, a high-rise bridge exited at the same intersection he was rapidly approaching. His eyes shifted from the water to the road ahead, and then out of the corner of his right eye, he, and Cooper at the exact moment, caught a glimpse of an eighteen-wheeler that appeared to be barreling down the exit way too fast.

Immediately dismissing everything else in his surroundings, Andrew focused on the truck. The speed in which it seemed to be traveling reminded him of a runaway truck on a mountain—only there was no emergency runaway-truck sand ramp to bring it to a halt—there was nothing—except his freshly painted Land Rover. The vehicle, though, he cared nothing about. His concern shifted to the woman sitting to his right.

Instinctively, Cooper slammed her foot into the floorboard as though she were the instructor in a driver's education car. The sound of the impact made by her foot and, in unison, the one made by Andrew's, traveled through the silence inside the spacious SUV. Andrew felt his heart begin to pound fiercely. Cooper leaned in his direction, wanting to be as far away from the grill of that frightening looking eighteen-wheeler as possible. At first she clinched the door handle but then quickly ducked down close to Andrew's lap, gripping the center console with both arms for dear life.

A nightmare, this had to be a nightmare—Andrew slammed his foot down three more times, but the brakes did nothing. They didn't squeal, and they didn't work. At this point, he realized it was too late to pull the emergency brake. Even if it did work, there was no way the vehicle would stop short of that intersection.

At that moment with death staring Andrew Callaway and Cooper McKay in the face instincts kicked in—Andrew gunned the gas pedal to the floorboard, closed his eyes, and breathed a prayer.

Just across the bridge, Meredith, waiting patiently on the park bench—the bench she had always referred to as *Our Bench*, meaning her and Andrew's—heard the deafening sound of metal crashing against metal. Every person in the entire park stopped what they were doing and tried to look across the river, but from their viewpoint no one could really see anything that had happened.

A dozen blocks away, firefighters began sliding down poles and in less than two minutes were fully geared and into the three trucks the main station housed.

Less than twenty yards had separated Andrew and Cooper from the oncoming big rig when they first realized that neither of them would make it to Union Point Park today . . . or maybe any day. The pedal remained wedged between Andrew's foot and the floorboard, but the eight-cylinder engine failed to pull its own weight out of harm's way. The adrenaline rush Andrew felt reminded him of the many brushes with death during his high school years—stomping the gas to outrun oncoming trains and breaking triple-digits to make curfew. How he hadn't killed himself or someone else during his reckless driving stage was nothing more than pure luck—and the hand of God. Unfortunately, his Land Rover lacked the acceleration speed of the Camaro he used to drive. This time, unlike the days of old, he'd done nothing wrong, he'd broken no laws, but it seemed as though today, fate had so quickly turned against him.

23

Minutes ago, the driver of the semi that had barreled into Andrew's vehicle, now overturned in a steep canal, shouted, "Oh, my God," as he ran toward the spinning wheels protruding from the ditch.

"Call an ambulance!" another man screamed.

Each of the men expected the worst.

The short, stocky fellow—who'd been in the car behind Andrew and had gotten an up close view of the accident—screamed at the trucker: "What were you thinking?"

Feeling terrible for what his actions had caused, the trucker didn't respond; he was terrified at the thought that he might have killed someone. He didn't need to be scolded, not now anyway. To make matters worse, until impact, he had no recollection of the catastrophe. Not having slept in sixty hours, he had dozed off at the wheel. He'd pushed himself over the limit in an attempt to finish his deliveries ahead of schedule, so he could make it home to his wife and daughter. His baby girl would turn one-year-old tomorrow, and he had promised her he would be there . . . no matter what. When he'd made that promise, he didn't anticipate something like this happening. He'd driven without sleep before. Most all truck drivers had, but that didn't excuse him, he knew that. What if his wife and little girl had been the ones in the vehicle at the bottom of the embankment he was now standing over while reliving the harrowing sound of the collision in his mind.

The Land Rover had come to a rest on its side and the driver's side door was jammed into the deepest part of the ditch. If there was anything to be thankful of at this moment, the driver of the car that had been behind Andrew and Cooper thought, it was that it hadn't rained as much as the forecast had predicted last night. Thank God there was little water standing in the steep trench. If they got down there and found the driver trapped in three foot of water that would only add to the severity of the situation. The man noticed that every window had shattered upon impact; basically, the vehicle had been turned into a pile of rubble quicker than it could have been at a junkyard where people smashed cars for a living.

"Call 911!" the truck driver shouted from the ditch, yelling to anyone within the sound of his panicking voice.

"We're here to help!" the other man shouted in Andrew's and Cooper's direction, not yet sure if there was anything he could do or if anyone in the vehicle was even alive to hear him. Without thinking twice, he attempted to climb onto the vehicle, but when his hand touched the bloody hand that began to emerge through the passenger side window, he lost his balance and toppled back down into the ditch.

Still at the bench with no idea that less than half a mile away Andrew was clinging to life, Meredith watched the first Highway Patrol car whiz past, blue lights swiveling and siren sounding. Once again she searched the park for Andrew's Land Rover. She'd been here for two hours now although it seemed like four. He would come, though; she knew Andrew would come.

"Stay in the car, Daddy's going to help some people," a tall and slender middle-aged man instructed his two children. For nearly an hour he'd been driving behind the eighteen-wheeler that now blocked the entire intersection at the bottom of the ramp. From the top of the exit, he had watched helplessly as the accident unfolded. Now, his car parked on the shoulder, he snatched what resembled a briefcase from his trunk and sprinted toward the frantic scene.

Traffic had begun to back up. People were out of their cars, trying to figure out what had happened. Those close by stood motionless, their hands covering their opened mouths. Others began to crowd, asking what had happened.

"Help, somebody please help!" the truck driver continuously screamed from the bottom of the ditch.

"I'm a doctor," exclaimed the man carrying the black case, scampering down the embankment.

From the back seat of the doctor's white Mercedes station wagon, his two small children watched as their father attempted to save Andrew Callaway's and Cooper McKay's lives. He discovered that Cooper had managed to pull her upper body through the shattered glass of the passenger window. The sharp edges had scraped her flesh, penetrating the skin. From head to toe, she had sustained multiple wounds and was bleeding profusely. When she'd slung her body from the window, she'd slid down the bashed in roof painting it red with blood.

Sitting quietly in the busy park, Meredith recalled the many evenings she and Andrew had spent running together along the sidewalk between her and the river's edge on hot days like today. Every time, without even speaking a word to one another, they would stop to rest on this wooden bench and watch the sailboats pass by while dreaming of owning their own one day. But today, as she waited impatiently, she wondered if that day was any closer than it had been on the day Andrew dropped to his knee in this very spot and asked her to marry him.

The sound of another patrol car speeding by, followed closely by an ambulance, diverted her attention, and not until *that* moment did she realize how serious the accident she had heard must have been. At least ten emergency vehicles had sped across the bridge. Meredith dropped her head and began to whisper a quick prayer, unaware that she was praying for the same person on which she was waiting.

Then as if God spoke directly to her, she imagined the worst. "Oh my God—Andrew!" she shouted, her voice crackling. "God," she begged out loud as she began to run toward the bridge, "please don't let it be him."

When she reached the drawbridge on foot, she chased the second ambulance that was using the desolate oncoming lane to get to the scene of the accident. As its lights faded in the distance, she sprinted past car after car although it seemed to her as though she was getting nowhere quickly. When she finally reached the bridge's peak, she spotted a mirage of red and blue lights flooding the horizon.

Earlier, before the paramedics arrived and after helping push Cooper out of the vehicle, Andrew climbed through the same window she had come out of. He attempted to raise his body from the mud-filled ditch, but after only one step he fell face first into the mud covering its bottom, and then looked up to find three men huddled above him.

"Don't try to walk," the doctor from the Mercedes called out.

It appeared the impact had broken Andrew's leg and shards of glass were protruding from his skin.

The doctor kneeled beside him. "Sir, remain still. I'm a doctor."

From the top of the embankment, dozens watched as the doctor worked. In this small southern town, many residents stopped at accidents, chances being good that they would know someone involved. Everyone stood in awe as Andrew lay in the bottom of the ditch, but a couple of ladies who worked in the shop next to his office began to choke up once they realized it was him.

The doctor began to inform Andrew of the injuries he'd sustained, since he seemed a little delusional. "Sir, your left leg might be broken," he started, "and you're going to need stitches on your forehead."

A gash, the length of a pen, ran along Andrew's hairline, and a T-shirt that had been wrapped around his head now looked as though it had been dipped in a pool of blood.

"While we're waiting for the paramedics we'll need to tidy up these other cuts," the doctor added, replacing the blood stained shirt with a towel and gauze before tending to the other not so major wounds.

"Okay," Andrew replied, his fingers twitching. He squinted his eyes, trying to endure what felt like the worst headache he'd ever had. "Where is Cooper?"

"I'm sorry—I'm so sorry," the trucker repeated, over and over, interrupting Andrew's question.

When no one responded, Andrew began to look for her.

"Sir," the doctor said sternly, "you are going to have to stay still. We need to keep your back and your neck straight until a stretcher gets here."

Andrew didn't say anything, and if he *had* been moving, he didn't realize it. And now, either his eyes were playing tricks on him or the images up above were getting further away. For some reason, he couldn't help but wonder if the wetness beneath his head was from the blood trickling down his face. If it was, he thought, it might well be the last feeling he ever felt.

As Andrew's breathing drew heavier, the doctor continued

talking, asking him question after question. "Do you know what day it is? Do you know where you are? What is your name?"

Andrew mumbled his name, but that was as far as he got.

If he didn't know the answers to the other questions, the doctor decided it would be best for him not to know he was lying in a pool of his own blood. "Focus on my eyes," he instructed.

A few men, who'd already given the shirts from their backs, asked if there was anything more they could do to help.

"Find Cooper—and Meredith," Andrew pleaded, all of a sudden remembering where he was headed and why he was headed there, but not quite sure if he'd made it.

"Who?" a man who'd given up his blue shirt with his name embroidered on it, asked, thrown off by two names since only one woman and Andrew had been in the vehicle.

For a moment, Andrew seemed to be doing much better. "Will someone please go to Union Point Park? Find my fiancée, Meredith. Tell her I want to marry her—"

As soon as those words exited Andrew's mouth, Sheriff Ronnie Ringer hustled down the ditch to his aid.

Andrew recognized him immediately. "What took you so long, Ronnie?" he asked, almost seeming drunk.

"You know this man?" the doctor asked the sheriff.

"Yes."

Ronnie reached for Andrew's hand and focused his attention solely on his eyes. "Hey," he reminded Andrew, "I'm the first responder here, aren't I?" He paused, quickly evaluating Andrew's injuries. "How many fingers am I—"

The doctor interrupted again, introducing himself and eloquently explaining the precautions he'd already taken. Moments later, volunteer firefighters swarmed the scene. Some began directing traffic and others came to where Andrew was lying. Along with another police officer, two of the firefighters helped clear the crowds to make a path for the ambulance. The paramedics quickly wheeled a stretcher toward the ditch and strapped a neck brace on Andrew. After carefully hoisting him onto the stretcher, Ronnie helped carry it up the steep embankment. Slowly, they made their way to flat ground and then rolled the gurney to the ambulance.

❦

Even though she was gasping for air, Meredith didn't slow until she reached the side of the bridge where the accident had happened. She quickly pushed her way through the crowd, thicker than the one that gathered at this very spot every 4th of July to watch the firework show.

When she spotted Andrew's overturned vehicle, she began running toward it. "Where is Andrew?" she demanded to know, searching for someone, anyone who could answer her question. "Where is the man who was driving this vehicle?"

"I'm not sure," one of the volunteer firefighters said after Meredith tugged at his suit.

She shouted again, even louder this time. "Does anyone know where Andrew is?"

"Ma'am," a firm voice called out.

Meredith turned. Ronnie had been sent to calm the woman who was screaming at the top her lungs, but when he realized it was Meredith, he felt a knot in his stomach. "Meredith, come with me," is all he said, grabbing her by the hand.

24

The Next Saturday

"*I* do," Andrew agreed, as the preacher lowered his Bible and smiled. He leaned forward to kiss the most beautiful brown-eyed bride he'd ever seen—his bride. The woman he vowed to spend the rest of his life with. The woman whose children he wanted to father. The woman he couldn't wait to honeymoon with in Cancun. She was wearing a flowing white gown with sequins sparkling around the sleeveless shoulders, and he hadn't been able to quit staring, not until he closed his eyes for this kiss. Even though his neck felt stiff from the accident, he kept his head tilted until a steady string of oohs and ahs erupted from the thirty-six people in attendance—which included one person who had not been on the original guest list that he and Meredith put together six months ago.

On the back row, wearing a simple blue summer dress, a tear rolled down Cooper McKay's face as the ceremony came to an end. Even though she'd wished she'd been the one standing up there next to Andrew as Brooke sang the most beautiful rendition of Alison Krause's *When You Say Nothing At All*, she forced a smile as Andrew in a white tuxedo and a pink tie walked Meredith back down the aisle. When Meredith winked at her on the way out of the cutest and most quaint church she'd ever stepped foot in, Cooper had to admit that she was genuinely happy for both Andrew and Meredith.

Holding Meredith's hand, Andrew smiled back as they passed by Cooper. For a moment, he held her gaze, but even then he still couldn't believe that Meredith had been the one who'd wanted to invite Cooper. It seemed awkward, but in an odd sort of way, it seemed right at the same time. He just hoped the two of them wouldn't exchange phone numbers and become best friends. That would be too weird. The fact that they already had each other's email addresses—thanks to Meredith's mother and brother who had apologized over and over for sending the emails and taking the photographs—was more than enough, too much, actually.

When Barry—Andrew's best man—and Brooke—Meredith's maid of honor—held open the two wooden doors that led Andrew and Meredith into their first breath of fresh air as a married couple, Andrew knew he could walk out of the church with absolutely no secrets to keep hidden. After eating the absolute worst hospital meal he'd ever experienced, Andrew had cleared his conscious by telling Meredith every single detail about the most dramatic week of his life. Later that night, Cooper, Ronnie, Meredith, and himself had all sat down over a cup of coffee and talked about the crash—including Chris's involvement.

The new hire that Greg had been praising in the note on Andrew's windshield had turned out to be none other than Mr. Chris Selzer himself. Ronnie had found this out after piecing together all the clues and was actually speeding toward Andrew's house with Chris Selzer cuffed in the backseat when the call of an accident near the drawbridge came across his radio. Using tactics he dared not admit to anyone, Ronnie had coerced Chris into a taped confession of spray painting Andrew's Land Rover, hiding out in the backseat of Cooper's car and attacking Andrew. And the big kicker—two counts of attempted murder for rigging the brakes in Andrew's vehicle to give out. Needless to say, he would be locked up for quite some time.

As for the honeymoon, Andrew was glad the doctor from the Mercedes had been wrong about his broken leg. After the accident, when he'd made it to the hospital under the influence of a concussion, he'd woken up to find Meredith sitting to his left and Cooper to his right—miraculously, the only injury Cooper had sustained from the accident was sewn together with three stitches below her left ear. At the time, Andrew thought he'd died and gone to heaven, not because the only two women he'd ever loved were sitting in the same room with him but because they weren't at each other's throats. He was glad to hear they had talked out the troubles Sylvia and Chris had caused, but he still couldn't believe they didn't hate each other.

With a banged up leg, Andrew made the most out of five nights stay in Cancun. Along with some souvenirs, he'd come home with a whole new perspective on the art of making love—or at least a new sense of creativity when it came to positioning.

Thanks to the modern medicine—for scratches, scrapes, and bruises—called make-up, which Andrew swore he would never allow anyone to put on his face again, the wedding pictures turned out beautiful. In the weeks following the wedding, it seemed like he and Meredith sent at least one photograph to every person they had ever met. When they weren't working on thank-you notes, the two of them spent countless hours lying in bed talking and giggling like little children. A tender touch would often spark an episode of passionate lovemaking, and every time Andrew held Meredith's naked body in his arms it felt like the first. He could finally put to rest the curiosity behind the myth of how fabulous it was to make love with a pregnant woman—"Wow" was the word he usually used when he fell back onto his pillow.

Andrew's mother was thrilled to get a call from him to inform her that she would be a grandmother, and so was Meredith's mom—whom Andrew had forgiven and actually grown to like now that she'd had a change of heart and decided to accept him as part of the family. She hadn't made him happy with every decision, however, and he stayed mad at her for almost a week when she broke up with Charles, his security guard friend from the airport.

Andrew even let Eric talk him into going hunting with him once although he doubted he would ever do that again. Six hours in a deer stand with nothing to show for it other than sweat dripping from the tight camouflage jumpsuit Eric had let him borrow wasn't his idea of fun, especially since Eric hit a deer with his truck on the way home. Imagine that, Andrew had thought, and then he spent the next thirty minutes pleading with Eric not to bring the animal home so they could spend another hour gutting it before storing it in the cooler on his mother's back porch.

Meredith continued to receive roses at work. All of her co-workers ogled over them as usual as Andrew sent one for every month they had been married, which was very sweet and thoughtful but at the same time, she liked to joke about him resetting the counter. On top of that, he cooked dinner for her every Friday night and made sure to be dressed in his pajamas every Monday night in time to watch *Castle*. On other nights they watched movies, played cards, and went grocery shopping, which for some weird reason seemed to have become their favorite hobby.

Marriage, Andrew decided, was definitely much more beneficial than society seemed to make it out to be, but maybe that is because he and Meredith were in many ways old-fashioned.

They went to church on Sundays and often caravanned with Barry and Marie and a group of friends to eat fried chicken and all the other southern delicacies that ended up on a banquet style table in someone's backyard every weekend.

Epilogue

March 14, 2014

As Andrew thought about the possibility of losing one of the most important people in his life, he cried until he couldn't muster up another tear. When the pain that accompanied the thought of losing his mother on March 14, 2014—the same day his son would be born—began to eat at his stomach, the constant hum of the monitors produced the only sound in the room. He reached for her hand and held it tighter than he ever had, even tighter than the day his father died of a heart attack.

Mounted in the corner, the blank television accurately represented the mood in the room. It felt like the most remote place on earth. The shades had been drawn shut, allowing little light to enter the small space, and a thin white sheet had been draped across Andrew's mother's aged body; the thin gray hair on her head was being supported with two pillows, and at sixty-two-years-old Rosemary Callaway looked as peaceful as she ever had, Andrew thought. He kissed her hand, glad that she wasn't suffering.

A little later, Barry and Marie returned hand-in-hand, and Andrew headed for room 209. Marie had told him that Meredith's contractions were getting closer, and she thought Andrew should be with her. He was torn between staying with his mother and going to be with his wife, but he knew he had to be there when his son was born. With all the commotion, there was no telling if that would be sooner or later. At least there was someone else to sit at his mother's side so that she would have something other than a cold drift to wake up to if the fifty percent prediction the doctor had given happened to fall in their favor.

Andrew pushed through the door and watched his wife smile for the first time since the doctor hooked her up to the sonogram machine earlier this morning. Since Barry had called with bad news, no one had smiled, not even the doctor or the nurses. Word seemed to travel pretty quickly around the small hospital, and even the nurse who'd been giving Andrew a hard time had offered to say a prayer for his mother. She asked if there was anything else she could do too, and now to add to every other feeling the human heart was capable of experiencing, Andrew felt guilty about being snippy with her in the first place.

"How is your mother holding up?" Meredith asked.

"The doctor is still saying 50/50," he said, his lips curling inward.

She searched his brown eyes appearing as heavy as rain clouds in the summertime, and it was at that moment, when she thought his eyes were about to burst open, that her water broke. Andrew couldn't see it beneath the covers he had fetched hours ago, but he could tell it was time even though he'd never done this before. He ran to his wife then back to the door, yelling at the top of his lungs for the doctor.

Twenty minutes of labor later, Andrew watched the head of a baby boy come out of the woman that his son would get to call Mommy for the rest of his life. There were no words that could explain the miracle that had just occurred in front of his very eyes. He had just witnessed a newborn baby—his newborn baby—enter this world. Even though he'd read countless books on childbirth throughout the last nine months of his life, none of the experts had even come close to touching the heartstrings that were playing within his soul at this very moment. When the doctor handed him little Caleb Callaway and Andrew held him in his arms for the very first time, he actually forgot for a split second about everything that was going on two floors above.

"Hey little man," Andrew said in his new *daddy* voice. "I'm your dad. And that is your mom," he said, facing Caleb toward his mother. He was so tiny.

This was better than falling in love, better than making love; Andrew knew there was not a description of a feeling he would ever be able to use to describe this moment to a man who had not experienced it for himself.

When the delivery room team eventually cleared the room, Andrew sat down next to his wife, and with a fatherly touch stroked the thin, oily feeling hair on their son's head. "Look at what we did," he smiled, a tear sliding down his face.

"He's ours," Meredith replied proudly, rubbing her bloodshot eyes, yet enjoying their first moments alone as parents. At the same time, she wasn't sure which had been more painful, the birth of an 8lb. 7oz. baby boy or the worry she had bottled inside since Andrew told her about his mother. As she watched him hold their son against his chest, all of a sudden the door unexpectedly flung open, and an instinct Andrew didn't even know he had been equipped with took over. The muscles in his forearms flexed as he wrapped his arms around his son, protecting him from any harm that might come their way.

"Andrew!" Barry said loudly, barreling into the room with a frantic look covering his face.

The doctor had said visitors were now welcomed, but Andrew hadn't expected this type of entrance; but once the initial shock wore off, he knew he probably should have.

Andrew took his eyes off his son for the first time since he'd come out of the womb and studied the expression on Barry's face. The messenger, he now knew, hadn't come to harm anyone. He was simply the bearer of bad news.

Barry paused for a moment, standing in the doorway, and taking in the sight in Andrew's arm. "Oh, my God. Andrew, oh, my God."

Barry didn't know what to say next or if he should even say what he had come to say. Without speaking another word, he watched Andrew kiss Caleb on the forehead and quickly yet gently hand him to his mother.

"What is it?" Andrew asked in a squeaky tone, fearful that he was about to find out his mother had died the very hour his son had come into this world.

Some things are genetic, and others . . . well . . . *tragic.* That was the best word Andrew had been able to come up with for what God let happen on March 14, 2014.

For years, he had wondered what his father had gone through on the day he was born, the day his grandmother died . . . now he knew, first hand. He knew that Caleb would never know his grandmother. She would never get to hold him in her arms or tell him that she loved him. She wouldn't be able to spoil him with new clothes or let him stay up past his bedtime. He wouldn't even be able to spend one night at her house.

A month after that day, Andrew cried for what seemed like the millionth time when he put a home filled with his very own childhood memories on the market. As hard as it had been on him, he knew he either had to sell his parent's house or let it rot away like he often wished he could. The house sold in less than a month, and he and Barry split what was left of their mother's portfolio. Andrew used his portion to open a college fund for Caleb. An education was priceless, and he knew that would give his son at least one thing to remember his grandmother by.

Walking into Carolina Bank to open that account had been more difficult than Andrew imagined. Two months after the fact on a day much like that rainy Monday morning, he could still remember the way each of the tellers looked at him, like he was a ghost yet like he couldn't see them staring at him while they pretended to focus on their work. He didn't say a word to any of them, not even the ones he knew by name. He only walked to the door that had always led him to Meredith.

But after March 14, 2014, there were no doors that led to Meredith. Not since he'd run through the clouded and claustrophobic feeling hallway back toward Room 209. The doctor had sent a nurse for Andrew that day moments after his mother slipped away in front of his very eyes, but he didn't make it back to the room in time to say goodbye to his wife. He didn't get to hold her hand as she breathed her very last breath. He didn't get to tell her he loved her more than anything in this world. He didn't get to promise that he would make sure their baby boy grew up knowing what a wonderful mother he had.

That room, cold and dreary, had stolen that from him . . . from her. He remembered wishing he could bottle up the air and bring it home with him. He had even considered going back for the pillow that supported her head; the sheet that covered her body; even that darn green chair that he thought about every day since he last sat in it. As uncomfortable as it was, he would sit it in every day for the rest of his life if he could have her back. He wouldn't complain either, about anything, not even about changing diapers. He'd told Meredith he didn't look forward to changing diapers—but that didn't matter anymore. He would change every diaper Caleb could dirty. She could read or watch television or just relax. It would be fine with him if she breastfed, too. A lot of the books he'd read before Caleb was born talked about breastfed children becoming extremely dependent on their mother, but Caleb could spend as much time with her as he wanted. He could even be a mama's boy. Instead of playing baseball and soccer like all the other little boys, he could take piano lessons or even dance.

One of the hardest things had been walking into the house for the first time without Meredith. With Caleb wrapped in a blanket secured tightly against his chest, Andrew had walked through the door all alone that day. He'd lowered Caleb into his crib while his own tears rained down all around his newborn son. After watching him sleep for hours, he'd ventured out to the deck and sat on the benches that he and Barry had finished a few months after the wedding, but never again did he step foot on the sailboat that he watched sway in the wind that day. It was going to be a surprise for Meredith. She would have loved it, he knew that. It was small and old, but it was gorgeous. The previous owner, a retired gentleman, had kept her in great shape and had even become a little teary-eyed when he sold it to Andrew. He hadn't wanted to sell, but he had to, he said, to pay for his wife's doctor bills. Andrew hadn't asked what was wrong with her, but a week after Meredith passed he watched the man cry once more when he returned the boat and told him to keep the money, too. "I don't have any use for this anymore," Andrew had said and walked away.

Money didn't matter anymore. Neither did work. Andrew let Brooke take over the office, and he told her to keep every penny that the business earned until he figured things out, but every two weeks she showed up at his doorstep with a check for him. A really big one after she sold the Tyndall mansion to an attorney from

Texas. Brooke often brought her son and let him play in the floor with Caleb while she and Andrew sipped cappuccinos and reminisced about the days when Meredith was still alive.

✦

The obituary in the newspaper had read that Meredith Anne Callaway was only twenty-seven years old when complications from pregnancy took her out of this world on the same day Andrew lost his mother. He hated that day, but he loved it, too. It was his son's birthday.

Thinking such thoughts brought on other thoughts. Meredith wouldn't be there for their son's first birthday, just like she hadn't been there for his first visit to the doctor. While the other mothers in the waiting room held their babies, Andrew had closed his eyes and pictured Meredith, holding Caleb, playing with him in the corner near the building blocks. She would have been a natural mother, he knew that. She would have been wonderful if she could be there for his first word, his first step, and his first day of school. She would know all the right things to say and do. Andrew was afraid he would do something wrong. He would forget to pack Caleb's lunch or catch him when he fell.

The one thing he knew he wouldn't forget was how to love his son—but tucked away in his heart, right next to that love, was anger. Andrew was mad at God and had been since March 14, 2014. At the same time, he thanked God that Caleb was healthy, and he still took him to church every Sunday and prayed with him each night before he kissed his forehead. When Andrew would go into his own room, he would curl up in the fetal position, and while crying himself to sleep, he would scream at God.

Screaming and crying, it seemed, was the only way to lessen the sting as the hands on the clock continued to move; but time, to Andrew, stood still. Minutes—Hours—Days—Months—Time didn't matter anymore. Nor did it matter that when someone would ring his doorbell to offer their condolences his hair was matted and his breath smelled like the last thing he'd eaten—a Dorito, probably, since he rarely had much of an appetite for anything of substance.

Over time his eyes adjusted to the darkness within the house, the darkness that had become his life. The only light he ever saw was in Caleb's eyes. Even though Andrew had been unable to take care of himself the way he once did, he made sure to take care of his and Meredith's baby boy. He fed and dressed him well, bought him the safest car seat, stroller, crib, and toys on the market. Those were the things a family was supposed to do together, things he and Meredith had chosen to wait to do until after their son was born, but now Andrew's family consisted of only him and his son. Caleb would never know his mother. He would never witness the twinkle in her beautiful brown eyes.

Andrew made sure to give his son all the love and attention that he knew Meredith would have. He spent most of his time with Caleb. Every now and then he would venture over to Barry's and Marie's, but even then, he would often leave Caleb with them and head for Cedar Grove Cemetery to sit at Meredith's graveside where he would cry for hours on end.

After eight months passed, Andrew let Brooke take him out for pizza. She'd been dropping by at least once a week for quite some time to help out around the house. She often brought Caleb a new toy, cooked dinner once in a while, and found herself cleaning up after a man who had once been the tidiest straight man she'd ever known, but Brooke was the only woman Andrew would allow to get close. Barry and Marie had encouraged him to start dating again, but he wouldn't hear it. He told them it would be wrong.

No woman could ever take the place of his wife. He'd made the mistake of taking down photos of her once, but he made a pact with himself that he would never let that happen again. Every night when he carried Caleb to his room, he would stop in the hallway to tell his son stories about his mother. The first photograph on the wall was of him and Meredith on their first date. The second, their engagement photo. The third was of them exchanging their vows. She looked so beautiful and so happy. Her white dress still hung in a prominent place in his closet. It helped him remember that day, not that he could ever forget it. And the fourth photograph, the one just outside Caleb's door, was a maternity photo. The last photo taken of her. The photographer had caught Andrew kissing her stomach, and he and Meredith both loved that picture more than any of the staged shots. That was the one he stared at the longest. Caleb always seemed to smile when Andrew told him that he was in the photo, too. At least Caleb would always have that picture of him and his mother, Andrew often thought. Even though Caleb would never be able to see his mother's face next to his own face—which resembled his mother's more every day—he would always have that photo.

On Caleb's first birthday, Andrew sat in the spot he had sat in so many times in the past year that the maintenance man at Cedar Grove Cemetery no longer tried to grow grass there although it seemed the many tears that he had left behind could have probably sprung a seed in the middle of the Sahara desert.

About an hour ago, he had loaded Caleb into his car seat and driven across the drawbridge—the same bridge Meredith had sprinted across to reach him on the day she had agreed to put his mistakes behind them and start a new life. Today was the first time Andrew had brought Caleb here with him, and now and every time Andrew had visited her gravesite in the past year, he was reminded of that day, of Meredith's decision—and of his decision to tell Cooper that she was one of the most wonderful people in this world, and that if Meredith wasn't already *his* world, he would give up everything he had in life just to be with her. But every time he thought of that decision, of the amazing son it had brought him and the wife and best friend he had lost along the way, he knew, if given the chance to make the decision all over again, he would still be sitting right here in this very spot at this very moment.

Weeping harder, Andrew drew Caleb close to his chest. He watched his son's tiny fingers trace the engraved epitaph: *We're Only A Bridge Apart*, the bottom line on Meredith's stone read.

He had chosen that saying for so many reasons. The obvious because Meredith's instincts had drawn her to cross the drawbridge to find him the day of the accident, but also because he felt that both his and his son's life were merely a bridge that would lead them to heaven—to be with her again.

The thing that hurt Andrew the most was knowing that his son would never experience even one memory of the mother he would have to grow up without. But, as he leaned against Meredith's tombstone, instead of "Dad" being the first real word to ever trickle out of Caleb Callaway's mouth, Andrew felt the hand of God reach through his chest and squeeze his heart as his son uttered the word "Mama." Most kids had already spoken a word by twelve months, which had worried Andrew a little, but it was as if Caleb had been waiting for this very moment like he knew it was coming all along.

Mama. Caleb had said the word as clear as the day.

Andrew smiled at him and hugged him tightly. Then Caleb, looking over Andrew's shoulder and pointing, said it again, "Mama."

Andrew turned his head to see what his son was pointing at.

When he saw her standing there, he couldn't believe his eyes. The last time he'd seen Cooper McKay she'd been standing in that exact spot—near the old rusted gate, her arms folded as Andrew kissed his wife's casket and then made his way through a crowd of close friends and loved ones.

Admiring Andrew with his son for the first time, Cooper smiled and lifted her hand to wave. She hadn't stuck around after the funeral that day because she didn't want to be another one of those people who hugged Andrew's neck and said *I know what you're going through.* The truth was she didn't know what he was going through, not then and not now. She had no idea how it felt to lose a spouse. What she did know, however, both then and now, was what it felt like to lose him—the man she hadn't stopped loving since the day her eyes met his in the local video store.

"I've wanted to call you every day since I left this place," she said, the gap between her and Andrew growing smaller as she stepped slowly toward him and his son.

For a moment Andrew wondered if she was referring to New Bern—or this place—the place where they were now. He watched her glance around as if checking to see if anything had changed and then he knew this was the place she was talking about, the last place she had seen him. An entire year had passed since that day, and although it seemed more like a decade, he was glad Cooper had not called or come to see him before today. Even one day less would have been too soon. But this morning, when Andrew had knelt at his bedside to pray, he'd asked God to send him and Caleb someone to walk along with them across the bridge.

"This is Caleb," Andrew said. "Today is his birthday."

"Happy birthday, Caleb," Cooper said without missing a beat.

"Cooper," Andrew said honestly, "I would love to stay here and catch up, but Caleb and I are already late to his first birthday party."

"Oh," she said. "I'm sorry. Don't let me hold you up." She paused for a moment, and almost turned away, temporarily forgetting that the reason for her visit to the cemetery was to set the flowers in her hand at Meredith's tombstone. She hadn't expected to run into Andrew here, but she had come back to New Bern knowing that she wanted to see him. Taking her eyes off

Andrew for a moment, wondering what he thought about her being here, she stepped toward the gravesite. "I just wanted to bring these flowers for Meredith; she was a very special woman."

Andrew smiled and glanced at Caleb. "I tell him that all the time."

It was very sweet that Cooper had remembered the significance of today and thought enough of Meredith to bring flowers.

The air grew silent for a moment except for birds chirping and a light breeze blowing. Andrew could tell that Cooper didn't know what else to say, and honestly, he didn't either. He started to say *Goodbye, Cooper* and walk away.

Thinking similar thoughts, Cooper wasn't sure how to take the next step, but she knew what she had left Fort Worth for, and she decided to say it even if it ended up meaning that these were the last words she ever spoke to Andrew Callaway.

"I had to come back to make sure you were okay," she said softly, ". . . are you okay?" she asked, openly concerned for his well-being.

Andrew thought about forcing a smile; he'd become pretty good at that.

"No," he admitted. "And yes," he added, which left only one thing to say. "Will you come with us to Caleb's party? He needs someone to help him blow out the candles."

"And what about you?" Cooper asked.

"I need someone to help me with the dishes," Andrew said smiling for real as he let Caleb down and held his hand to steady his walk.

As if Caleb knew what was supposed to come next, he stretched his free hand toward Cooper and grinned the cutest grin she'd ever seen.

Reaching down to let Caleb hold her fingers, Cooper knew she'd made the right decision. "I would love to," she confirmed.

The three of them walked slowly out of Cedar Grove Cemetery, hand in hand, like the perfect family if seen from a stranger's eyes. Andrew had no idea why Caleb had called Cooper "Mama," but he knew that if there was anyone other than Meredith Callaway whom he would ever want his son to call "Mama," Cooper McKay was that person.

THE END

A Note from the Author

Thank you for reading *A Bridge Apart*! I am honored that you invested your time in my debut novel. I hope you will rush out to pick up your copy of my next novels, *Losing London* and *A Field of Fireflies*. If you enjoyed the story you just experienced, please consider helping me spread the novel to others in the following ways:

- REVIEW the novel online at Amazon.com, goodreads.com, bn.com, bamm.com, etc.
- RECOMMEND this book to friends (social groups, workplace, book club, church, school, etc.).
- VISIT my website: www.Joey-Jones.com
- SUBSCRIBE to my Email Newsletter for insider information on upcoming novels, behind-the-scenes looks, promotions, charities, and other exciting news.
- CONNECT with me on Social Media: "Like" Facebook.com/JoeyJonesWriter (post a comment about the novel). "Follow" me at Instagram.com/JoeyJonesWriter and Twitter.com/JoeyJonesWriter (#ABridgeApartNovel). "Pin" on Pinterest. Write a blog post about the novel.
- GIVE a copy of the novel to someone you know who you think would enjoy the story. Books make great presents (Birthday, Christmas, Teacher's Gifts, etc.).

Sincerely,
Joey Jones

About the Author

Joey Jones has fifteen years of creative and professional writing experience. He fell in love with creative writing at an early age and decided in his early twenties that he wanted to write a novel. *A Bridge Apart* is a love story that was years in the making, as he tinkered with the book off and on while working full-time in the marketing field. He holds a Bachelor of Arts in Business Communications from the University of Maryland University College, where he earned a 3.8 GPA.

He lives in North Carolina with his family. In his spare time, he enjoys spending time with his family, playing sports, reading, and writing inspirational quotes. His favorite meal is a New York Style Pizza with a Mt. Dew. He won the 8th-grade spelling bee at his school, but if you ask him how many students participated, he'll say, "Such minor details are not important!"

Joey Jones is currently writing his second novel, and he invites you to connect with him online to find out more about the upcoming book, giveaways, exciting news, and more:

Joey-Jones.com

Facebook.com/JoeyJonesWriter

Instagram.com/JoeyJonesWriter

Twitter.com/JoeyJonesWriter

Book Club/Group Discussion Questions

1. Were you immediately engaged in the novel?
2. What emotions did you experience as you read the book?
3. Which character is your favorite? Why?
4. What do you like most about the story as a whole?
5. What is your favorite part/scene in the novel?
6. Are there any particular passages from the book that stand out to you?
7. As you read, what are some of the things that you thought might happen, but didn't?
8. Is there anything you would have liked to see turn out differently?
9. Is the ending satisfying? If so, why? If not, why not . . . and how would you change it?
10. Why might the author have chosen to tell the story the way he did?
11. If you could ask the author a question, what would you ask?
12. What author(s) would you compare to Joey Jones?
13. Have you ever read or heard a story anything like this one?
14. In what ways does this novel relate to your own life?
15. Would you read this novel again?

Turn the page for a preview of

Losing London

- A Novel by -
Joey Jones

Available at Joey-Jones.com

1

*L*osing London had caused more tears to stream down Harper Adams' face than all of her previous life experiences combined. Losing James had proven to be a distant second. Losing two people she loved more than anything in the world within a one-month period was a reality she would have never imagined possible. There was, however, a difference.

Now that the initial sting of rejection had passed, she couldn't care less if she ever saw the face of her ex-husband again. Eleven months ago, James had slammed the door on his way out of their townhouse in Silver Spring, Maryland, and she hadn't heard from him since. The jerk hadn't so much as picked up the phone or even taken five minutes to drop a sympathy card in the mail.

When the mailman knocked on her door today, Thursday, June 4th, she was surprised to find him there. Most days, she found herself waving as he drove off from the row of boxes out by the road. Harper reached for the package in his hand, and as he walked to his truck in the parking lot, her hazel eyes remained fixated on the name in the top left corner: Dr. Harold Thorpe. Dr. Thorpe, a slender and overworked gentleman in his mid-sixties—twice her age—had been a close friend to her sister. In fact, he was the main reason London had moved to Emerald Isle, North Carolina two years ago.

Why in the world would he send me a package? she wondered. She had met the man many years ago, but that was about it. They'd never even had a real, adult conversation.

The 8x12 inch padded envelope felt light in her hand. Beyond curious about the contents, Harper hurried inside and dug through the drawer next to the sink, searching for a pair of scissors. "Where does all this stuff come from?" she asked an empty room as she dug through the mess.

Harper halted the search for an instant and sighed, taking a moment to study the pair of tweezers in front of her face. Where had those been yesterday when she'd spent twenty minutes hunting for them? Dumb question, she quickly realized. Next, she came across the tape dispenser that she'd needed last week. But no scissors. Out of everything in this drawer, she found it hard to believe that there wasn't a single sharp object inside.

Keys, she decided, *I'll just use a key.*

The set on the keyring jingled when she plucked them from a nail—a nail that James had tacked into the wall when they'd first moved into the townhouse after their honeymoon five years ago. A second nail, just above her spot, remained empty. Harper stood there long enough to remember what that meant. No one else had taken his place—that's exactly what *that* meant. And to be honest, she'd recently started to wonder if she would ever find a man who would be able to sweep her off her feet the way James once had. But maybe the real question was: Would any man worth a darn want to be with a twenty-nine-year-old divorced woman who had gained fifteen pounds since graduating college?

At such a silly thought, Harper turned her attention back to the package, which she had decided contained a book, and tried to shake off the ridiculous ideas running through her aching head. That, she suddenly remembered, is what she'd been doing when the doorbell rang . . . she'd been on her way to the medicine cabinet.

Harper chuckled. Finding someone she'd trust to hang his keys on that nail . . . who was she kidding? She hadn't even been on a real date since James ran off with that bimbo. Why should she even have any interest in a serious relationship at this point in her life, anyway? How could she ever trust a man again? When she had needed her husband the most, he had packed his bags and left her with an empty townhouse and two pairs of his dress shoes. Those ended up flying out of the second story window. She'd hoped to hit his car, but the taillights moved a little too quickly as she'd cocked her arm and launched each one like a football.

The key cut right through the tape. Harper then used her fingers to separate the flaps on the envelope, and she nearly fainted when she held one of the most beautiful books she'd ever seen in front of her eyes. The cover design was absolutely amazing. One she knew she would have picked up if she were browsing the local bookstore shelves for a good read. But it wasn't the silhouette of a couple sitting in an antique convertible car overlooking the ocean in the dusk that tugged at her heart. It was the name below the title.

How?

When?

These one word questions led her on a search for any clues she might be able to find immediately.

Wedged into the cream-colored pages, she noticed a single sheet of paper, barely protruding from the top of the book. Wondering if it held some answers, she found herself tugging at it with her fingertips.

Unfolding the letter, she instantly recognized the handwriting . . . London's handwriting.

Made in the USA
Middletown, DE
29 November 2022

16404736R00154